THE SECOND MRS. PRICE

Also by Toni Fuhrman

One Who Loves

The Second Mrs. Price

A NOVEL

TONI FUHRMAN

LAGOON HOUSE PRESS

The Second Mrs. Price

Copyright © 2018 by Toni Fuhrman

ISBN: 978-0-9972609-3-9

Cover and interior book design by Marcia Barbour
Cover image by Getty Images
Author photo by Jennifer Skelly & Auston James

Anna Akhmatova, ["Waiting for you gives me more pleasure"] from *Complete Poems of Anna Akhmatova*, translated by Judith Hemschemeyer, edited and introduced by Roberta Reeder. Copyright © 1989, 1992, 1997 by Judith Hemschemeyer. Reprinted with the permission of The Permissions Company, Inc., on behalf of Zephyr Press, www.zephyrpress.org, as well as with the permission of Canongate Books Ltd.

"Fern Hill" © The Trustees for the Copyrights of Dylan Thomas, published in *The Collected Poems of Dylan Thomas* (New Directions), reprinted by permission of David Higham Associates and New Directions Publishing Corp.

For more about Dylan Thomas and "Fern Hill," visit www.discoverdylanthomas.com.

For more about the author, visit tonifuhrman.com.

Note to the reader:
This is a work of fiction. Names, characters, businesses or companies, locales, and incidents are products of the author's imagination, or are used fictitiously. Any resemblance to actual persons, living or dead, or actual events, is purely coincidental.

Lagoon House Press
Long Beach, CA
lagoonhousepress.com

For David and Jennifer, with love.

Waiting for him gives me more pleasure
Than feasting with another.

Anna Akhmatova

translated by Judith Hemschemeyer

The Second
Mrs. Price

CHAPTER 1

In The Midwest, in the spring, there are a few days so warm and soft, so gently in motion, so tenderly inviting, that we forget the ravages of the winter just behind us, the heavy, breathless summer days just ahead; we accept that we are home, that we are where we belong.

It was on such a Sunday afternoon, in the year 1999, in the small town of Sylvan Springs, Ohio, that Selene Fugate Price first met Griff. He was about to enter her house, not expected but not unwelcome. He was standing on the porch with her husband, Alex, as she pulled into the driveway, got out of her silver Honda, glanced at the dusty red Chevy pickup truck parked across the street, and walked up the front steps. She stood between them for a moment, turning with pleasure toward one and then the other, while Nippy, their lively mixed-breed terrier, bounced and bounded around them.

She loved her husband, so she looked first at him, catching the smile that he reserved for her, expressed mostly in the play of expression around his eyes. That smile, part welcoming, part possessive, part questioning—where have you been? who have you seen? should I be worried?—was as familiar to her as his kiss, and the touch of his hands, and equally satisfying and frustrating.

"Selene, meet Griff, the ne'er-do-well of the family. Griff, you bastard, it's about time you said hello to my wife."

"Hello, Selene," he said.

She looked at him then, lifting her chin, for he was tall—taller than her husband—broader across the shoulders, and younger, his coloring lighter, his nose somewhat smaller, his mouth more generous.

"Hello, Griff," she said.

"All right," said Alex, "now that that's taken care of, let's get the hell out of the doorway and go inside. Griff just got here. He says he can't stay but I'm sure we can talk him into having a beer with us."

"Yes," she said. "Please stay."

He nodded, and they went inside. She rubbed her bare arms, feeling the chill of the house after the pleasant heat of the sun. Alex and Griff followed her through the living and dining rooms and into the kitchen. They watched her as she took beer out of the refrigerator and put the sweating cans on the table.

"Sit down, you two," she said. "I'll see what there is to go with this."

"That's okay," said Griff. "The beer's enough."

"Bullshit," said Alex. "We could both use some high-octane fuel. How about it, Sele?"

"There's ham—"

"There you are. Let's have a ham sandwich. How about it, Griff?"

"Sure. Thanks."

It was then that it began. It was, perhaps, five minutes in all. When she sat down at the table with them, having brought out bread and butter, ham, mustard, pickles, there was no more to be done. The stream of her existence had been diverted.

Alex was being "hearty," a condition she had come to recognize as rising out of anger, embarrassment, or uncertainty. In the present situation, it seemed to be a combination of those feelings. He hadn't seen Griff for years. She knew of him only as Alex's half-brother, some years younger than her husband, the one who let years pass between phone calls, the one who dropped him an occasional postcard from Oregon or Arkansas as he moved from one job to another, from one address to another.

"He's a bum," Alex had told her. "No home. No job to speak of. And what kind of a life? I can't even tell him we're married. I don't know where he is."

Now, he sat across from her, painting the soft white bread with mustard, layering it with paper-thin slices of ham, lifting it to his mouth, biting into it with the indifference of an appetite already satiated, smiling at them, patting Nippy's upturned head, nodding to Selene in polite acknowledgment of her presence and hospitality.

"Where are you staying?" said Alex. "Do you need a place to unroll your sleeping bag? You can bunk here, you know."

"Thanks. I'm at Sue Smoller's, for tonight at least."

"Sue Smoller? You mean Sue Jackson? From high school? Did she get divorced? Where does she live?"

"She has a place between here and Ryeburg. She's been divorced for years. Works as a hairdresser and at Spangleman's part-time, I think she said. We ran into each other."

"But we're your family, Griff," said Alex. "You should be with Mom, or here with us."

"I'm okay where I am," said Griff, with a sudden grim and unexpected combativeness.

"Hey," said Alex, lifting both hands in mock surrender. "Just want you to know you're welcome here."

Griff nodded and smiled, acknowledging them as family and rejecting Alex's invitation with the same polite indifference with which he ate at their table. Selene moved her uneaten sandwich to the exact center of the plate. Her stomach churned.

She realized that she was jealous of a woman she didn't know, because this woman was sheltering a man she had never seen until a few minutes ago.

"Well," said Alex, "Now that you're back with us, what are your plans?"

"Plans? I don't have plans. You should know that, Alex."

"Some things never change, right, pal?"

Selene cringed, smarting under the remark, as though the sarcasm had been directed at her. "That's *his* business, Alex," she said.

Griff looked at her then, as though she had just entered the room. She couldn't quite meet his eyes, although she saw that they were blue and direct, with a slight squint.

"So it is," said Alex. He grinned. "I'm finding it harder and harder to argue with my wife. She's always so damned—right."

"Since when does that count?" said Griff.

They laughed, self-consciously. Alex said, "How long has it been, Griff? Six years? More?"

"Yeah. About."

"Are you staying for a while this time?"

"Yeah. Probably."

There was a brief silence; then Alex said, with sudden warmth, "I'm glad you're here, Griff."

The three of them seemed to relax then, as if by permission. Selene smiled at Alex, and put her hand over his. "Yes," she said. "We're both glad you're here."

Having met the challenge of a strained first quarter of an hour, they slid through the next three quarters with relative ease. Griff talked a little about his travels—the southwestern states, then Alaska, Wyoming, Montana—always within the borders of the country—doing outdoor work, construction, manual labor, odd jobs whenever, wherever, he could get them—he was good with his hands; he could ride a horse. Alex urged him on. Selene recovered her composure enough to make a few polite comments while she studied him.

Why the brother? she asked herself. *They share the same last name; they emerged, bloody and enraged, from the same womb. There's something similar in the stacking up of the features, the way the ears fit snugly against the head; but how at odds they are, otherwise. Alex so solid, so grounded, so cocksure of himself; this other one so tentative, so unsettled, perched on his chair as though waiting for, expecting, an alarm—a signal to flap his wings noisily, heavy and awkward as he lifts himself up and flies away.*

She acknowledged that she didn't want him to leave. She said, apropos to nothing, "Won't you stay here with us, Griff?" Hearing the plea in her voice, she added a more formal, "You'd be more than welcome."

Again, he looked directly at her.

"Thanks," he said. "Maybe later."

Seeing only the glaze of courtesy on her face, Alex said, "Whenever you're ready, Griff."

*   *   *

Alex and Selene had been married for five years, after a love affair—culminating in a divorce from his first wife, Carolyn— that had lasted almost as long as their marriage. Selene was 33 years old; her husband, 45. Alex was Selene's lover, her advisor, her companion. She considered their relationship, which had survived his divorce and the upheaval surrounding it, solid, comfortable—softened by wear.

She loved her husband, and tolerated his quirks. His aversion to anything cheap, and his contradictory compulsion to pick up anything on sale. His outrageous bouts of jealousy. His mania for organization. His joyful, antic sense of humor. The sentimentality he was so careful to hide, and she was so quick to ferret out.

"I'm crazy about you, Sele," Alex called out from the shower that evening, "but what did you do with my robe?"

Selene was in bed. She turned her head toward the bathroom that adjoined their bedroom.

"You mean the one you left on the bedroom floor?"

"You know I only have one robe."

"Well, then, Nippy scrunched it up and made a nest for himself with it."

"You mean Nippy's sleeping on my robe?"

"Very contentedly."

"Will you bring it to me, please?"

"I would have to disturb Nippy."

"If you don't, you'll disturb me."

"I can live with that."

"Nippy?" Alex said. "Here, boy."

Nippy sighed and burrowed into the robe. Smooth-coated, compact, mostly white, with black V-shaped ears folded delicately over the ear canal, a black patch around his left eye, and a slightly curled tail that pointed to a black patch on his back, Nippy's Jack Russell ancestry dominated the softer, milder terrier traits on his family tree. Selene and Alex had adopted him as a ten-weeks-old puppy, shortly after they married.

There was a brief silence, punctuated by the sound of dripping water.

"Selene? Here, girl."

"That's not funny."

"There's not even a dry washcloth in here."

"Oh, all right."

Reluctantly, Selene got up from the bed, grabbed a towel from a basket of clean laundry, tossed it to Alex from the doorway.

"Ah. Better," he said, rubbing his face and hair with the towel, then working down from there.

"You're welcome."

"Did I ever tell you you're a pain in the ass?"

"You know I'm more than you deserve," she said, leaning against the doorway, away from the heat and steam. She lifted a narrow strap of her shortie nightgown—black, splashed with pink roses—and flipped it off her shoulder.

He pushed her against the doorjamb. "Do me, woman." He turned around, and she rubbed his back with the towel.

"A little lower. To the right. Yeah, baby, right there."

"You want more? Come to bed," she said, wrapping the towel around his shoulders.

Alex lay down beside her on the bed. She positioned herself against him, her head on his shoulder, his arm around her, his fingers lightly cupping her left breast.

"Do I love you," he said softly.

"Mmm."

They turned toward each other then and slowly, with pleasure and the mounting desire that had sustained their relationship for almost a decade, they made love. It was only some time later, when they lay in the same position again, her head on his shoulder, his arm around her, that Selene permitted herself to think about Griff.

"Tell me about Griff," she said, moving his name around on her tongue, liking the taste of it.

She felt no guilt in speaking to her husband of this other man, this stranger, who had entered her life unexpectedly, with immediate ascendancy.

"Yes. Griff," said Alex. "Back in our lives."

"Back in your life. New in my life."

"The bastard."

"You said that before. Is he?"

"Maybe I am. We're too unlike to be Price brothers."

"You don't look alike."

"Superficially, no. But we're both ruggedly handsome, devastatingly attractive to the opposite sex."

"You're much darker."

"I cull most of my genes from the Price lineage. Griff, on the other hand, favors the maternal side of the family."

"The Cavillons."

"Yes."

"He's very quiet."

"Thoughtful, I would say. Like the mother."

"Why do you always say, 'the mother'? Nan is your mother too."

"She gave birth to me. Otherwise—" He took a breath. "My dear, you know my family history as well as I do."

"I do, but—"

"She favored him."

"Griff?"

"Yes."

She savored this. It tasted good, this possibility. She wanted to distance the brothers, set them apart from each other, make Griff the favored child, give him another father, another lineage. Howard, Alex's father, had died before Selene and Alex met.

"Why are you saying this? Where is it coming from?"

"Seeing Griff, I guess. Christ, I don't know. I haven't even thought about this since—"

"Since?"

"Well, since Griff left the last time and Mom got so—"

"You never said—"

"She got all quiet. Withdrawn. She was like that for months. Then she—"

"She's very proud of you."

"Her eyes always follow Griff, as though she's afraid he'll disappear. And then he does. You'll see."

Selene pushed herself against the warmth of her husband, fitting him to her as they lulled themselves to sleep with the sound of their voices. On the floor near the foot of the bed she heard Nippy—still nested in Alex's robe—sigh and turn in his sleep.

She murmured, "I can't imagine Nan—"

"You know that photograph of her? The one that's in the study?"

"Yes, of course. It's lovely. She's lovely."

"I think he was with her then."

"Who?"

"The other man. The one that Griff comes from."

CHAPTER 2

The next morning, after Alex left, Selene sat at her dressing table and studied herself in the mirror. She lifted her hair away from her face, traced her cheekbones and jaw line with her fingers, as though she were a stranger to herself.

"This is me," she said, quietly but out loud. "This is what I have to give you."

When she was born, her mother had looked at her pink face and transparent silvery hair and said to her father, "Let's call her Selene, our little moon child. She'll watch over us in our evening hours." They had reminded her of this, fondly, as she was growing up. But she had been conceived late in their lives; they didn't live long enough for Selene to fulfill their wishful plan. Irene and Thomas Fugate had slipped away, dying within a few months of each other, and Selene was left with an obligation she could neither forget nor fulfill. She had kept the house, however, renting it out because letting go of the house would be like letting go of her parents, her childhood.

After their marriage, Selene and Alex had moved into her parents' house. Now, both she and Alex watched over her parents' furnace, their lawn, their gutter spouts.

Her pink face had turned pale; her blue-black eyes had turned gray; her hair had grown out white blond and then, over the years, turned to ash blond. She smoothed her hair away

11

from her face, gathering it at the nape of her neck so that she could study her face—the face that Griff had looked at only yesterday. Did he admire this face, as his brother Alex admired it? Did he at least want to see it again as she wanted—longed—to see *his* face?

The face that looked back at her was clean, creamed, without makeup, pleasing to look at, as a well composed but not dramatic watercolor is pleasing to the eye. The beauty was not in any individual feature but in the blend of light and color in the whole. Would that be enough for Griff, who had already chosen, at least temporarily, the face and body of another woman?

Selene applied makeup quickly but with the sure strokes of a practiced hand, then smiled at the effect. "Yes," she said in a whisper, "he'll want to see me again. He'll want to know something about the woman Alex takes to bed every night." She fluffed out her hair so that it framed her face, sprayed a light musk scent beneath her ears and at her wrists, stood up. "He'll want me," she said to her image.

Downstairs, in the kitchen, still fragrant from the toast and coffee Alex had prepared earlier, Selene poured coffee into a mug, slid bread into the toaster, and urged Nippy outside for a final inspection of the fresh morning scents. By 8:15, her Honda was propelling her toward the freeway, following the route her husband had taken an hour earlier—he to make executive decisions, to dominate, to assert his will, at Stampler Communications—she to look at manuscripts and manipulate words on paper at Cotter Publishing.

How unlike they are, she thought, *Alex and Griff*. Griff did not dominate—he eluded. He was eluding her at this moment, even as she tried to bring up his image and look at it, touch it. *I must see him again*, she thought, as she launched herself onto the freeway.

Twenty minutes later, she was off the freeway and turning into the Cotter Publishing parking lot. She could scarcely remember the commute, so vivid had been her thoughts of Griff. She slid smoothly into her parking space, waved at the parking attendant, and walked quickly to the Cotter Building, her heels clicking rhythmically on the pavement, the sun warming her, a light breeze lifting her hair away from her face. She pushed through the revolving door, nodded to the security guard, then strode to the elevator, checking her watch.

On the fourth floor, she greeted her coworkers, thinking, *How different I am this morning. I am a different person. Over the weekend–just since yesterday–I have become the lover–in effect, if not yet in fact–of Griff, my husband's half brother. And I'm not sorry; I'm not ashamed; I'm full up with this feeling. It's overflowing; it's splashing onto the micro-tufted green carpeting of Cotter Publishing; it's bouncing off the faces of the people I'm looking at, smiling at, as I toss out the patter that opens the day. "Goomorning." "Howareya." "Howasyurweekend?" "Beatifuday." They're smiling back at me, following me with their eyes, as they try to pin down the change in Selene Price, the alteration that is more than a weekend of rest and sex with her husband; that is, in fact, a subtle sea change, another woman walking past them–cocky, self-assured–in the familiar pinstriped pant suit, pink ruffled shirt, small silver earrings swinging from pierced ears, a lift to the chin that wasn't there on Friday. Must have been really good sex, they're saying to themselves.*

As she sat down in her cubicle, as she turned on the computer, as she checked the screen for email messages and appointment reminders, what she wanted, what she looked forward to, was the end of the day, the ride home, that little oasis of time in which she could think about Griff, visualize him, be with him in her mind, in her nerve ends.

* * *

Evening. Alex in the kitchen, astride the dinner hour, constructing a meat sauce with his usual assurance, while Selene acts as *sous chef*, chopping onions, tearing lettuce leaves, dropping bits of tomato, like communion wafers, into Nippy's upturned mouth.

"He's a dog. He needs meat," says Alex, rolling a small ball of ground chuck, tossing it at him. Nippy deftly catches it, swallows it, then looks up at Selene. She places another thin edge of tomato in his mouth. His teeth gently graze her fingers.

"He needs his veggies," she says.

She is content. She is with her husband, who is loving, and comfortable, and a good cook. Images of Griff—images she called up and nourished as she drove home from work—float just beneath the surface, tickling her now and then, but she pushes them away. They are for later. She wants to be with Alex, whose eyes glance over her with relish. Who makes her laugh.

"Where did you get that shirt?" he says.

"It's yours."

"I know. I've been looking for it."

"Would you like it back?"

She opens the shirt, a soft and faded plaid flannel, flashes her bare breasts.

"Shameless hussy," he says, pulling her up against him. She likes the smell of him, the gritty feel of his cheek against hers.

"You need a shave," she says.

"I always need a shave." He rubs his face against hers. "My five o'clock shadow comes in around noon." He pulls away to look at her, his dark eyes close to hers. She sees herself reflected in them, twin images, miniscule.

He says, dramatically, "Kiss me, you fool."

She kisses him. They stand close together, her bare breasts pressing against his chest until the meat sauce bubbles and hisses. He releases her to turn toward the stove. She buttons her

THE SECOND MRS. PRICE

shirt, pushes up the sleeves, prepares a vinaigrette dressing for the salad.

The phone rings. "Don't answer it," says Alex. "It's a solicitation." It rings again. He picks up the cordless handset, turning his back to her.

"Hullo? Yes? No. No, I can't. I can't talk now. How many times have I asked you not to call me at home. What? No. I'm sorry, but it's out of the question. What's that? Well, all right. I'll see." He turns around and hands the phone to Selene. "It's for you," he says, and goes back to his sauce.

"Hello? Selene?" The voice in the phone is tolerant, amused.

"Hi, Nan. Your son is out of control. I think he's high."

"Can you have dinner with us on Saturday? Sort of a welcome home for Griff. Just us. Dad and Griff and me. Are you free?"

"Yes," she says, turning away from Alex to hide her blush of delight. "Yes, of course. Seven? Yes. We'll be there. Thanks, Nan."

She sets the phone in its cradle on the wall, pulling the flannel shirt close to her and shivering, though it's warm in the kitchen. She looks at Alex, who is tasting the sauce and smacking his lips in satisfaction. She looks down at Nippy, whose tail waves back and forth; then, uncertain of her expression, the tail pauses, mid-wave.

"Good dog," she says, pitching her voice high. Nippy's tail dances, pulling his hindquarters rhythmically back and forth.

Alex mimics Nippy's dancing rear. Selene uses a dishtowel to swat him as he raises a wooden spoon dripping with sauce to his mouth.

"Bad dog," she says, close to Alex's ear, her voice a deep growl.

*　*　*

Nan opens the door. Smiling, gesturing with her hands, she invites Selene and Alex inside.

"Come in. Come in. How good it is to see you both. Griff is here. We're all here. Just waiting for you. Come in. Selene, you look lovely."

Nan is elegant in a favorite outfit—long black hostess skirt and white silk shirt, open at the throat. Her graying blond hair is pulled back; onyx earrings in a silver filigree setting dangle from her ears. Her voice is soft, eager, pleasant to the ear, seldom raised.

She hugs Selene, then turns to her son. "Hello, my dear," she says, putting her hands on his face, drawing him down to her so she can kiss his cheek. "How are you?"

"Hello, you gorgeous creature, you."

Alex gives her a bear hug, releases her. She laughs up at him, shaking her head. She has collected compliments all her life, but she never tires of them.

"Come along, you two," she says, leading them into the large, comfortable living room, gracefully modernized but still retaining vestiges of its mid-century colonial style. "Here's Griff. Dad, here's Selene, your favorite granddaughter-in-law."

"Not to mention your *only* granddaughter-in-law," says Selene, walking up to the old man as he slowly rises from his chair.

Bernard Cavillon is in his late 80s, moderately tall, gray, slightly stooped, with the same elegance—impressive but not imposing—as his daughter. He wears an old maroon dinner jacket with flair.

Griff stands up. Selene sees him but doesn't look directly at him.

Alex grasps Griff's hand, clasping his elbow in a grip that is friendly but keeps him at arm's length. He turns to the old man. "Hi, Gramps, you old fart."

Bernard laughs. "How you been, sport?"

Selene turns to Griff, says, "Hello again," holds out her hand. He takes it. She feels the momentary pressure of his grip before he sets her free. They don't quite look at each other. Selene breathes out, cradling her right hand with her left, wanting to hold onto the warmth of him.

Nan pours wine, refills glasses, dribbles the conversational ball while they stumble through the first awkward minutes. They are family, normally comfortable with each other, but tonight they are uneasy, apprehensive. Griff sits among them, appropriately dressed but informal in dark pants and blue, long-sleeved shirt open at the collar. His large presence disturbs them, as it did Alex when Griff was in their home the Sunday before. Griff is silent, except to answer direct questions. He is courteous, without making the slightest effort to put himself forward or lead the conversation.

"So," says Alex to Griff, "how's it going? Are you settling in okay?"

"Oh, yeah."

"There's always room for you here, you know," says Nan.

"I know, Mom."

"You can have my suite, if you want it," says Bernard.

Griff laughs. "Your *suite*?"

"Privacy. Picture window. Garden view. Luxury under the eaves."

"In other words, your attic apartment."

Bernard huffs in mock insult, then laughs with the others.

"That's okay, Gramps. I'm comfortable where I am."

"How is Sue?" says Selene, determined to mention her by name.

"She's fine."

There's a silence, then everyone—except Griff—tosses out a conversational ball, which everyone—except Griff—attempts to answer.

They patch through, waiting for Nan, who has left the room, to call them to dinner. When she does, they stand up, welcoming the invitation to move and regroup, to take their places at the dining room table, fragrant with food, Nan's food, every glass and spoon carefully arranged, every dish flavored with Nan's care and attention.

Bernard sits at the head of the table, where the roast resides supreme, sharpening the carving knife with a sharpening sword that has whispered the beginning of a special meal for as long as those present can remember. Even Selene remembers her first family meal here, the same knife sliding rhythmically against the sword—*whoosh* along one side; *whoosh* against the other.

They murmur their appreciation of the carefully chosen red and white wines; the fragrant pork loin roast with its accompaniment of thick brown gravy; red potatoes garnished with parsley; buttered green beans; French bread warm and inviting in a linen-lined wicker basket.

"Fit for a king," says Bernard, looking down the table as he slides the knife end against the sword. *Whoosh. Whoosh.*

"Not if we wait much longer," says Nan.

"C'mon, old man," says Alex. "Let's not put too fine an edge on it, as they say. Carve the beast!"

They laugh, still self-conscious, as Bernard wipes the blade, steadies the roast with a long-pronged fork, then slices into it. The juice bubbles out, seeps down onto the platter, as he carves with expert strokes. Selene looks across the table at Griff. He is studying the fork in his hand, as if it is an object new to him. He turns it over, studies it, turns it over again. Then, he looks up, at her, his glance bouncing off her like an electric shock. His face is neutral, expressionless. He turns to Bernard, who is handing him a platter of meat. He passes the platter to Nan, who takes a slice and hands it to Alex. The air is thick with the buzz of polite conversation, the aroma of food. Selene shivers as Alex hands her the meat platter.

"You doin' okay, sweetheart?" he says to her.

"Better than okay," she says, automatically.

"Griff," says Alex, "hand around the potatoes. Those redskins look tempting."

Griff hands the serving bowl to Nan, refusing to take any food before she does. She nods, smiles at him, a loving smile without the amused tolerance she reserves for Alex. She moves the hot dishes around the table; when they return to Griff, he helps himself.

When all the food has been passed around, Alex lifts his glass of wine, looking directly at Griff. "Good to have you back in the fold," he says. Griff nods his thanks. They all sip at the wine, murmuring, "Hear, hear."

"Welcome back, my dear," says Nan.

Selene looks at Griff over the rim of her wine glass. He seems mildly embarrassed, as though he has stumbled into the wrong house, sat down with strangers. He eats with gusto, though, catching Nan's eye, so that she nods, her cheeks coloring faintly.

They dispatch the first round of food, simultaneously discussing the weather and touching on the political climate. They agree that they have been anointed with an unusually mild and prolonged spring, and clamorously disagree with each other on everything else—including Bill Clinton's impeachment acquittal and Monica Lewinsky's culpability—still fresh in everyone's mind, although supposedly resolved several months earlier.

Alex defends Clinton, insisting the whole affair was "extraneous" to the business at hand, which is running the country.

"It *is* possible to separate the political from the personal," Alex says.

"Not in this case," says Nan.

"It was not an impeachable offense," responds Alex.

"He lied under oath," Nan counters. "He's our president, and he lied under oath."

Alex sighed. "I say we put the whole thing aside and get on with politics as usual."

"I think that *was* politics as usual," says Selene.

"Hear, hear," says Bernard.

"Maybe he did skirt around the truth a little," Alex concedes, winking at his own pun. "But he was telling the truth according to his lights."

"Alex, when did you become a flaming liberal?" says Bernard. "Pass me that platter. What you need is a little more meat and a lot less attitude."

"It takes an arch conservative to call me that," says Alex, handing the platter to Selene, who gives it to Bernard. "Most of my friends accuse me of being too middle-of-the-road."

"If you were aboard ship, you'd be sinking on the port side," says Bernard, slicing into the roast. "Who's ready for more?"

Everyone accepts another slice of meat, exclaiming again over the meal, allowing the conversation to drift away from politics.

"So how's the big executive?" says Bernard, heaping his plate as the serving bowls move around the table once again. "You running the company yet?"

"Not yet, Gramps," says Alex. "Probably not ever."

Nan turns to Griff. She says, confidingly, "Alex is a senior executive vice president now."

Griff looks at her for a moment, smiling as though at a private joke, then says to Alex, "And what does a senior executive vice president do?"

Alex glances up from his food, quickly, as if to gauge the question, and the questioner, then calmly continues to chew his food, as if considering his answer.

"It's not that incomprehensible," he says, "even for the likes of you and Bernard. An executive is just a decision-maker. The higher you move in the ranks, the bigger the decisions."

"But bigger decisions are harder to make," says Nan.

"I don't know that they are," says Alex. "There's not much difference between making big decisions and making small decisions. It's the same process. It's just that there are more consequences when you make big decisions—broader consequences. That's the hard part."

"That's right, my boy," says Bernard, complacently. "When you get to be president and chief executive of this great country of ours, the consequences can be mighty earth shattering."

Everyone murmurs agreement; then, Selene says, "Here I was, so impressed with my husband, and now I find out he's just worked out a formula for making a living."

"Not so simple, I'm sure," says Nan.

"Don't hold back, Alex," says Bernard. "There's more to that job than you're letting on."

"You're right, all of you," says Alex. "There's a formula, of sorts. Actually, an executive has to do two things: make decisions; then persuade or con or bully everybody into accepting his—or her—authority. Sometimes the persuasion part is more important than the decision making."

"That's it?" says Griff, as though challenging him.

"You make it sound so easy," says Nan.

"It's not that hard, once you have your moves down." Alex frowns in concentration. "You need to know the lexicon. The business-speak. You need to exude confidence like a sweat. You need to drip with it. Otherwise, the people you're working with and for won't buy into your act."

"It makes me tired just to think of it," says Nan.

"You nailed it, Mom," says Alex, lightly. He adds, his voice serious, thoughtful, "That's the thing about it. It takes so much out of you. The responsibility, the crises, the finanical reports, the travel, the planning." He pauses. "In fact, it takes just about everything you've got. It's like going into battle every day and coming out exhausted, maybe even wounded."

Selene giggles. "I know. I've seen the wounds."

They laugh. Alex presses her hand. "This is my healer," he says. "I come home to her warm tent and loving arms. Before I know it, I'm good as new."

Selene is about to respond that the tent is sometimes cold because she's out working herself, when Alex turns to Griff, saying, abruptly, "So, what about you, Griff? What have you been doing?"

Griff looks at him for a few moments before answering. Then he says, "Slinging burgers. Delivering pizzas. Pumping gas. Driving a truck. Loading and unloading. Moving furniture around the country. Hauling trash out of companies like yours. Pretty much anything to make a buck, so I can grab a little time for myself, to do whatever the hell I want to do."

Alex says, "Don't you have any desire to—to—"

Griff says, "No."

There's a silence, prolonged, uncomfortable. Then, once again, Selene giggles. Nan looks at her fondly, then laughs. Bernard laughs at the two of them, then Alex laughs.

Griff shakes his head, evidently amused.

*　*　*

Later, over coffee in the living room, Selene indulges in the urge she has had all evening—the urge to look at Griff, to study him. He has said so little all evening that she has had little opportunity to look at him without being obvious. But she has chosen her seat deliberately, so that he is in her line of vision as she chats easily with Bernard and Nan.

Just once, under cover of laughter and a hearty exchange of insults between Bernard and Alex, Griff turns to her.

"What's *your* work?" he says.

It is the first time he has questioned her, singled her out. She speaks quickly, her words tripping over each other as she tries to explain herself to him, to compress into a few words her work, what she has so recently done to change her life, how she and Alex differ in their views.

"I'm an editor. I work for a publishing house in Ryeburg. But lately I've been working at home a lot. One of those flex-time deals. It's my parents' home. Was. Ours now, of course. It's been my home all of my life. I'm comfortable there. More so than in an office. In a corporate environment, that is. Surrounded by office politics. I don't like the going-into-battle part."

He listens to her, his expression polite, his eyes—so intensely blue—distant. Then he nods and turns back to Nan, who sits next to him on the couch. Nan leans toward him, takes his arm, hugging him to her before she releases him. She reaches up, grazing his face with her hand, then turns again to Alex and Bernard. Selene watches this, envying their ease with each other, longing to draw him close, to touch his face.

If he is aware of her silent watchfulness, he makes no sign of it. He is attentive to Nan; he grins now and then at Bernard who, full of wine and good food, is relaxed, talkative; he listens soberly to Alex, as if trying to remember who he is. Now and then, he shakes his head in disagreement, or looks as though he'd like to make a comment, but mostly the conversation moves along without him, or draws him in only to answer such questions as, "Isn't that right, my dear?" or "I've got his number, right, my boy?" Griff has only to nod his agreement.

The phone rings. Nan leaves the room to answer it. She comes back, hesitating in the doorway, looking at Griff.

"It's Sue," she says.

Griff gets up, his face flushing as if in anger, or embarrassment, before he turns away from them, saying to Nan, "Okay. Thanks."

Only Nan and Selene see his reaction. After a pause, Alex and Bernard return to their discussion. Griff comes back into the room a few minutes later, mumbles, "Sorry." He sits down, busying himself with pouring coffee from the thermal carafe.

Selene watches his hands as he pours and stirs. Heavy on the cream. Two teaspoons of sugar. Big hands, used to hard work, the hairs on the back golden, catching the light, the nails clipped short, very white, as though scrubbed. She allows herself to imagine bringing those hands to her lips, momentarily, then guiding them down over her body ...

She wonders if Sue Smoller will do that tonight, when he returns to her. *Is she so hungry for him she has to call him back to her, hurry him home to her warm bed?*

Nan asks her something. Selene starts.

"Sorry, Nan, I was drifting," she says.

* * *

The evening is drawing to a close. Bernard is winding down. Alex is talking quietly with Nan and Selene, sometimes drawing Griff in, sometimes granting him his long silences. Selene finds his silence more tolerable than does Alex—almost comfortable. It is a listening, attentive silence, with no sullenness. What Alex finds irritating in his wordless attention, Selene finds spacious, promising.

"We're keeping Gramps up," says Alex, standing up. "We'd better be on our way."

24

"Wha—? No. No. Not at all," says Bernard, rousing himself. "It's all that good food and wine. Just nodded off for a minute. Stay, you two. Stay. The night is young."

"And you're so beautiful," says Alex, cuffing him. "Go to bed, Gramps. We know you get up with the birds."

"I do. Why would anybody stay in bed on a spring morning, with the birds singing and the air like a little bit of heaven?"

"Enjoy it, old man," says Alex. "It's the only bit of heaven you're going to get."

They all get up, smoothing their clothes, flicking away stray crumbs from Nan's rich dessert cake, Alex teasing, Bernard gruff, sentimental, hugging Nan and Selene to him, one on each arm, calling them, "My beautiful girls."

Griff stands a little apart from them, somewhat awkwardly, his hands in his pockets. Then Bernard releases Nan and Selene so that he can stand directly in front of Griff, grasping his upper arms.

"Griff, my boy, my grandson, you make our family circle complete. Welcome back."

For a moment, Griff's eyes well up. Then he squints, blinks, returns Bernard's grasp.

"Thanks," he says. "I missed you, Gramps."

Nan and Bernard stand in the doorway as they walk out together—Selene, Alex, Griff—into night air that is so soft and mellow they catch their breath, then inhale deeply. Selene watches Griff as he stands at the foot of the front steps, looking up at the new moon in a clear sky, then looking around at the trees, rustling in their sleep. He glances at her for a moment, then shrugs his shoulders, as if apologetically.

"G'night," he says.

"Night," says Selene.

He turns away, walking toward the pickup truck parked down the street.

"Don't be a stranger," Alex calls after him.

Without looking back, Griff raises an arm and waves.

Alex loops his arm around Selene, drawing her to him.

"Can't fathom the guy," he says, as Griff disappears into the truck, which starts up with a heavy, choking gasp. Then it settles into gear and purrs. The truck pulls away.

Selene and Alex wave at Nan and Bernard, who are still standing in the doorway. Then they climb into Alex's dark blue Buick sedan.

"Good time?" he says, pulling away from the curb, squeezing her knee.

"Good time," she echoes, thinking of Griff as he walked across the dewy lawn, moving comfortably in his large, loose-limbed frame, his arm raised in a gesture at once friendly and dismissive. Not bothering to look back at them.

CHAPTER 3

Selene usually looks forward to Sunday morning with her husband. It's a quiet time, uninterrupted by phone calls, with no set schedule to impede its progress from early-morning lovemaking to coffee and newspapers, followed by a late, leisurely, breakfast. This Sunday, however, Selene is preoccupied, responding to Alex somewhat mechanically as they make love, wanting to be downstairs, behind a newspaper, steam from her mug of coffee rising into her nostrils, her thoughts focused on last evening—Griff's raspy voice, the touch of his big rough hand as it held hers, so briefly, at the beginning of the evening.

I love his hands, she thinks. *They are made to touch, to touch me, to touch me all over.*

She wants to feed on the minutiae her mind calls up—as though she were a fish in a tank, gulping morsels of food as they drift down from the surface.

"You okay?" says Alex as they emerge from the shower, a ritual of mutual soaping and scrubbing they indulge in only on Sunday morning, after they've made love.

"Yes, of course. Why?" says Selene, rubbing her hair with a thick towel, glancing at Alex as he pulls on shorts, undershirt, his thick white terry cloth robe.

"You seem—preoccupied."

She turns away from him to the high chest of drawers, pulls out a sports bra, skimpy panties, clean sweats.

"I'm just fine," she says, damning his perception. "Let's go down and have some coffee."

Downstairs, behind the swinging door that opens to the kitchen, Nippy rises from his wicker bed, stretches luxuriously in a perfect downward dog pose, then greets them with high-pitched whimpers and gyrating hindquarters. Alex opens the back door for Nippy, then steps outside to the fenced yard, radiant with sunshine, while Selene heats the water and grinds the coffee beans.

By the time man and dog reenter the house, the kitchen is fragrant with the aroma of coffee, the coffee pot is on a tray, together with mugs, sugar and cream. Nippy's food is in his bowl, where he pounces on it. Selene props open the swinging door, Alex carries the tray, and they proceed to the living room. Alex brings in *The New York Times* and the local paper from the front porch. They settle down to read, sip coffee, nudge each other with commentary and occasional asides—Alex in the easy chair, Selene curled up on the couch.

"Anything special you'd like to do today?"

"I'd like not to move."

"That can be arranged. Tired, are you?"

Selene yawns. "No. Just lazy."

"I'll see to it that your laziness is indulged to the fullest."

"Thanks."

"Think nothing of it."

Silence. The crackling of newspapers. An occasional mutter from Alex as he scans the news. A sigh from Selene. A series of crunching sounds as Nippy navigates his way through the strewn papers, then drops down on the comics, near Alex.

Selene looks up from the local real estate section.

"What do you suppose our house is worth?"

"Right now, or after we do all the fixing up we keep meaning to do?"

"I mean right now, this minute."

"Itching to move, are you?"

"No—but we've never even looked around. We've always lived here. *I've* always lived here, except when I had renters."

"You've been lucky."

Selene persists.

"But what about you? Wouldn't you like to live in a super-modern tri-level with decks, a pool, landscaping? I mean, just for a change?"

"Sounds confusing, all those levels and decks. What's wrong with an upstairs and a downstairs?"

"Nothing, I guess."

"Then let's stay on here for now."

Alex refolds the news section and places it, tent-like, over Nippy, who exhales contentedly through his nostrils, rippling the sides of the tent. Selene throws the real estate section on the floor, reaches for *The New York Times Book Review*. Alex scans the local entertainment, turning the crisp pages decisively.

"In the mood for a movie?" says Alex.

"What's on?"

"Not much."

"Then I guess I'm not in the mood."

Long silence. Sipping of coffee. Selene immerses herself in the reviews, thinking of Griff casually rolling up his sleeves late in the evening, the way the light from a nearby lamp caught the hairs on his forearms, turning them golden. Alex systematically rifles through the newspapers. Nippy snores softly inside his tent.

"You're preoccupied," Alex says at last.

"I am," says Selene; then, looking up, "I am?"

"Nippy's more company than you are."

Hearing his name, Nippy stops snoring.

"I'm not feeling well, I guess."

"Tell me," he says, throwing the newspaper aside, leaning forward.

"I don't know. A headache. PMS. General fatigue. Nothing serious."

"Tell me," he says.

Nippy crawls out from beneath his tent, stretches, sits, alert, his head to one side.

"There's nothing to—"

"Tell me."

Selene closes the *Book Review* on her lap. She has Alex's full attention, in a way she doesn't when they are going about the routine of their life together. His look is loving, but severe—drawing her in, yet distancing her.

She is afraid of that look, but she has been expecting it.

"It's—just my job," she says, plunging into a diversionary tactic.

Alex visibly relaxes. He leans back in his chair, places his left ankle on his right knee, his well-shaped bare foot dangling. He nods his head. He glances around the room as he considers this. Then he says, "What about your job?"

Now, in turn, Selene looks around the room, picking out familiar objects—her parents' vintage upholstered armchair, its ultra-modern side table and lamp, the intricately framed mirror over the fireplace.

She has never underestimated Alex's intelligence. He is quick, perceptive, disarmingly sympathetic, skilled at drawing people out—able to turn an interview or a performance review into a therapy session. Selene knows that people confide in him, on and off the job, because he invites their confidence, while keeping to himself the harsh cynicism of his evaluation, his judgment. All they see and hear is what Alex wants them to see and hear: the understanding in his eyes; the faint, encouraging nod of the head; the compassion in his voice. Knowing this, she's wary. She loves to confide in Alex, as does almost everyone, but she knows the invitation is two-edged.

Alex, in his wisdom, has told her more than once that the best lie is a half truth, so she says, hastily pulling her thoughts together, "I'm—thinking of quitting."

"Oh?"

Alex does not look surprised, although Selene knows he is. She is surprised herself, having given little conscious consideration to the matter until this moment.

"Yes," she says, rushing forward. "I've thought of it a lot. I'd like to quit. Well, not quit exactly. I'd like not to go to work every day."

"In that you are not unique," says Alex, dryly.

"I mean," she says, taking a breath, "I'd like to work—on my own."

Here, she thinks, *where I'm close to Griff, available to him, where I can wait for him.*

"You already work on your own," says Alex.

He is studying her—her face, her gestures, her body language. Assessing her.

"Yes, of course I do, but it's not the same. I'm expected to be at work most of the time. For meetings and assignments. Most of the time, I'm sitting at my desk, in my cubicle, doing my thing from nine to five."

"And what, sweetheart, would you like to be doing? And where would you like to be doing it?"

Unbidden, the answers come to her. *I'd like to be lying on the bed upstairs, where you and I made love this morning, my legs wrapped around Griff, looking up at the expression on his face while he fucks me.*

"What I'm thinking of doing," she says to Alex, forcing herself to be calm, reasonable, "is quitting my job as editor and working for Cotter on a contract basis. Book by book. I can do most of the research and writing here. Meet with the managing editors periodically—"

"Sounds like a plan," Alex says, his voice carefully nonchalant. "Will it be enough for you?"

"What do you mean, 'enough'?" Selene senses that he is looking behind her words for a motive. "It's not that much different from what I'm doing now."

"But you'll be doing it here. Alone. You've never worked that way."

"But I've always wanted to," she says, pumping enthusiasm into her voice. "I've worked at Cotter Publishing for years. It's the only real job I've ever had. I finally got myself to where I want to be—an editor. What I don't want is what surrounds the job. Robin is an okay manager, but she's so unsure of herself and her territory. She thinks I'm out to get her, or her job. You know I'm not."

She and Alex exchange war stories in the evening, after work. Alex knows her coworkers almost as well as he knows his own, even though he hasn't met many of them.

"And Jeff—well—he's threatening to retire early, or leave the company. Riley will probably step up and—you know we don't get along."

At one time, Riley had been the subject of many evening discussions, as he had pursued Selene with unrelenting persistence. She had considered bringing a suit against him.

"Men are going to make moves on you wherever you go," says Alex. "I'll continue to ward them off with a baseball bat."

Selene laughs, trying to relax into his mood.

"Thanks, love, but you know what I'm saying. It's all politics—and I can't handle it the way you do. I try to avoid it, but it's always there, all around me, like—like air pollution."

"An interesting analogy," Alex says.

He gets up from his chair, stepping around the strewn papers and over Nippy, who has been listening with great care, his head tilting, his drooping V-shaped ears moving back and forth delicately, as he absorbs each intonation. As soon as Alex sits down close to Selene and wraps an arm around her, Nippy jumps up on the couch, squeezing between them. They fuss over him until he settles down, sighing with contentment.

"I know you thrive on that sort of thing," Selene continues, "but I'm not good at it, or comfortable with it. I just want to do—what I do."

"Then do it," says Alex. "I'll fight the wars while you stay here in the castle, weaving books and warding off suitors until your man returns."

* * *

Nan tapped on Bernard's door.

"Good morning, Dad," she said.

"Come in. Come in," Bernard called out.

Bernard lived on the third floor of Nan's house, in a roomy loft that she and Howard used to rent out to college students and itinerant instructors. It consisted of a living area with a kitchen at the far end, a bedroom, a bathroom. Bernard had always liked the sunny, open space. He had moved in several years ago. He had been a widower for some time, and Nan persuaded him to sell his house. At his insistence, she accepted a nominal rent from him.

Nan worried about the climb to the third floor, and the time he spent alone there. But she understood how important the illusion of independence was to him. She accepted that this would be the arrangement until such time as his knees, and his strength, gave out.

"Another beautiful day," she said, kissing the soft, sagging skin of his cheek, accepting the mug of coffee he poured and held out to her. "Shall we go downstairs and sit outside?"

"In a minute," he said, sitting down in his armchair, inviting her with a motion of his hand to sit across from him. "The sun feels good here."

The living area, which faced east, was dominated by a leaded glass window arching toward the roof and overlooking the back yard. Bernard rested his head against the back of the chair, sighing contentedly as the sun warmed his face and arms.

Nan sat down in the rocker facing him. She had learned to accept him as he was, to cope with or overlook his many foibles—especially since he'd come to live with her. She had decided to enjoy, to appreciate, her father's company while she could. When the stairs became too much of a burden for him, he might have to move downstairs—or he might have to leave her, much as she wanted him to stay.

"Well," said Bernard, sipping his coffee. "You finally got him back."

"Yes," she said, "although I doubt he'll stay long."

"You hatched a wanderer in that one."

Nan leaned forward in the bentwood rocker that used to be in her parents' living room. The few pieces of furniture that Bernard had kept were rich with asssociation. "What does he want, Dad? What didn't we give him when he needed it?"

"Wanderers are born, not made," said Bernard. "He came into the world what he is."

"I don't believe that. He came into the world soft and malleable. We shaped him."

"If that's so," Bernard replied sharply, "and I don't say it is, what's wrong with the shape he's taken?"

Nan leaned back, rocked for a few moments, before she said, "He's not happy. I don't know why."

Bernard looked at the face that many men, himself included, thought beautiful. It was her mother's face, reinvented but recognizable, if he looked hard enough.

They sat in silence, Nan thinking of Griff, Bērnard thinking of Anna.

"Last night—" Nan began, then stopped.

Bernard waited for her to continue.

"There was something—"

She stopped again.

"Did you notice—"

She shook her head, smiling at her want of words.

There! Bernard said to himself. *Anna smiled just like that when she couldn't find the words for what she wanted to say.* How often she had smiled like that, shaking her head. How many thoughts she had suppressed because the words wouldn't come. How he longed for those words now, like a miser who regrets the coins that slipped through his hands.

"If you're talking about Selene, the way she looked at Griff," he said, forcing his thoughts back to the present, back to Nan, her progeny, her concerns, "yes. I noticed."

"Was it just—curiosity, do you think? Because she's never met him, we've not seen him for so long, and she wonders—"

"Maybe," he said. "Probably."

"Oh, Dad," she said, "what's wrong with me? Why am I even thinking these things?"

Bernard set his mug of coffee on the table beside him. He held his hands out to her. She stopped rocking, leaned forward, taking his hands in hers.

"When are you going to forgive yourself, Nan?" he said.

* * *

Selene sat at her kitchen table, bare legged, barefoot, watching a lazy black fly crawl across the screened window over the sink. It was late Sunday afternoon. She was weary of the day, which seemed to crawl by as slowly as the fly, picking its way from one rhombus of mesh to the next. She was satiated with food, sex, sunshine—unable to begin preparations for the day's conclusion: another meal, followed by a companionable evening of television or a movie, perhaps a final round of sex. She could hear Alex whistling tunelessly as he adjusted the lawnmower, then the whir and sputter of the engine, then the whistling again as he readjusted, then again the whir and sputter.

At last, when she thought she would scream to him to stop the fucking whistling and buy a new lawnmower, the engine roared triumphantly. She saw Alex march off across the lawn, cutting a swath in the bright green carpet of grass. She closed her eyes, exhaling in relief.

When she opened her eyes, the fly was gone. She thought, idly, *Who is Griff? What has he been doing all these years? Who has he been with?* She realized she didn't really care, even as she puzzled over these questions. She cared only about where he was, and who he was with, at this moment. *Who was listening to that rough, raspy voice? Was it Sue Smoller?*

Selene had been jealous only a few times in her life—mostly of Carolyn, Alex's former wife. Even that was different from what she felt now. She had possessed Alex's body, mind, heart, long

36

before his divorce. She had wanted only that Carolyn acknowledge this and release him. She had wanted only that Alex come home to her, not to Carolyn; that he live in her house, not in Carolyn's house, sleep in her bedroom every night, share her weekends and her taxes, mow her lawn.

Now, Alex was hers, Saturdays and Sundays included—and she could think only of Griff who, though he and Alex shared Nan's blood, was as much a stranger to Alex as he was to her—maybe more so.

Her thoughts hummed and buzzed like the lawnmower, picturing Griff with Sue, talking to her, laughing with her, touching her—then snatching him away from Sue, picturing him with her, Selene. She couldn't find enough moments in the day, it seemed, to satisfy her need to focus her thoughts on him, to daydream about him, to fantasize ...

I want him, she thought. *I want him.*

She had always been the one pursued. Now, with any opportunity, she would pursue. If the opportunity didn't come to her, she would make it come. She was not a manipulator, but she knew she could be, would be, for Griff. Her need for him—so sudden, so unexpected, so elemental—was like her need for food, for warmth. She could no more turn off this greedy onslaught of feeling than she could stop breathing. What she felt was the only truth. She would guard those feelings, nurture them, at any cost.

How strange, she thought, *to meditate so much potential destruction with so little guilt.* She felt, indeed, almost no guilt— and she was used to guilt. She had worn guilt like a hair shirt for years before she married Alex, when their affair was just that— an affair. She wore it still, to some extent, when she thought of Carolyn, of the children Alex and Carolyn had made and raised. Wendy and Kevin were young adults now, both living away from home, but she had deprived them of an unbroken span of years with both their parents—she who had lost her parents when she was barely an adult herself. She still felt the pain, the loss, that they must have felt, must still feel, when she thought about her parents, what her life might have been like had they not died. At least, Carolyn and Alex were alive ...

Sue Jackson, now Sue Smoller, with her slightly upturned brown eyes and frizzy brown hair, her rough, somewhat pitted complexion, her tight sweaters and short skirts, had been several years ahead of her in high school, but Selene knew her by reputation. Everybody at school knew her by reputation. She had sex, it was said, with any boy who asked. Selene wondered how much that tendency had carried over into her adulthood. Although Selene thought her only moderately attractive, it was her eyes that she worried about most. Those eyes were riveting.

If I knew how, she thought, *I'd make a demon doll with eyes like hers, stick pins in it, in its eyes, its cheeks, its small breasts, its twat, the bottom of its little feet.*

The sound of the lawnmower stopped. The fly buzzed at the screen door, like a mower in miniature. Selene got up from the table, pushed open the door, swishing at the fly until it found its way out. Nippy trotted in from the back steps, where he had been enjoying a nap in the sun until the sudden quiet had awakened him. He lapped up some water from his bowl in the corner, sat on his haunches, scratched at an ear, then looked up at Selene expectantly. She cuffed him lightly with a bare foot; he seemed satisfied.

She opened the refrigerator, pondering its contents. Nippy followed her, sniffed politely at the bottom shelf. While they were thus engaged, Alex came in from the back yard, slamming the screen door, the agreeable scent of fresh mown grass, sunshine, and sweat wafting in with him.

"Yard work done, ma'am. Yard man mighty hungry."

He grasped her shoulders from behind, planting a kiss on the back of her neck.

"What's for dinner?"

"I was just contemplating that," said Selene. "See anything here you like?"

She kept her voice light, cool, affectionate.

He closed in behind her, tucking his chin against her neck, fondling her breasts.

"Plenty," he said. "Care to join me in the shower?"

"You go ahead," she said, turning toward him, pushing him away from her. "I'll get things going here."

"If you change your mind, you know where I'll be."

He pushed open the swinging door, whistling something from his tuneless repertoire as he went out.

Looking at the door as it swung shut, she realized that she still loved Alex, just as she always had.

Griff hasn't changed that, she thought.

*   *   *

Sue Smoller lay in bed next to Griff, listening to his soft, rhythmic snore. It soothed her, made her feel close to him, as even sex with him could not do. Sex with Griff was spectacular—better than she had had for years. But Griff always seemed to be somewhere else, especially tonight.

Sue, who in high school had had sex with more boys than she cared to remember, realized, not for the first time, that she wanted more than sex. She had made some distinctions, even as a reckless teenager; now, she was much more particular. She was 37—closing in on 40. She had a kid to support. Jimbo was experimenting with drugs, probably screwing every girl in his junior class. He hadn't come home last night, and he was openly hostile to Griff, who didn't seem to take offense. Sue wanted some stability for Jimbo, for herself. But here comes Griff, "a blast from the past," leaning out the window of his dusty red pickup truck, waving, smiling, offering her a ride, a burger—back in her life, back in her bed. She still didn't know where he'd been before he came back. She probably never would. He brushed off her questions as though they were pesky gnats. She kept backing off, not wanting to lose what she had.

What she had was this tall, big-boned, fair-haired stranger sleeping beside her, his snores rising and falling with his breathing, which quickened, then slowed, with quiet regularity. He had been silent most of the evening, after she got back from the mall, where she had worked until six. She was exhausted after a week on her feet at Hair Today. She hated her part-time job at Spangleman's Department Store. She hated the pampered married women with their demands, their complaints—hated the young girls with their budding breasts, their giggles, their insatiable need for more—more clothes, more baubles, more artificial excitement, more attention. But she stayed at Spangleman's because her job as a hair stylist didn't cover expenses for her and Jimbo. She had no other skill—only her skill in bed—and for that she had never been paid.

That evening, when they turned off the television and went upstairs to bed, Griff responded to her almost by rote—*like he was my tenant, like he was paying the rent.* It bothered her enough to keep her awake, but not enough for her to wake him up, demand that he talk to her like a real person—the person he was living with, sleeping with. Sue had never had any success when she made demands on men. Jimbo's father had married her when she'd gotten pregnant and had refused to get another abortion, but he had been nothing but a noose around her neck. She and Jimbo were well rid of him.

Men came to her when they needed something—sex or a roof over their heads—and she took them in, mothered them, sheltered them, fucked them. Then they left. Always, when they left, she said, "Never again."

Before Griff pulled up beside her in his pickup truck, she had pretty much resigned herself to a sexless life. She saw few men at Hair Today, where she rented a chair and eked out a modest living with her "regulars." Aside from a sprinkling of alluring, often irritating, young things, she was surrounded by middle-aged and older women, lamenting their scanty hair, their straying husbands, their lonely, idle "sunset" years. She saw fewer men still at Spangleman's, where she rotated from department to department on weekends and holidays.

Griff stirred in his sleep, opened his eyes for a moment, closed them again, then turned on his side, away from her. In that moment, she saw his recognition of her, of his surroundings—and his rejection—as though he had forgotten, in his sleep, that he was with her, that he was sharing her bed.

She put her hand out to touch his back, then stopped, dropping her hand on the bed. In the darkness, she looked at her polished nails with their crescent of square, extremely white tips—admiring them for a moment, as though they belonged to someone else, before she too turned on her side, away from him.

CHAPTER 4

Two weeks later, Selene has — almost — achieved her independence from Cotter Publishing. She is to fill out her exit forms today and, at almost the same time, sign a contract with Cotter to edit a new book by Kirby Woods. Kirby liked the work she did on his last book, *Being Who You Are*. He had recently asked to work with her on his new project, a book on extrasensory perception. He's a sloppy and careless writer, with a Ph.D. after his name and a finger firmly on the pulse of the reading, inquiring public. Her managing editor, Jeff Wolinski, promised him Selene and Selene only, so her sudden decision to leave the company has upset both Kirby and Jeff.

"Don't try to get around me with this independence crap," says Jeff, who is a little bit in love with Selene. "I want you in here once a week."

Jeff Wolinski is thin, nervous, wiry, past middle age, his blue eyes magnified behind thick glasses, the nose that holds them large, his manner acerbic, his voice gravelly.

"So you're not going to leave," says Selene, leaning back in her chair, across the desk from Jeff, and crossing her legs. "You're not going to take an early retirement."

Jeff looks appreciatively at the silky legs encased in black hose before he says, "Hell, no. Not with Riley licking at my heels."

43

"I'm relieved," says Selene. "Riley is—"

"He's a slime ball," says Jeff. "But he has abilities, and we're stuck with him. For now. Let's talk about the Kirby Woods manuscript. We've got three months to get this baby born."

* * *

By six o'clock, Selene is on the freeway, headed home, Kirby's manuscript in her briefcase. She's feeling buoyant, heady.

"I'm free!"

There's no one to hear her so she says this out loud, for emphasis, smiling at the man shooting past her in a small green convertible. He smiles back and then arcs into the right lane ahead of her. She sees him checking her out in his rearview mirror. He raises his arm in a salute, perhaps to her friendly expression, perhaps to her beauty. After a moment, he pulls ahead, weaving in and out until he disappears. She is trailing a semi with its left turn signal winking uselessly.

"Now for it!"

"*It*" is the new life she has designed for herself, in which she continues to forge her reputation as an editor, but from her own home turf.

"*It*" is the freedom she has given herself to be with Griff, or around Griff, or at least in the same neighborhood as Griff.

"*It*" is whatever lies ahead, intriguing because unknown, enticing because possible, because she has *made* it possible.

She thinks, as she always does when she is able to focus her mind, of the mysterious force and intensity of her feelings toward Griff.

What do I do with these feelings? They don't fit into my life, and yet ... It's as natural for me to think of him as it is to breathe in and out ...

In less than a month, she has altered the course of her life, in part for a man she does not know, who has barely acknowledged her existence, who is half-brother to the husband she loves and respects. She does not love this man, this stranger. She doesn't know him well enough to love him. She suspects that knowing him would not give rise to loving him.

But I want him. I want that first kiss, that drowning touch ...

She looks quickly over her shoulder, then shoots out into the middle lane, slowing down long enough to let the semi move into her lane, then into the left lane, where it lumbers off onto a connecting state route. She picks up speed, passes the two or three commuters dawdling in front of her, then darts into the right lane again, where she can ease up enough to enjoy her own thoughts.

Even while I'm working, talking, meeting with people, I want him ...

Then, honking her horn in triumph, she says out loud, "He is as good as mine!"

Startled, the man cruising ahead of her accelerates in response. She is left with a comparatively bare stretch of road.

Except for her, he is as good as mine.

She thinks of Sue Smoller.

I'll look her up in the yearbooks, she thinks. *She can't have changed that much. She had dull brown hair and blotchy skin. And those eyes.*

In high school, there was always a boy jockeying for space around her, waiting his turn, knowing his time would come. Griff was about her age, so he must have known her from school, dances, and games. Alex seemed to know her by reputation. Selene was reluctant to ask Alex about her, not wanting to appear too curious.

Perhaps he ...

I won't go there, she thinks. *It's bad enough thinking of Griff in bed with Sue. I won't give her Alex as well.*

Alex was older, and much wiser. Even as a young man, Alex must have been cautious, discerning. So unlike Griff, who is, perhaps, not discerning enough.

Or is he? How would I know? He is so elusive, so—

Her exit looms ahead. Distracted by her thoughts, she realizes she's in the wrong lane. She checks the solid line of traffic in her rearview mirror, flicks on her turn signal. Seeing a driver acknowledging her signal with a momentary hesitation, she shoots out ahead of him, accelerates, sweeps into the right lane just in time to make her exit. She exhales in relief, ignoring the angry honk of the SUV just behind her.

A few minutes later, she pulls into the parking lot of Grossman's, the area's largest supermarket. She and Alex call it "Monster Mart." They avoid it as much as they can, but it's on her way home. Selene wants to buy whitefish and asparagus for dinner, and a bottle of bubbly.

She cruises up and down the lanes, looking for an opening in the endless stretch of asphalt, cars packed rump to rump in the late afternoon sun, abandoned shopping carts aimlessly littering the few open spaces. She spots a woman loading groceries into her trunk. She prepares to pull up behind her when she sees a red pickup truck approaching the woman from the other direction, its blinkers on. It's Griff at the wheel of his truck, with Sue beside him. They're watching the woman as she puts the last bag in the trunk, slams down the lid, pushes the cart out of her way. Selene stops, not knowing if she should acknowledge them or move on before they notice her.

At that moment, Griff sees her. Sue is talking to him but she isn't looking at him, so she doesn't see his face change. Selene nods, then raises her hand to him. His arm is resting on the open window of the truck; he raises it in response. Selene eases her car to the right, passing between him and the woman who is about to pull out. Sue is still talking, her head turned away from him. Griff is looking at Selene, his face blank.

In comparative privacy, on the far side of the parking lot, Selene pulls into an empty space, turns off the engine, and stares blindly ahead, gripping the wheel as though she were still on the freeway. She tries to sort out the tangle of feelings pushing to the surface—joy at coming on him so unexpectedly, anger at seeing him with Sue, disappointment with his neutral response to her, relief that Sue hadn't seen her. She isn't sure why it matters that Sue hadn't seen her. It's unlikely that Sue would have recognized her. Perhaps she's afraid she might have seen something in Sue's face that would have crushed her. Something smug, possessive. Something exultant.

*   *   *

Sue and Griff wait for the woman to load her car and pull out of the parking space. Sue is talking about Jimbo.

"He's out of control, Griff, and what's more, he doesn't give a shit about anything. If he listens to me at all, it's because he wants something—money for drugs, most likely, though he won't own up to it. Otherwise, he just tells me to fuck off. I tell him he should respect me, I'm his mother, and he says, what for? For frizzing old women's hair and selling pantyhose at Spangleman's? I say, no, for taking care of your sorry ass and putting a roof over your head until you get out of school and get yourself a job. Then he says I don't need you to take care of me. I don't give a shit about school. Why don't you go and fuck that cowboy you're living with and leave me the fuck alone."

Griff grins suddenly, pulling sharply into the vacant parking space. "So I'm a cowboy, am I?" He turns off the ignition.

"You don't want to hear what else he calls you."

Sue rolls up the window on her side.

"I wish you'd of known him when he was just a kid, Griff. He was so sweet and affectionate—and we're not talking about a long time ago, either. He just changed when he hit puberty. Changed schools. Changed friends. Became a whole other person. I wish his no-good deadbeat dad was around. Even he would be better than nothing."

"Am I 'nothing'?" says Griff.

"He's never gonna take to you, honey," says Sue. "He hates all my boyfriends. Always has." She drawls, deliberately, "He don't want no truck with my men," running her hand down his bare arm, resting it on his thigh. She grips the hard muscles there and moves close to him, turning her face up to his. "Especially this man."

"Why me, especially?"

He turns away from her, reaching for the door handle.

Sue grips his thigh until her red nails pinch the skin beneath his jeans. He turns back to her. She presses her red mouth against his, pushes her tongue between his lips. He is unresponsive.

She says, sliding away from him, pushing open the door, "Maybe because you're such a cold, unfeeling bastard."

She gets out, slamming the door so hard the truck rocks.

* * *

"Chicken again?" says Alex, standing behind Selene, kissing her hair as he holds her.

"I didn't have time for the Monster Mart."

Selene unwraps the frozen, boneless chicken breasts, shoving them into the microwave for a quick defrost. "I'll think of something."

"How about chicken Kiev? Do we have butter and chives? Get the oil going. I'll pound the flesh."

He gets out the kitchen mallet and wax paper. Selene pours oil onto a skillet, turns on the heat. She gets butter, parsley, chives out of the refrigerator, inspects the limp broccoli that she bought several days ago. She puts out flour, bread crumbs, an egg for the coating, garlic cloves, garlic press, salt, white pepper grinder. She's rinsing the broccoli under the faucet, pinching off yellowing florets, when the sound of the pounding stops.

Alex says, "Do we have any bubbly in the house? Let's pop open a bottle."

Selene turns off the faucet and leans against the sink, gripping its edge, sudden tears filling her eyes, spilling over onto her cheeks, her hands.

"I meant to get some. I wanted to stop—"

Alex turns her around, so that she's facing him. "Honey? What is it? What's the matter, baby?" He takes her in his arms.

She cries silently against him, loving his tenderness but wishing the arms around her were Griff's, wishing she had pulled Sue out of the truck, pushed her aside, then climbed into the truck with Griff and said, "Let's get the hell out of here."

"I'm just—just so—I wish—I want—"

Selene stops, then says, her head resting on his shoulder, "This is supposed to be a celebration. I'm a free agent, as of today. I stopped at Monster Mart for whitefish and asparagus and bubbly, but I couldn't find a parking space. I got so disgusted cruising up and down waiting for somebody to leave I just—took off. I'm sorry we have to have frozen chicken and three-day-old broccoli and—no bubbly."

"There, there," he says, patting her back. "It's nothing but a little separation anxiety you're feeling. You've left the comfortable security of your job. You're wondering if you'll like all this freedom you've given yourself. You'll be all right. I know. Trust me. You'll be all right."

Selene relaxes in his arms. The tears stop. He is so soothing, so comforting, her Alex, even if he doesn't know what she's thinking, what she's feeling. She remembers the tears she shed when he and Carolyn were separating, then divorcing. How guilty she felt! How guilty she still feels about that divorce. Why, then, is there no guilt for Griff? Was all of her allotted guilt expended on the family she shattered? Or is it that what she feels for Griff is separate, apart from her life with Alex? She wanted a future with Alex; she was willing to hurt him and his family to get it. When she thinks of Griff, she doesn't think of spending her life with him. There is no future with Griff. He is her present.

"Better now?" says Alex, holding her away from him, inspecting her tear-blotched face.

"Better."

He wipes away some of the wetness under her eyes.

"I look ghastly, I'm sure."

"Go upstairs and splash some water on your face. I'll take care of dinner. And don't worry about the bubbly. There's some white wine in the refrigerator. It'll do just as well."

He kisses her lightly on the mouth, turns her toward the swinging door, gives her a push, slapping her affectionately on the rump. Selene hears his tuneless whistling, the spatter of hot oil, as she walks through the dining room and into the living room, the sinking sun casting softly swaying shadows across the hardwood floor, the comfortably dowdy furniture.

I love this house, and I love the man in the kitchen, she thinks, climbing the stairs slowly, her hand caressing the carved oak banister.

She stops, looking down at the vibrant sunlight and shadows crisscrossing the living room. She hears Nippy scratching and

whining at the back door, not wanting to miss dinner preparations, the screen door slamming as Alex lets him in, saying, "Hi,
pal. How was *your* day?"

She turns, runs lightly up the stairs, not wanting to miss
dinner preparations herself.

*　*　*

Carolyn O'Leary Price poked at her dinner with disgust,
pushing aside the tired looking green beans that had so recently
resided in her freezer, scooping up a forkful of white meat covered with a gooey sauce that had been labeled "Chicken *Cordon
Bleu.*"

"To think I used to be considered a gourmet cook," she said
out loud, then looked up, self-conscious at the sound of her
voice.

The television news anchor looked back at her, reeling off
the day's disasters and political maneuverings, seemingly talking
to her alone as his eyes scanned the monitor, confidently traveling to the camera eye, then fetching more lines with a barely
perceptible glance before he skewered her again with his handsome middle-aged smile.

*He's making millions and all he does is sit and read off the
news,* she thought. She reached for the remote, switched to
the CNN channel. The anchor was an attractive woman with
long dark hair carefully arranged around her shoulders, a hyp-
notically soothing voice. Although she was reading the same
dire, calamitous news as the network anchor, trouble and cares
seemed to melt away at the sound of her voice—like a mother
telling her children a bedtime story.

Carolyn put down the remote, picked up her fork, cut into
the pliant, overcooked chicken breast with distaste. She looked
around the living area of her condo as she chewed the salty,
oddly tasteless meat. Although she had lived here for several

years, she still wasn't used to the impersonal white-walled apartment. But she liked the easy informality of apartment living, the sense that she was taken care of, the lack of responsibility for upkeep and maintenance. Periodically, she drove past the house that she had shared with Alex, where they had raised Kevin and Wendy, where they had been, supposedly, happy. It had been a new development when they moved in, with a sign at the entrance that said "Twin Oaks," the namesakes the only mature trees within sight. Now it had a settled, permanent look, its young trees anchoring the well-tended half-acre lots.

She always cried when she drove past their former home, glimpsing toddlers and young children as they climbed on colorful plastic play sets, scooted up and down the drives on tricycles, skates, skateboards—the latest rendition of preschool and preadolescent transportation. It wasn't that she wanted to live there again, among the young mothers, weekend fathers, pampered, assertive children. There was no place there for a divorced woman with grown children, who lived on alimony and taught elementary school on a substitute basis. It wasn't even that she wanted to be the young wife and mother who had complacently trusted that her husband would return to them each time she sent him off to work, trusted that her role as a full-time homemaker had an indefinite run. She cried because her season as a wife and mother at the top of her game was over. She had been a star player, born for the role.

She picked up the remote, switched to a rerun of a situation comedy involving family matters. *Are there any families left?* she thought, spearing limp green beans onto her fork, chewing them listlessly. *Yes, of course, there are. They're living in our old neighborhood, in our house.* There must be a lot of them because they kept razing farmland, building new houses in new developments. Recently, she had heard that only 25 percent of American households consisted of married couples with children, that one in four households consisted of one person living alone. Old people. Middle-aged career people. Young people tasting independence for the first time. Abandoned wives.

She picked up the remote once again and switched off the TV. The television fare was as disgusting as her dinner. She shoved the food away from her, listening to the silence. Not even a whistle or a curse from her neighboring condo residents. It was strange hearing and being heard by her neighbors. She had always taken her privacy for granted when she was living at Twin Oaks. Now she had to regulate the sound on her television and stereo, stifle her groans and cries when Alex made love to her.

She went into the kitchen, scraped the leftovers on her plate into the sink, switched on the garbage disposal. She wondered, as she often did, what Selene would do if she knew that Alex was cheating on her with his former wife. She had been tempted, at one time, to tell her, in some shockingly abrupt or quietly subtle way, how Alex came to her on occasion, supposedly to talk about the children, staying for a casual meal and, as he jokingly called it, "a roll in the hay." But she didn't want those spontaneous, satisfying sessions to end, so she said nothing to anyone, keeping what remained of their relationship to herself, as though *she* were the adulterer, not that brazen bitch who had stolen her husband, then married him.

The phone rang. She reached for the white cordless on the wall next to the sink, hoping it was Wendy calling from Texas A&M, where she was studying computer programming. She knew it wouldn't be Kevin. It never was. But when she heard the familiar click that signaled the telemarketer at the other end, she hung up, not willing to listen to the scripted call.

It's all her doing, she thought, tidying up the already spotless kitchen. *I would have Alex, and I would have Kevin, if it were not for her. I should kill her, cause a media sensation, plead insanity, rot in prison waiting for my appeal, while the TV vultures produce a made-for-television movie called "Revenge of the Homemaker: The Carolyn Price Story."*

She took the phone out of its cradle. *I'll call Wendy,* she thought, *calculating the time difference in Texas. She's probably out of her classes by now. We'll have a mother-daughter chat. It will get me to the close of my evening.*

*   *   *

"Damn Griff for coming back," says Alex, sitting at Nan's kitchen table several days later, the early evening sun blazing in on him from the window over the sink. "Why didn't he just stay wherever the hell he was."

"I wanted him back," says Nan simply, stirring cream into her mug, then sipping the hot coffee, her eyes on Alex. "I'm glad he's back."

"Sorry, Mom," says Alex. "Of course you are. It's just that— what in Christ's name are we supposed to do with him?"

Nan puts down her mug. She puts her hand over the fist he is unconsciously clenching on the table. "We'll think of something," she says, quietly.

"What? What does he do? What does he want?"

He hits the table with his fist as Nan's hand slides away from him.

"I think—just to live his life."

"Just to fuck up his life is more like it."

Seeing the downward glance, the puckered brow—Alex says, "Sorry, Mom. Sorry I said it. Sorry for the way I said it. Griff is—he has some good qualities."

Nan watches Alex's face as he struggles to identify Griff's "good" qualities.

"You won't get very far on your own with that list," she says, teasing him. "You're too unlike each other."

"Why is that, Mom?"

Alex leans back in his chair and skewers her with his searching-for-information look, the look—head slightly tilted, eyes kind, alert—he undoubtedly uses on recalcitrant employees.

"We're brothers, after all," he says, thoughtfully, when Nan doesn't respond. "There aren't that many years between us. We were brought up in the same home, with the same parents and grandparents. We went to the same schools, got dragged to the same church on Sunday. We played softball and basketball on the same teams, went fishing with Gramps on the same lake, hung out downtown, smashed up Dad's cars as soon as we could, did our best to—sorry, Mom—screw the local girls, got the hell out of here as soon as we could—"

"And came back as soon as you were able," says Nan.

"Well, I came back. Griff hasn't been around all that much."

"Then why should you resent that he's back now?"

"*Resent?*" Alex throws the word back at her. "I don't know that I—"

A fierce little frown etches Nan's face.

"You resent Griff because you don't understand him."

Alex's voice softens. "What's there to understand, Mom?"

Nan says, tentatively, "Griff is—different."

"You can say that again."

"Griff is different."

She says it firmly this time, fixing him with her eyes.

Leaning forward, trying for humor, he says, "Be different and be damned," and then, getting no response, "*Vive la différence?*" Nan laughs, suddenly.

"What I'm trying to say is, Griff has come back for a reason."

"And what might that be?"

"I don't know yet. But I want to find out. In the meantime, I don't want you to drive him away with your—"

"My—?"

"Your—sarcasm. Your questions. Your unreasonable expectations."

"Why 'unreasonable'?" he says, stung. "What's unreasonable? That he have some direction, some goals? That he put his oars in the water, instead of drifting endlessly? That he make some effort to articulate what it is he wants, where it is he's going?"

Nan gets up, walks over to the window above the sink. She watches Bernard as he putters with his flowers. He stops, looks up. She waves. He nods, perfunctorily, and resumes his task.

Nan's response is curt, impatient. "He can't—'articulate.' He can't write a business plan around who he is. Don't you understand? You can't judge him by your standards."

"I didn't make up the standards," Alex says.

"He's your brother, not your clone. And he's not even—"

She stops, confused.

"Not even—what?"

Alex repeats her words, politely, because he knows he can't goad her. Nan won't be maneuvered into saying what she doesn't want to say.

"Never mind."

He wonders why she closes in on herself the moment she gets too close to the truth. *Why is she so determined to keep her secret, even though we all know what it is? Dad is dead. Griff's father—whoever he is—is gone. What does it matter if Griff is "not even" my full blood brother, "not even" my father's son?* But he knows that it matters to Nan. Matters so much that she has never been able to talk about it openly, to confront it completely—at least with him. Perhaps, if she did, he could accept Griff—maybe even help him.

Well, what the hell. He had a secret or two himself he wasn't about to share. *What would Mom think of me if she knew I still sleep with Carolyn?* Aside from the moral ramifications, he is aware that, although Nan had accepted Carolyn as his wife, she loves Selene from her heart. Strange, that. Selene is what is commonly referred to as a home wrecker, who drove Kevin and Wendy—my kids, her grandchildren—out of town, and who estranged Kevin from the entire family. Yet, Nan loves her, had always loved her. *I don't know shit about women,* he thinks. He grins suddenly.

Nan says, "What's so funny?"

Alex puts his hands in his pants pockets, leans back in his chair until his chest expands and the front legs of the chair lift off the floor.

"Mom, I don't understand you, I don't know where you're going with this, but I love you to pieces. I want to make you happy. So just tell me what you want me to do. Barkus is willing."

Nan sits down again across from him.

"Just this," she says, leaning toward him. "I want you to accept Griff into your life—into our lives—as long as he's here with us. I want you to make him feel—loved—at home. I want you to help him, if you can, but I don't want you to direct him. Griff hates directives."

"What does he want, Mom?" Alex sits up straight. The front chair legs hit the floor with a small crash. "I'd really like to know what Griff wants."

"I think he wants to rest here for a while."

There's a pleading note in her voice as she offers this up to him, as though she knows it's inadequate, but it's all she can give him.

"I think he has been hurt by something or—someone."

Alex looks at her for a moment; then, he nods. He nods several times, fixing his eyes on the warm oak of the table, picking out nicks, stains, discolorations that are as old as his memories of this house, older than his own nicks, bumps, and scars.

"Okay, Mom," he says at last. "Okay."

When he looks up, she is smiling at him.

Bernard comes in from the back yard, the smell of fresh grass and fragrant plants clinging to his clothes, his hands.

"Hey, what'd I miss?" he says, clapping Alex on the shoulder.

*   *   *

"Am I oversexed?" says Sue, turning on her side and rubbing Griff's back. Early morning light turns the window shades golden.

Griff's voice is muffled by his pillow.

"Yeah. I've been meaning to talk to you about that."

"I'm serious, Griff. I seem to want you a lot more than you want me. Why is that?"

He is still for a moment, then he says, "Look, Sue. I'm just camping out here. We didn't take any vows."

He sits up, swings his long legs over the side of the bed. His back is still toward her as he says, "You want me to leave, just say so."

"I won't say that. I don't want you to leave."

Why did I say that, she thinks. *What if he gets up and leaves right now? He almost left me the other day at the supermarket.*

She pulls herself up, reaches out to him, but he doesn't turn toward her or acknowledge her touch, except for a small muscle spasm where her hand is against his back. She drops her hand and looks at his broad back. She can still see a few faint red marks where her long fingernails pressed into his skin. She is still damp and throbbing where he pushed into her, relentlessly, until she called out in wordless panic and release.

"It's just that—well—I feel like I could be any woman and it would be just the same with you."

She tries to stop herself but the words come out, wheedling, pleading.

"Could I be? Am I?"

"Shit," he says, almost to himself.

He gets up, pulls on his jeans. "Is Jimbo home?"

"Don't know," she says, her voice trembling. "Didn't hear him come in last night."

He opens the door and, without looking back, shuts it quietly behind him as he goes out.

Sue listens to the sound of the toilet flushing, the shower running, the water splashing into the sink as he brushes his teeth and shaves his light brown stubble. She clenches her fists. Her long, carefully filed red nails dig into the palms of her hands. She wants to follow him into the bathroom and sit on the side of the tub, in the steamy room, while he scrapes his skin with a razor, pushing his tongue against the inside of his cheek to guide the blade. But she knows the door is closed against her, the cheap metal hook fastened, the man looking at his face in the fogged-over medicine cabinet mirror unknown to her. Unknowable.

What does he want? Who does he want?

She reaches down and pushes a finger inside herself, feeling the warm slippery ooze, wishing it were Griff's ooze as well. But he is careful, always careful, the condom in place before he touches her there. She won't get knocked up, not with him, not ever.

She brings her hand up to her nose and sniffs at her finger, thoughtfully. Then she wipes her hand on the sheet and gets out of bed, stretching, her fingernails reaching toward the ceiling.

* * *

When Selene saw, from the window of her newly arranged first-floor home office, the red Chevy pickup truck pull into her driveway and stop, the afternoon sun glancing off its hood, her heart thudded with such suddenness she thought she would vomit. She pushed back the gorge at the front of her throat and waited.

Griff was sitting at the wheel, looking down, as if deep in thought. After a breathless time, which might have been half a minute, the truck came to life again with a muffled rumble. Griff turned to look behind him as he backed the truck out of the drive. Selene was outside, at the bottom of the steps, when he faced forward again.

"Hello," she called to him. "Hello."

She waved feebly, not sure what to do but determined to stop him before he got away. She walked over to the truck, still waving, until the truck stopped moving.

"Hi," he said, not quite meeting her eyes; then, after a lengthy pause, "I was in the neighborhood."

"Yes. So I see."

She put her hand on the open window, as if to hold him there.

"How are you?"

He nodded, not answering her. He looked at her hand, as though wanting to pry her fingers away from the window.

"Won't you come in?"

She studied his face—the blue eyes, the wide, generous mouth—in case he refused her and she had to move on with her life, again, without him.

He nodded.

She released her hand from the window so that he could open the door and get out. He swung his long legs down to the ground effortlessly. He slammed the door and stood waiting, close to her, his hands jammed into the pockets of his jeans so that his shoulders humped slightly.

She turned away from him, walked across the small patch of lawn to the front steps, up the steps to the porch, feeling his eyes on her as she moved—moving for him, her buttocks swaying beneath her shorts. She pulled open the screen door and went inside, hearing him catch the door as it swung back, feeling him just behind her in the hallway, gloomy after the sunshine.

"Come in," she said.

He let the screen door slam behind him.

They stood in the hallway while Selene hesitated, catching her breath. She was winded, as though she had been running. She gripped the banister, glanced up the stairs, wanting to take his hand and lead him up, step by step, to her bed—to the bed she shared with Alex. She shivered, shrugged, suddenly shy, afraid to move.

Griff said, "Maybe this isn't a good time."

She said, almost angrily, "This is a very good time."

He grinned, suddenly; her curt response seemed to amuse him. She led him through the house to the kitchen, because she didn't know where else to put him.

Behind the swinging door, Nippy rose up from his wicker nest, greeting them tentatively, wagging his tail at Selene, sniffing in the area of Griff's knees.

Griff looked down at him without much interest.

"He's checking you out," said Selene, to say something. "You seem to have passed his litmus test. Or maybe he remembers you from your first visit."

"Maybe," said Griff. He put his hand out. Nippy jumped up, sniffed at his fingertips. "He sure is a little thing."

"Terriers generally are, and he's all terrier, as far as we know," said Selene, happy to hear him talk.

"I like dogs I can pat without bending over," said Griff. "He doesn't even come close."

Selene pushed open the screen door that led to the back yard.

"Nippy, go outside and see if you can grow a little. You're not wanted here."

Nippy trotted outside without a backward glance.

"Sorry," said Griff. "I didn't mean to hurt his feelings, or yours."

"You didn't. Nippy is very tough and resilient. He'll win you over eventually because he doesn't know how to give up."

Griff was standing close to her. She forced herself to look directly at him, at the almost startling blue of his eyes, before she added, "We have that in common."

When it became necessary to say something into the silence that followed, she said, "Can I get you a beer?"

"You can, but I'd rather have a soda."

She opened the refrigerator, bent over to find a chilled bottle of 7-Up, feeling his eyes on her again, pleased that she was wearing a flattering pink T-shirt and her new denim shorts, that beneath her shorts her legs were shapely, flawless, that her feet were bare.

"Shouldn't you be at work?" he said, as she reached into the freezer for loose ice cubes from the icemaker.

"I am at work," she said, dropping the cubes into a tall glass, waiting for the ice to settle as she poured the fizzy beverage over the cubes, handing him the glass. "That is, I was working when you came by. I'm working at home now."

He nodded as he took the glass from her; then he drank deeply. She waited for him to question her about her work, but he didn't. He seemed to be waiting for her to talk, but in a polite, incurious way.

"What about you?" she said.

He looked her over briefly, as if assessing her worth, then glanced around the kitchen, assessing everything around her in the same way. She felt the almost offhand insult of his deliberate appraisal.

"I'm always working," he said, at last. "Living is my work."

"Oh," she said.

He wasn't looking at her, but he was watching her, his eyes moving around the room, then glancing off her, like light off water. She leaned back against the counter, allowing him to watch her. Through the window she glimpsed sunlit trees nodding beneath a clear blue sky.

"Oh," she said again.

He lifted the glass to his mouth. The ice cubes clinked as he drank the soda.

She watched his throat move as he swallowed, then drank, swallowed, then drank some more. She thought she heard a small gurgle in his stomach as he put the glass down on the table.

"Thanks," he said. "I'd better be going."

"Why?" She wanted to grab his arm, push him into a chair. "There's no hurry."

"You were working."

"Yes, but—"

She stopped, not knowing what to say, afraid of the words she wanted to say: *But I want you to stay.* Afraid he would shy away from the words, from her.

"Can I go out this way?" he said, gesturing toward the screen door.

She nodded, feeling like a disappointed child. If only she could stomp her bare foot and say, *No, you can't go out this way or any other way. Not now. Not yet.* But she let him push open the screen door and walk outside, following him down the steps.

Nippy trotted up, expectant, but Griff, who seemed anxious to leave, barely glanced at him.

"The gate's right over there," Selene said, pointing.

"See you," said Griff, putting his hand up to his forehead in a brief salute.

"Please come back," said Selene, almost under her breath, almost pleading.

She didn't know if he heard her. He unlatched the gate, walked through, nodded as he latched the gate from the outside. Then he was gone, out of sight.

She listened to the sound of the truck door slamming shut, then the rumble of the engine, the crunch of loose gravel as he backed out of the driveway, the muffled roar as he drove away.

CHAPTER 5

Bernard got up from the lawn chair and walked slowly over to Nan and Griff, who were standing near the back porch. He lifted his visored cap to let the morning air dry the sweat on his forehead, then settled the cap snugly on his head again. The three of them surveyed the moist, freshly turned black soil.

"Let's put the impatiens over there, up against the fence, near the roses," said Bernard. "They'll need the shade."

"There's still a bare spot here by the porch, Dad," said Nan. "We should have picked up more flats."

"I'll go back to the nursery and get some more," said Griff. "I'll fill up the truck."

"Hang on, Griff," said Bernard. "We've got enough plants here to start our own nursery. Your mom's planting everything two inches apart, as usual. Nan, give those roots some room to grow."

"They've got plenty of room, Dad," Nan said, mildly. "But we need more marigolds and salvia, and maybe some snapdragons, for this sunny area around the porch."

They stood there, three generations of Cavillons, with the same expression of intense concentration on their faces, the same breadth of forehead, fair skin tones, fine hair, harmony of feature; so that Alex, when he approached them from the driveway, was struck by how much alike they were, and how unlike them he was.

"Morning, all," he called. "How does your garden grow?"

The three looked up, identical frowns on their faces.

Nan's frown was wiped away in an instant as she walked up to him. She put her cheek against his. Bernard was just behind her, clapping him on the back. Griff stood his ground, his hands in his jeans pockets, nodding a greeting.

"I'm so glad you stopped by," said Nan. "We need a critical eye. Is Selene with you?"

Alex put his arm around his mother. "She's bringing some sweet rolls and croissants. She says I'll just mash them together if I carry them. I can be trusted to grind the coffee beans, however. Got anything exotic?"

Alex and Nan went inside. Bernard waited for Selene. She came around the side of the house, holding the bakery box carefully out in front of her. She was wearing skintight jeans and a white halter top that stopped just above her waistline. Bernard, taking the box from her, pecking her on the cheek, admired the ribbon of exposed skin.

"How are you?" she said to Bernard.

Bernard saw her look quickly at Griff, who stood close by, then toward the kitchen, where they could hear Nan's murmur and Alex's deep, jovial bass.

"Better, now that I see you," said Bernard. "You're the prettiest flower in this garden."

"Thanks, Bernard," she said. Then, "Hello, Griff."

Griff nodded, not moving. Bernard, looking first at one, then at the other, felt a moment of envy, a fleeting, scarcely acknowledged, stirring in his loins. They were so young, such healthy, beautiful young plants.

He thought of Anna, the young Anna, before he had married her and made her his. How his body had ached for her.

What a time that was, just before and just after we got married, when she opened herself up to me, like those little daisy-like plants with their pink and white petals that close up tight until the sun warms them. They're not showy. They're shy, modest. But how satisfying it is to see them shining in the sun after a day of rain and clouds—to know that they're strong, hardy, because they're able to close up tight against storm, wind, darkness.

Oh, Anna. If I could only warm you in my arms again, thought Bernard, as he continued to look absently at Selene and Griff, who were now standing close to each other, side by side in their scuffed, tight-fitting jeans.

"It's been a while since I've seen you," said Selene, her voice calm and neutral. "I thought you might stop by again."

Griff shrugged, his hands still in his pockets.

"Haven't been in the neighborhood," he said.

"Well, if you are—when you are—please come by. I'd like the company. I'm alone a lot these days."

There, thought Selene. *That was unequivocal, without being too brazen.*

"You chose to work alone, didn't you?" he said, responding to the obvious, ignoring the implication.

You bastard, she thought, but she said, "Yes. I chose it. But it takes getting used to. I've always worked in a business setting. I've always been motivated by the people around me."

He nodded, without showing much interest, looking past her to Bernard, who stood with the bakery box in his hands, watching them from a polite distance. "Need some help, Gramps?"

Bernard shook his head. "I think I can handle it," he said. "You stay there," he added, not wanting them to move or shift their positions until he could drink them in, in their matching jeans, their youth, their beauty.

Selene turned her head toward Bernard. He saw something in her face—hurt? anger? What had Griff said to her to make her look like that? Why would he want to hurt her, or to make her angry?

"It's okay, Dad. You can put them down now," said Nan as she came down the back steps to the flagstone patio.

He turned, plunking the bakery box down on the glass-topped table, annoyed that he was no longer able to watch them unobserved. Nan whisked a damp cloth over the surface, set down plates and cups. She came around the table, gently pressing him into a chair. "Sit for a while, Dad. You look a little tired. Too much sun?"

"I'm perfectly all right. Don't fuss so."

Seeing the same expression on Nan's face he'd seen on Selene's just a moment ago, Bernard patted her hand, saying, as he had wanted to say to Selene, "There, there. Don't worry. Smile for me."

Nan kissed him lightly on the forehead and went back inside. Griff came over and sat across from him. Selene, after a few moments, sat next to Bernard.

"How's my best girl?" said Bernard, taking her hand. Because he wanted to comfort her, because she was lovely, fragile, somehow injured, he raised her hand to his lips and kissed it.

Her gray eyes welled up for a moment.

"I'm fine, Bernard. Just fine."

He loved the sound of his name when she said it. He listened to it again in his mind, still holding her hand, until she withdrew it gently, patting the top of his hand where it lay, cupped and claw-like, on the table.

He looked down at his hand with its mottled, parchment-like skin and prominent veins, wondering if it were his. Was he as old as this hand? Was this him? As he considered this, his mind became blank, then spacious.

He was with Anna. He could feel her close to him. They were both young—so young!—and they were dancing. Anna was wearing a long gown. He thought it was red, a dark red. The material was soft, like velvet, like satin, like velvet and satin. It made a swishing sound as she moved. She was looking up at him. He could see her eyes. He could smell the sweet musky scent she liked to wear. Shalimar. He could hear the music. His head was swimming with bliss—with her nearness, the feel of her skin, the sweet smell of her, the soft red of her dress, the light in her hair, the light in her eyes.

Faint with emotion, he looked up, to catch his breath. He heard voices.

"Dad? Are you all right?"

"Can he hear you? Gramps? Can you hear us?"

"Of course, I can hear you. I'm not deaf—not yet, at least."

He looked around the table.

"Why are you standing there, gaping at me? Have a seat. Nan, I'll have some of that coffee. It smells good."

They sat down around the table, Nan next to Griff, Alex on the other side of Selene. Nan poured coffee. Everyone selected a sweet roll or a croissant from the plate in the center.

"We were worried there for a minute, Gramps," said Alex. "You looked like you saw a ghost."

"I did. I saw Anna," said Bernard matter-of-factly, biting into a frosted, jelly-filled roll that was so sweet it made his teeth ache.

"You mean—you mean you—"

Alex, for once, seemed at a loss for words.

"I mean just what I said. She was wearing a long red dress. I remember that dress. We were dancing. Selene, honey, hand me that half-and-half."

"So, you were remembering—"

"Nope. She was there."

Bernard poured a liberal amount of cream into his coffee, stirring it thoughtfully. No one spoke.

"I could see her. I could touch her. I could smell her."

There was a long pause, during which Bernard drank down his coffee with a resounding slurp.

Griff said, "How was she, Gramps?"

"She was fine, my boy," said Bernard. "She was looking like a million dollars." He added, after a moment, "She sure was one fine woman."

There was a murmur of assent, then Bernard said, "You can't live with a woman that long and then just—let her go." He paused. "Or, maybe it's the other way around. I don't know. All I know is, there she was, big as life, all decked out for a dance."

"You and Mom were such good dancers," said Nan. "I loved to watch you dance."

"We were that," said Bernard, nodding his head as he bit into the roll again.

"She was—dainty," said Nan.

"She was that. My dainty rose."

"'Dainty.' There's a word you don't hear anymore," said Alex.

"We don't have women like that anymore," said Bernard. "Present company excepted."

"Now, we have women like Monica Lewinsky," said Alex.

"What do you mean?" said Selene, suddenly defensive.

"I mean women with brazen sexual appetites and aggressive behavior," said Alex calmly.

"Alex, don't be absurd," said Nan. "This generation didn't invent sexually aggressive women."

"No, but this generation has embraced them," said Alex. "This generation has made them stars."

"We still expel them; we still punish them," said Selene, her breath quickening. "One way or another."

"Oh, yes, of course we do," said Alex. "We give them a sound pat on the butt, a few million dollars, tell them to go to their rooms, and not to come out till they've written a book."

"While their partners in seduction go about the business of ruling the world," Selene snapped back.

"That has yet to be determined," said Nan. "Clinton was acquitted, but he was far more guilty than she was. Can he continue to rule the world? Will the world let him?"

Selene shook her head. "It's already been determined. It's been determined from the beginning of time. The only thing that's changed is our level of acceptance, our confessional bent. It's very Catholic, actually. All is forgiven, if we confess our sins and do a token penance."

"Are you saying we shouldn't be forgiven?" said Alex.

"If we no longer believe in the sanctity of the marriage vow," said Bernard slowly, chewing the last of his jelly roll, "why punish adulterers? Without a code of conduct, there is no crime."

"We still have values," said Alex, pouring more coffee from the thermal pot. He raised his eyebrows at the others to indicate his willingness to serve them.

Bernard held out his mug, nodding his thanks. "We may have *values*, but somewhere along the way we lost the concept of *sin*."

"What do you mean, Gramps?" said Griff, who had been a silent auditor of the conversation.

"I mean, my boy, that, when I was growing up, I knew what was right and what was wrong. It was drilled into me, at home, at school, at church. When I was wrong, there was no discussion.

There was no gentle admonition. It was the back of a hand, a slap of the ruler, a nun or a priest telling me I was on my way to hell in a handcart. It was corporal punishment and *fear*. And it worked for most of us. It at least kept young scrappers like me in line."

"We can't go back to that, Dad," said Nan. "We're light years beyond that."

"That's right, Mom," said Alex, folding a flakey morsel of croissant, popping it into his mouth. "We're way beyond that. We can't fit the punishment to the crime anymore, because our notion of what's right and what's wrong is so screwed up."

"What does any of this have to do with Monica Lewinsky?" said Selene, irritably.

"She did what she felt like doing," said Alex, chin down, eyes leveled at her across the brief expanse of table. "That's my point."

Selene felt her mouth quiver, as if she were a child, as if she had been rebuked. She looked out across the yard.

"Bernard," she said, "your flowers are beautiful. Look at your rosebuds. How especially lovely they are."

Bernard recited, his eyes fixed on Selene: "*I will not have the mad Clytie, Whose head is turned by the sun; The tulip is a courtly queen, Whom therefore I will shun; The cowslip is a country wench, The violet is a nun;—But I will woo the dainty rose, The queen of every one.*"

"I remember your saying that to Mom," said Nan. "You would appease her with that little verse when she was angry or upset."

"Yep. It worked like a goddamn charm," said Bernard, reflectively.

Everyone laughed. There was a general shuffle as chairs were pushed back, the table cleared.

Bernard took Selene by the arm. They went off on a tour of the garden. Alex helped Nan with the dishes. Griff sat where he was, leaning back in his chair, his hands pushed into the pockets of his jeans, looking thoughtfully at the old man and the young woman bending over a bed of roses.

* * *

A few days later, Alex lay beside Carolyn in her bed, indulging in a rare cigarette. He inhaled, pulled the cigarette away from his lips, watched the ash cool from pink to gray while he held his breath. Then he exhaled luxuriously, the smoke wafting into the air in front of him, tickling his nose as he expelled it. He held it out to Carolyn. She took a quick puff and handed it back to him.

"We really should be smoking grass," she said, settling herself closer to him. "This is so old hat."

"I'm just a conservative guy, I guess," said Alex blandly, inhaling until the pink ash glowed, the white cylinder of the cigarette diminished itself.

"Oddly enough, you are," she said.

"Why is that odd?"

"Well—you've made some pretty radical moves in your time."

"Like?"

"Well—you left me, and Kevin, and Wendy."

Alex shifted impatiently.

"I left you. I never left the kids. And I'm here with you now."

"So, now we're the adulterers."

"But you were my wife. It doesn't feel like adultery."

"It does to me. There's another Mrs. Price."

"I'll leave, if you're uncomfortable."

He turned away from her, stamping out his cigarette in the ashtray next to the bed, blowing out the last of the smoke.

"No," she said, grasping his arm, pressing herself against him, even though he made no move to get up. "I don't want you to leave. I like having you here—in our bed—again."

He pulled his arm out of her grasp, putting it around her, drawing her closer to him. She fit herself against him, her head snug against his shoulder. He ruffled her short, curly brown hair.

"I like being here, with you, Olyn," he said, calling her by a pet name. "Sometimes ..." He thought for a moment, then said, "Sometimes, Selene is so—*young.*"

"How so?" she said, her voice carefully neutral.

"Well, quitting her job, for one. That was a dumb move. I think she'll regret it, but I can't tell her so. She's so proud of herself for doing it. And then—"

He paused. Carolyn felt him tense as he said, "There's this—thing—with Griff."

Carolyn turned her head, her mouth open in astonishment. "What 'thing' with Griff? What are you talking about?"

When he didn't reply, she said, again, "What are you talking about, Alex?"

He took a breath, exhaling forcibly.

"I don't know what I'm talking about. Just forget I said it."

She turned toward him, pushing herself up on her elbow. "How can I forget it? Selene and—Griff? Alex, what's going on?"

"Nothing. Nothing's going on. But I don't like the way she—looks at him. And I've noticed she gets all—quiet—when he's around. I don't know. Maybe I'm just imagining it. Maybe I'm just a jealous old fool."

"You're not old. Not by a long shot—at least, I hope you're not. If you're old, I'm old."

They were both in their mid-forties, Carolyn's birthday just a few months behind his. Alex's superior age and authority had been the subject of much teasing, many jokes, in their younger days.

She lay back down. She said, choosing her words, "I haven't seen you since Griff came back. How is he? Is he still—well—Griff?"

"He's still Griff, only more so. Nothing to say. Nothing to do. Coming from nowhere. Going nowhere."

Alex kept his voice low, calm, but Carolyn sensed the familiar restraint. She wondered, as she often had, what he would do if he didn't hold himself in almost perpetual check.

"I thought," she said tentatively, "you and he may have—mellowed."

"I thought so too, when he first came back. But it won't happen. I know that now. We're oil and water."

"You're the oil. He's the water."

Alex was quiet for a few moments.

"Yes. I think you're right, Olyn. I cling to people, to things. Then I can't let go, while Griff—"

She murmured, finishing his thought, "He evaporates if you try to hold on to him."

It feels familiar, this conversation, Carolyn thought. *It feels good to be here with Alex, able to translate, interpret, for him.*

She added, "He's very deep, very dark, like a pool in the woods."

After a moment, she said, "Do you remember that trip we took to Canada, when Kevin was eight and Wendy was seven? Remember that stop we made in upper New York state, before we crossed the border? Remember how we had to search for Kevin in the woods?

"We had a picnic in a state park," she continued, relishing the details as they came back to her, "trail bologna and cheese wrapped in butcher paper, a loaf of bakery bread, milk in pint-size glass bottles. We bought all of it at that little general store off the main route, remember? When we were through eating, we lay on a blanket, looking up at the leaves shining in the sun, too sleepy to move. Then Kevin went off on his own, into the wooded area close by.

"We got worried when he didn't come back, so we woke Wendy up from her nap and went looking for him, calling him. I was frantic with worry. You kept saying, 'He's okay. Don't worry, Olyn. Kevin is okay.' Then, he answered our call. We found him next to a pool in the woods, just sitting there, with his shoes and socks beside him, his feet in the water. Kevin said, 'I found it. All by myself. Look at it.' You said to him, giving me a look—that look you have—so I wouldn't cry out my relief, my alarm—you said, 'Nice find, Kevin. How cold is it?' And Kevin said, 'Cold as ice, Dad.'

"He looked proud. So proud. We all sat down beside him, peeled off our shoes and socks. Wendy fussed and fidgeted, but she put her feet in the water, too. We splashed each other, laughing. We stayed there until we were so cold we couldn't stand it.

"After that, we talked about that pool all through our trip."

Alex nodded. Her head against his shoulder, Carolyn felt his nod, which traveled down his body so that he rocked, gently.

This is why I come here, Alex thought, not for the first time. *This is why I make love to my wife, who is no longer my wife. Nobody else has our memories. Nobody else in the world. Nobody else can bring back my kids to me, as they were when they loved me, when they looked up to me, when they belonged to us, when we were the center of the world to them.*

He ached for Kevin, the Kevin that was gone from him. There was a time when that was an impossible thought.

"I'd better get going," he said.

"Where are you supposed to be?" she said, mildly curious.

"Running errands."

Alex sat up, turning his back to her, head down, gathering his energy. "Hardware. Home improvement depot. Selene has this notion I should be doing things around the house. Probably because she's at home so much now."

He got up, pulling on briefs, pants, a button-down shirt, then sat down again on the bed to put on his socks and shoes.

"About Griff," she said, to his back.

"What about Griff?" he said, as though he had forgotten all about him.

"Why don't you get to know him again? He's not such a bad guy."

He stood up, facing her, fully dressed, ready to go—suddenly impatient to get going—crossing his arms over his chest. "And what do you know about him that I don't know?"

"Just this." She beckoned to him. He leaned over the bed. She pulled him to her and kissed him. "He doesn't want to be you. Or anything like you."

He lingered there, his face close to her.

"And why not?" he asked, slowly, distinctly.

"Because you're exactly like your father."

Alex stood up, his arms crossed again.

"The hell you say."

"He needs to prove he's a Cavillon and not a Price. Why do you think he told you and Nan he'd dropped his last name? That he's now William Griffith Cavillon?"

"Because he's a damned fool," he said.

He paced the small bedroom. Then he walked to the window, pushing back the thick drapes.

Carolyn blinked as the bright afternoon sun flooded the room, watching him as he paced again.

"Why don't you let him help you?" she said.

"Help me? Help me how?"

"I don't know." She thought for a moment. "He could help fix up the house."

She couldn't bring herself to say "your house." It wasn't his house, just as Selene wasn't his wife, not really, not in the way she, Carolyn, was his wife, the mother of his children. His "real" wife.

"What in the hell are you talking about?"

He was angry now, still pacing, eyeing her with distrust.

"Well, you're so busy, and he's good at that sort of thing. He gets it from Bernard. He spent more time with Bernard than he did with his own—with Howard. It's natural with him. With you, it's—"

"Well?"

"—contrived," she said.

Then, liking the sound of it, enjoying his wrath because she had aroused it, 'With you, it's contrived. You're not that good with your hands. You're good with your head."

He stood beside her bed with his hands on his hips, his feet apart, as if ready to pounce on her.

"You used to be able to admit it," she went on. "You used to laugh about it. Remember how many times we put Griff to work when he came to see us? Even when he was a teenager? You said he should be a surgeon and he said—"

She stopped, frowning.

"And he said?"

Alex sat down on the side of the bed, her side, rocking her with his weight. He waited, forgetting his anger.

"He said—" She nodded, calling up the words. "He said he'd never use his hands to cut open people."

"Yes. He said that. How do you remember so much?"

She shook her head. "I don't know," she said softly.

She wanted to say, *Because that's my whole life, remembering. Because I don't have a new life to overlay my memories. Because I don't have a new love to wipe out my love for you.* But she just shook her head until Alex took her head between his hands to still it, kissing her quickly on the lips.

"Gotta go," he said. "See ya."

She wanted to say, "When?" Instead, she repeated, as casually as he had, "See ya," then listened for the sound of the door closing behind him.

The condo was quiet. So quiet. *I should get a cat,* she thought. But then she remembered that she didn't like animals in the house. She had tolerated a cat while Kevin and Wendy were growing up, but she was relieved when it finally died of old age.

"Mrs. Malaprop," we called it. Who knows why? Probably one of Alex's "heady" names. But the kids called it "Mal." Even Alex finally called it "Mal."

CHAPTER 6

Nan and Griff were in the country, south of Sylvan Springs, in Nan's comfortable Chrysler sedan, Griff driving she knew not where. It was the first time they had been alone for any extended time since Griff's return. They had been driving slowly, in near silence, for more than half an hour.

It was not an awkward silence; it had no overtones or undertones. Nan was, by far, the more vocal of the two, but she was capable of great stillness. She indulged herself when she was alone with Griff, who had little to say. Knowing him as she did, she could interpret him, anticipate him. But even she had limits. She lay awake at night, trying to fathom the Griff who had come home to her.

"Griff, I told myself I wouldn't ask you this. Not ever again. But—" Nan hesitated and then said, "Do you have any plans?"

"*Et tu*, Brutus?" Griff said, lightly.

"I know. I know."

Nan looked out of the open window at fields of young corn and soybeans, inhaling the earthy, grassy scents of spring after recent rains, the underlying smell of manure from a nearby farm, listening to the chorus of birds and bullfrogs, feeling the breeze against her face, in her hair.

She sat up straight, looked around her. "Why, I know this road. I guess I wasn't paying attention. I was daydreaming. This is ..."

"We used to drive out here a lot, you and me and—" Griff hesitated, as though the word came hard for him. "—and Dad. And Alex, when he was around."

Griff lifted his foot from the accelerator so that the car cruised like a ship in sail down the dirt road, gravel crunching under the tires. It was so quiet she could hear the slow-motion movement of the leaves as they passed under the trees along the roadside.

"I remember," she said.

She wondered what his childhood memories were, wondered if he had been happy then. Was it possible, even for a loving parent, to assess the life, the degree of happiness, experienced by another human being? Could she even assess her own life, the measure of bliss she had been allotted?

Yes, she thought. *Yes. Little enough, far away in time, but measurable.*

"I wish I knew you better," she said, without thinking, hoping he had not heard her.

"Nobody knows me better than you."

"I mean, as you are now, at this moment, not as you were when—when you were with us."

She knew, even as she said it, that he would call her on it, and he did.

"I was with *you*," he said, his voice carefully neutral—not raised, not angry. "When was I ever 'with' Dad? Or even Alex?"

"When we were driving down this road," Nan said, studying his profile, seeing, as if for the first time, Griff's father—the clean, even features, the high forehead, the arch of the eyebrow, the slightly downward-tilted nose, the strong, angular jaw. She caught her breath, surprised by the strength of what was, after all, just a memory.

He laughed, a short, bitter-edged laugh.

"Okay. I'll give you that. I liked those rides. We seemed so normal. Like a normal family. Especially when Alex was with us."

"Then you had someone to fight with in the back seat."

"We always ended up fighting. I don't know why. He'd say something and I'd—" Griff shook his head. "He knew all my trigger points."

"Alex has Howard's temperament," Nan said, thoughtfully. "Like his dad, he can be very charming—and very annoying. You're right. He seems to know all the pressure points."

"He's been on my case ever since I got back. I just wish we weren't too old for a fist fight. It would make me feel a hell of a lot better."

"You might lose," said Nan.

"The odds are better for me now. I'm not a skinny little kid any more. Alex Price's snotty-nosed little brother."

"He took care of you," Nan said.

Griff seemed to consider this.

"Up to a point, yes. Just like Dad took care of me—up to a point."

"Griff," she said, "What is it you want to know?"

He hesitated, again considering, then he said, "You asked me about my plans."

"Yes."

"I think you were asking me something else. I think everybody's been asking me something else."

"And what's that?"

"Why I came back."

"Oh, but I—"

"I know." He stopped her. "This isn't about my being welcome here."

Griff guided the car in its neutral course down the dirt road, considering his next words.

"I came back," he said, slowly, "because there's too much unanswered in my life. I think the answers—some of the answers—are here."

"My dear one, you shall have the answers, so far as I know them, and the truth—at least my version of the truth—from me."

He touched the accelerator. The car, which had been gliding to a stop, darted forward. Nan looked at the farms, neat and tidy; the fields, green, springing with life, carved into precise squares and rectangles. She thought about her life, neat and contained, for the most part, but with a few patches of wild growth in the distance, like the dark unclaimed woods behind the fields.

She was not a rebel spirit, like Selene. Nan knew her wild patch was shadowy, a dark, secret place she was hesitant to approach, even in memory. Selene, on the other hand, danced in the center of her wild patch.

Before Alex's divorce, Alex had introduced Selene to his mother as "a business acquaintance." Selene, Alex told Nan, had been assigned to edit the book that Alex was publishing on corporate management.

Nan and Selene had looked at each other in instant conspiracy. She and this lovely, vital young woman were together in acknowledging his naiveté in thinking he could pass off Selene as a mere "acquaintance."

Selene recognized Nan's insight. She made no attempt to deceive Nan. The look they exchanged was honest. That honesty had solidified their kinship ever since. It was Alex, that look said, who was clinging to his conservatism, a conservatism passed down to him his father, never far from the surface. But the women—his mother, Nan; his lover, Selene; even Carolyn, his wife, who was about to be undeceived—were realists. Life's cleanup crew.

Nan and Selene had grown to love each other down the years, and had protected Alex from too blinding a self-knowledge. But Griff, like his father, saw clearly. Nan could keep nothing from him that he wanted to know.

After a few minutes, Griff turned off onto another dirt road, tapping the brakes lightly, leaning forward, peering out the open window.

"It's a little farther down the road," said Nan. "Almost to the next intersection."

"That's right," Griff said. "I remember now."

They rounded a bend in the road and pulled up beside the mill.

Griff turned off the engine. In the sudden quiet, the sounds of the afternoon swept across them like waves—the churning of the shallow, rocky river, which widened and deepened a few miles farther on; the trees sighing, the birds clamoring intermittently, drowsy in the afternoon heat; the rustle of the small hidden community of creatures that crept close to the ground, away from prying eyes.

The mill, built to last for hundreds of years, then abandoned in the rush of progress, reproached them with the solidity of its stone walls, the stillness of its mammoth wheel. It rose up before them like a living thing, useless and comatose but not yet crumbling into nonexistence.

They opened their doors simultaneously and stepped outside.

"I think there's a blanket in the trunk," said Nan.

Griff opened the trunk and found the blanket. They walked together toward the same spot, a grassy patch near the river, close to a willow tree with graceful fronds touching the ground. Griff spread the blanket. They sat down, looking out at the river, its calm, endless journey, except where it collided with the rocks near the mill.

"We used to come here on Sunday afternoons," said Nan, knowing she was recounting what he remembered as clearly as she did, "—you, Alex, Howard and me. The trunk loaded with 'provisions.' You didn't want me to call it a 'picnic' for some reason. We set everything out right here. Then you and Alex explored the mill, the river bank, the woods. Howard and I, we just sat here, basking in the sun, waiting for the mighty explorers to return so that we could feast."

She smiled, enjoying the memory.

"When Alex didn't come with us, you went off by yourself. Sometimes, you didn't return for an hour or so. I know one time I—"

Griff stood up suddenly.

"I'll be back in a few minutes," he said.

He walked away toward the mill and the woods beyond. Nan looked after him, watching his long-legged stride cover the distance easily. In a few moments, she was alone, wondering at her son's inexplicable comings and goings, so like his father's.

Bill. Had she ever known him? She could call up his face and his body immediately. That half smile, a parenthesis-like indentation at either side of his mouth, which made her shiver, even in memory. His blue eyes, without a hint of green, so like Griff's. How he moved tentatively, as though not quite sure of himself, of his own height and strength. He had been her lover, briefly, the father of one of her sons, a man who was *unto himself*, utterly. So like Griff. But perhaps it was only a matter of degree, for how well had she known Howard, or he her? How could she begin to know the people who were important to her, let alone the people who came in and out of her life as friends and acquaintances, who told her everything—and nothing—about themselves, who impinged on her life, as she did on theirs, with so little genuine exchange of feelings?

How ignorant we are to think we know each other, she thought.

Nan sighed and lay down on the blanket. The buzzing, humming silence lulled her into a light sleep. She awoke to find Griff sitting beside her, looking out at the river.

"I must have fallen asleep," she said, in the way afternoon dozers announce the obvious. "Where did you go?"

"You said something that reminded me of a place in the woods I used to go to, when we came out here," Griff said, still gazing at the water. "It was a private place, a—secret place. I had almost forgotten about it."

Nan sat up and clasped her arms around her knees. "Did Alex know about it?"

"No. Nobody knew about it. I almost told him once or twice. But I didn't. He might have known about it. It's just a little clearing, and it isn't that big of a woods. But I always thought of it as mine alone. I was just a kid. Now, I know—"

He stopped. When he didn't continue, Nan urged him on. "Now you know what, Griff?"

"Now, I know how little we can claim for our own. Even our family can—evaporate."

"But it didn't." Nan heard the urgency in her voice, but she needed to say it. "You always had a family. Howard accepted you as his child."

"Didn't it bother him that I was named 'William'?"

"Maybe. Probably," said Nan. "I didn't ask his permission, and we always called you 'Griff.'"

"Wasn't it—hard—for him?"

"Of course. The hardest thing in our marriage. I don't know where he found the strength to forgive me, to absorb my affair, to absorb you, into our marriage. But he did—although the wound took years to heal over. Maybe it never healed. Maybe—"

Griff waited for her to continue.

"Maybe I shortened his life. Maybe that's why he had a heart attack. The stress. The false calm we tried to layer over everything. The silence. For some of our actions, you know, there are no words. No words that count. I could only tell him so much. After that, it was up to him. He chose to accept things as they were. I don't know if he ever forgave me, but he accepted things—as they were."

She thought for a moment. "He was a good father to you. The best he could be. He came to think of you, feel for you, as he would for a child he had adopted. Out of love. Out of forgiveness."

"He loved *you*," said Griff, quietly. "He tolerated me."

"He was more gentle with you than he was with Alex," said Nan. "He pitied you—maybe you felt that—or perhaps he pitied me, and it spilled over into his role as your father."

"It was a role for him," said Griff. "He was always playing the part."

"I don't think—"

"Alex is just like him."

"In many ways, yes, but—"

"They both resented me."

There was a finality in his words that stopped Nan's impulse to defend Alex and Howard, to make it all right for Griff, to revise his memories, to soften the blows of a childhood punctuated by the gradual realization that he was not the cherished center of a family but the one who was "tolerated."

"You blame me, I know," Nan said, her voice quavering.

"Not any more—I don't think." Griff frowned, considering. "There was a time when I was very angry. Now—it just makes me sad."

Nan said, chant-like, her voice still shaking, "But I don't want you to be sad. I want you to be happy! You're the child of my love, my passion. You were loved. You were wanted. Always. Even when I was frightened, alone. I never wanted you gone. I never wanted you not to be."

Griff turned his head away from her as she said this. Then he rose lightly to his feet, walking away from her, to the river bank.

She remembered, then, how utterly helpless he was when confronting someone else's emotion.

She got up, walked over to him, touched his arm. He nodded, without looking at her.

"You always made me feel peaceful," she said. 'Even when you were a baby, you would look at me, right into my eyes, and I would feel calm. Just like—"

He said, looking out at the river, "Tell me about him."

"You already know everything there is to know about him. I told you everything I know. You knew that before you—went away. What you want me to tell you is why I loved him. What drew me to him. Why I was willing to—"

She stopped.

"Yes," he said, into the silence. "I suppose so. I suppose that's what I want to know."

"Well, then, let me tell you, first of all, that nothing I say is going to satisfy you, Griff. You know the facts. You're asking for some kind of—justification. That's more than I can give you."

"Why?"

He said this almost in a whisper.

She looked up at him standing next to her, adult, mature, yet childlike in his need for answers, for the definitive.

He hasn't changed, she thought. *There's an innocence about him, a yearning to see all around a difficulty, as though it were a three-dimensional object. He has only to walk around it, measure it, study the lines of it, run his hands over it, feeling the texture of it with those big—but oddly delicate—hands. Those hands that can fix anything ...*

She turned toward him, took his right hand in both of hers, pressed it against her cheek, then released it.

"I'm so sorry I hurt you," she said.

"Hurt me?"

"In many ways. Yes."

"Maybe I hurt myself—by going away."

"Maybe. Probably. But I pushed the boat away from the dock. You just picked up the oars and steered a course. Oh, Griff! I caused a lot of damage. I can never make up for it. I can only hope for your forgiveness."

He looked at her in genuine surprise.

"You don't need my forgiveness. I didn't come back for— that. That's not what I—"

"All right," she said, soothingly. "I understand. This is not what you want to hear. It's selfish of me, I know. It's just that—" She stopped, took a breath. "You're like him. Very much like him."

He turned his head toward her, not to look at her, but to indicate he was listening to her. In that moment, she saw Bill— his oblique acknowledgment of her presence, her importance to him, combined with a careful distancing.

"When you left us, I wasn't sure. I couldn't tell. You looked like him but you were—unfinished. The mold hadn't quite set. It took years, those years when you came home, then went away again. But this time, when I saw you again, after—has it really been six years?—after all the waiting, and praying, and hoping, it was—it was as if I were seeing your father again for the first time. And it isn't so much that you look like him, although there's a strong resemblance. It's—you. The person, the man, you've become. All on your own. Without my intervention. Without my—imposing him on you."

She paused. She felt again, as she had all those years ago, the devastation of knowing Bill had left her, despite her love, perhaps because of her love—because her love was a burden he could not carry.

Then she said, musing, "What is it, I've often wondered, about strong men like you and your father that makes you want to run away—to escape, even from those who love you?"

Nan focused her eyes on the river as she spoke.

"I think about Alex and his father. Both strong men. Decisive, yet compassionate. Clear-eyed, level-headed, but capable of tenderness. Born executives. They know how to dominate, without being dominant. They know what to do in a crisis. You feel safe with them."

Griff stooped and began throwing flattened pebbles at the river. They both watched them cascading across the water.

"Then there's you and your father," Nan continued. "Both of you strong in a different way, a way that's almost imperceptible to men like Howard and Alex. You've chosen to be unencumbered. You've chosen to be free. You're capable of love, but only on your terms—so no one is safe with you. Your strength—and your great weakness—is your absolute autonomy."

Griff stood up. Nan faced her son squarely.

"So when I ask myself, what is it about men like you and your father that drives you away from responsibility, away from commitment, the answer is evident—at least to me. Your weakness is bound up with your strength, like the coils in a rope."

Nan shook her head, suddenly exhausted.

"Do you want to know who he was—your father? Then look to yourself, Griff. Look at who you are. You've hurt me—you've hurt all of us—in a way I couldn't have imagined when you were born, when you were a child. Your father left me—left us—once—before you were born, before he knew you existed. You've taken it one step further. You've made it a way of life. I love you, Griff,

but I'm afraid of you, afraid of what you'll do to me if you—
when—you leave again."

Nan walked away from him, not wanting to see his response,
not wanting to be softened by it. She got into the passenger side
of the car, her whole body trembling.

Well, she thought, *he wanted answers; he wanted to understand more about himself, who he is, who his father was ...*

He had brought her to this place of pleasant memories,
memories of family, wanting reassurance. Instead, knowing how
crushing it might be, she had given him what she had promised
to give him—the truth. Her truth.

It's too late for pretty stories, she thought, *for fiction.*

CHAPTER 7

Nippy is the first to hear him. The terrier, pressed against Selene's feet as she sits at her desk, raises his head, alert.

It's late afternoon. Selene, in her ground-floor study, is struggling with Kirby Woods' manuscript on extrasensory phenomena. It's not going well, this edit. Kirby seems to have thrown the material together while sitting with his laptop on a plane, en route from one speaking engagement to another. It's a jumble of facts, opinions, and ideas, some of it very good, most of it incoherent, repetitive.

Selene has her hand on the phone. She is about to call Kirby, or Jeff, her former boss (now her client), or both, when she hears what Nippy has already heard. She looks out the window to the driveway. Griff is pulling up in his truck, engine purring, gravel crunching softly. He rolls to a stop close to the window, his upper frame—all that is visible to her—absolutely still, as if deep in thought.

A low growl issues from Nippy's throat. Selene taps him with her foot, as if the sound might penetrate the walls of the house, carry over the sound of the engine, reach the ears of the man sitting in the truck as in a freeze frame, his hands gripping the steering wheel. This time, she knows, she cannot rush out to him. She cannot urge him to come into her house. She looks out the window at him, aware that he cannot see her.

If he put his hand on the horn and honked, just once, I'd get up from this desk and go out to him. I'd get in the truck and go off with him, forever, without looking back. I'd give up Alex, this house, my work, my life here in this town, for this man, this stranger, a man who would always be a stranger to me, as I would be to him.

A minute passes. Two minutes. Three minutes. Nippy, still at her feet, has relaxed, but Selene is tense, watchful, waiting for the next move, the move he must make, the decisive move. She bites her lip so hard she can taste blood. Her right hand is still on the phone. Her left hand is on the inside of her thigh, just beneath her shorts, the contact with her skin reassuring. Her fingers push into the flesh, yielding yet firm in her grip.

With a sudden swift movement, he shifts gear, turns his head, backs the truck out of the drive. He is gone in a few moments, the sound of the truck—surprisingly quiet—ebbing away. She listens to a basketball thudding against a nearby driveway. There's a pause while the ball is tossed in the air, then pinged against the basket. Then, another thud. Another ping. *Thud. Thud. Thud.*

"Go, damn you," she says out loud, lifting the phone still in her hand, slamming it down on the desk. "Go, you coward. You fucking coward. I don't want you. I don't need you. I've got what I want. I've got what I need. You're just a— You're just a piece of candy I'm craving. Nothing more. Don't kid yourself."

She looks down. Nippy is on his feet, tail down, consternation in his upturned eyes, as if he's being scolded. She laughs suddenly, harshly, saying to the dog, "He's not worth it. I know it. You know it. He probably knows it."

She gets up, walking back and forth between the desk and the file cabinet, the door and the bookshelf. She feeds her anger, afraid of the empty, panicky feeling that is beginning to take its place. "He's not worth it. He's not worth it," she says, again and again.

"C'mon, boy, let's go for a walk."

Nippy's tail gyrates, pulling his hindquarters into motion. He rushes out of the room and comes back a few moments later with his leash in his mouth. Selene fastens the leash to his collar. Nippy pulls her to the door, every molecule in his small frame drawing him toward the park a few blocks away, with its infinite variety of animal odors.

Selene puts her hand on the front door knob, then stops, while Nippy wriggles impatiently at her feet. The hallway is in deep shadow, the stairs behind her, the porch in front of her. She thinks of the first time she saw him, standing just outside the door, Alex beside him. She had walked up the steps from her car and there he was, talking to her husband. She had invited him in, knowing her danger, even then, in that first moment—accepting it, even then, without hesitation.

He will never come to me in that way. Without hesitation. He will always pull away from me because he doesn't want me as I want him. He has scruples, whereas I—I have none.

"You can't wait," she says to Nippy, opening the door, letting him pull her outside, "but I can."

Selene shuts the door behind her, following Nippy down the porch steps, onto the sidewalk. Nippy makes his way in the direction of the park, bounding at the end of the leash as though he were making his way through deep snow, his terrier instincts focused unerringly on what he knows is just ahead of him, if she will only move faster, faster.

"I can wait," she says, clutching the leash.

*   *   *

Jimbo had just slammed out of the house, cursing his mother in the foulest street language, making the walls shudder, the dishes in the kitchen sink tremble and clank against each other. Sue heard Jimbo's motorcycle rev up angrily, then charge down the street at full throttle. Then she heard Griff's truck purring in the driveway. After a while—a long while, it seemed to her—he turned the engine off.

"My kid's high as a kite," said Sue, as soon as Griff walked in. "I can't talk to him. He's got no business being on that bike in his condition, but it's like talking to a lamppost. All he wants is money. To hell with me and anything I have to say. Did you hear what he called me? No, you were out in your truck. Well, nobody should say to his mother what he said to me. What if he goes out and kills himself on that bike? What if he kills somebody else? How do I get through to him, Griff? He won't listen to me."

Without saying a word, Griff took hold of her wrist, firmly, leading her from the kitchen to the living room, then up the stairs.

Sue's house—the only thing, besides Jimbo, she had salvaged from her marriage—was small, cramped, with a kitchen and living room downstairs, two bedrooms and a bathroom upstairs. Griff led her into her bedroom, with its clothes strewn carelessly about—*her* clothes—Griff was careful with his few things. He shoved her unfolded laundry off the bed, and pushed her down on the rumpled sheets.

She was startled by his abruptness, but not unwilling. He never had much to say. Today, he had nothing to say. So what? She didn't understand him any more than she understood Jimbo, or Jimbo's lousy father, so what did it matter if they talked a blue streak or said nothing at all? Jimbo wanted her money, a place to come home to whenever it suited him to come home. Griff wanted a place to stay, a woman to fuck whenever it suited him to fuck her. Sue wanted—what did Sue want? She didn't know anymore. She had forgotten. What did other women want—women like Griff's mother, who lived in a big house in a fancy neighborhood, who had never met her, never asked to meet her, never invited her over? Or was that Griff's doing? Maybe he didn't want his mother to meet Sue Smoller, who rented a chair at Hair Today, and worked at Spangleman's whenever she could get the hours.

Griff pulled his clothes off. Sue, always obliging, did the same, undressing quickly as she sat on the bed. He found a condom in the drawer of the little table by the bed, put it on, entered her without preliminaries. She was ready for him, as she always was. He pushed into her impersonally, without looking at her, almost without noticing her. *So this is how it is,* she thought, responding to him despite herself, resentment and excitement mounting inside her simultaneously. *He's thinking of somebody, remembering somebody.*

He withdrew from her abruptly, turned her over so that her face and chest were pressed against the mattress, entering her from behind. *He doesn't want to see me. He wants to see her—whoever she is.* But it didn't matter now, now that she was almost there, now that she could no longer think, could only feel what he was making her feel, despite herself. *Use me. Use me. It doesn't matter now. Use me.* She repeated this to herself with every thrust, willing herself to connect with him, if only for a few moments.

After he came, he rolled away from her. She turned onto her back, a careful distance between them. There was nothing to say. She looked at the ceiling, following the cracks in the paint as they traveled down the walls.

This goddamn house is falling apart. Just like me. Getting old. Needing a facelift. Only how in the hell can I afford—

As if reading her thoughts, Griff said, "I'm going to paint this room."

Sue gasped, swallowed, said nothing.

"In fact," he continued, "I'm going to paint the whole house—except for Jimbo's room, unless he wants it. If you clear out the mess in here, I'll start tomorrow. I've already picked up some paint."

"What color—?"

"Forget it," he said. "I'm not putting up purple walls with pink trim."

"I don't—"

"I said, forget it. You're going to get your house painted, but I'm picking out the colors."

He got up and sat on the edge of the bed, his back to her. Sue looked at his broad back, the back of his head, with the light brown hair curling against his neck.

How vulnerable men are, just there, at the back of the neck, around the ears. How often I've thought that as I cut their hair—as I cut his hair. No matter how strong he is, no matter how strong he looks, he's soft there, like a baby. If I could just—

He got up, picked up his clothes and shoes off the floor, walked out of the bedroom without looking at her, having never really looked at her since he came in. He went into the bathroom, closed the door. Sue listened as he turned on the shower, pulling the shower curtain across its metal bar.

He always showers after we make love—have sex, fuck—whatever it is to him. Always. As though he can't wait to wash me away—the smell of me, the taste of me, the honey that I make inside of me. Who is she? Who does he want? It sure as shit isn't me.

The shower stopped. She listened as he dried himself, then—*He's brushing his teeth! I'm now expelled from every orifice.* She heard him open the door to let the steam escape while he dressed. She heard the zip of his jeans, the clunk of his boots as he tied them, walked quickly down the stairs—not quite running, as if restraining himself—across the living room to the kitchen, where he let himself out the back door, closing it quietly behind him. Griff never slammed the door.

What in the fucking hell am I supposed to do now, she thought, still lying flat on her back on her bed, now more

rumpled than it was before. *Kick him out? Can't. The sex is—
And he's so— Get some straight answers from him? Can't. Don't
know the questions. Take what I can get? That's what I'm doing.
Where are we going with this? Can't tell. Don't care. He's the best
thing that's happened to me since—*

Sue pulled herself up, bracing her back with pillows.

*Jimbo. He's out there on his bike, probably no helmet, high
on—what? What did it matter? He wasn't in control. Nobody in
his path was safe. And here am I, his mother, getting laid while
he—*

She got out of bed, looked around the small bedroom.

"This room is a fucking disaster," she said, out loud.

Naked, gluey with sweat, she began to pick up her clothes,
the clean towels and sheets Griff had shoved onto the floor to
make room on the bed.

"I wasn't going to say purple and pink," she said, again out
loud, looking around the room. "More like—lilac, to match the
flower pattern in the curtains. Or maybe I should get new curtains. Then I'd like—sky blue. And sea green in the bathroom. A
light sand brown in the hallway and—downstairs? Yellow in the
kitchen. A light, light blue in the living room, and—oh, fuck it.
He'll do what he wants to do."

She stopped, her arms full of clothes, towels, sheets.

"And Jimbo will do what *he* wants to do."

She threw the tangled heap on the floor and walked out of
the room, slamming the door behind her.

*   *   *

From his large sunny window at the top of the house,
Bernard can see Nan and Selene in the garden. They're walking
among the flowers and plants, on the wood-chip paths that he
and Nan laid out, so that the back yard is not a grassy expanse to

be mowed every week, but a small wilderness of fern and flower, edged in bushes and trees, with a fence behind, almost hidden from view but ensuring their privacy, their separateness from neighboring houses, neighboring yards.

Selene's little mixed terrier—Scrappy? Scruffy?—is nosing among the bushes at the outer edge of the property, his excitement evident even from three stories above. Bernard smiles, thinking of the family dogs of his youth—one a fox terrier named Toby, smooth-coated, white, like Selene's dog, with a few brown and black spots splashed on his compact body.

When Bernard was a boy, Toby had been his companion, following him all over town, whether Bernard was on foot or on his bike, always ready to carry a ball, a stick, or a pair of rolled-up swim shorts. He could catch a fly ball or fetch a stray tennis ball, swim in the river, the quarry, the lake ...

He danced on his hind feet, now I think of it. Just like a circus dog. Toby. Do I have a photo of him somewhere in my things? I'd like to see it. I'll ask Nan to help me look for it ...

Bernard looks down at the two women in the garden. They are intent on the roses and impatiens planted near the porch. They are talking, talking. *They're as pretty as the flowers surrounding them,* Bernard thinks, *and as colorful. What bright colors women wear nowadays!* Selene's shirt is the color of fresh celery. She's wearing a long greenish purplish skirt that seems to wrap around her. She has sandals on her feet. Even with his sharp eyes, Bernard can't see her toenails, but he's sure they're dabbed with color. Nan is in pink shorts, a pink sleeveless top. Her feet are bare. She looks fresh, young. Bernard is proud of her, of her beauty, which comes from him but, especially, from Anna.

He'd like to go downstairs and look at them more closely, as they stand talking in the garden, but he dreads the stairs. He will only admit this to himself, never to Nan, but it is getting harder and harder to journey down those three flights of stairs, even with the railings Nan installed on both sides of the stairway. He loves his little eyrie, but he wonders if it isn't becoming more of a cage than a nest.

I'll have to do what Nan keeps urging me to do, he thinks, gloomily. *I'll have to move downstairs into that back room that Howard used to use for a study. It was a bedroom a long time ago, with the bathroom next to it, off the kitchen, like the house I grew up in. Maybe it won't be so bad, after all. But Nan will lose her privacy—and I'll lose mine. Maybe I should just move out.*

Bernard moves from the window to his high-backed easy chair, sits down, settling into its worn, comfortable cushions, its textured hollows fitted to his body and the back of his head by years of use.

I could go to one of those apartments—what do they call them?—that are set up for old farts like me. He smiles, thinking of Alex's affectionately insulting soubriquet. *Well, that's what I am now. An old fart. Sitting in an old chair with my old memories. Waiting to die.*

He reaches into his back pocket for a handkerchief, wiping his eyes, his nose. *Feeling sorry for myself again,* he thinks, pushing the handkerchief back in his pocket, leaning his head back so that his chin is thrust up and he is looking at the ceiling.

Goddamn crybaby. Crying for what's lost and gone. For my youth, my vigor, my health. For Anna. For my old friends, now dead and buried. For the good times I had with them. An old man's tears. An old fart.

Very slowly, he leans forward, pushing down on the arms of the chair, taking some of the weight off his legs. He rises to his feet in slow motion, with great care. Only when he's alone does he allow himself to groan aloud with the effort. He goes to the window, glancing down to make sure the two women are still in the garden, then walks over to his kitchen area, against the back wall. He opens a cupboard, pushing aside cans, bottles, boxes, until he finds what he wants—the fifth of whiskey smuggled up from Nan's pantry, then shoved out of sight. He opens another cupboard, takes out a glass, pours out the whiskey—a generous portion. Then he lumbers back to his chair, his slippered feet heavy, dragging beneath him. He sits down again with a groan, a sigh.

After the first few sips, the sadness begins to recede.

I'm still alive, he thinks, relishing the warmth of the whiskey, shivering slightly with the pleasure. *It's harder and harder to keep warm, but I'm not dead. Cold and dead. That's what cold means to me now. Dead. Interred. Ugly word. Sealed inside a coffin. Earth on top of me. Earth all around me. And no air.*

Life!

Air to breathe. Each sunrise a blessing. Sun on my skin, a little whiskey in my veins. The feel of soil squeezed through my fingers. The smell of rain, things growing, grass, good food, an occasional cigar. Beautiful women to admire ...

How do I give it all up? How do I say goodbye?

Warm now, mellow, Bernard rests his head against the back of the chair, closing his eyes. A pleasant drowsiness seeps through him. Without opening his eyes, he feels for the table next to him, puts down the empty glass.

I'll go downstairs in a few minutes. I just need to close my eyes. I don't want to miss Selene, so lovely. Nan and Selene together, in the garden. Like flowers themselves, in the flower garden.

The sun, emerging from behind white clouds, shines through the window, on his face and hands, on his legs, on his feet, which are always cold. He slides out of his slippers, puts his feet on the hassock, carefully placed to catch the rays of the sun. He wriggles his toes. He feels blissfully warm, inside and out.

Ah, if only I had another drink at my side, and a pretty woman sitting across from me. Selene. I must go down to her and Nan.

But he is asleep before the thought can prick him into exertion.

* * *

"He's depressed," says Nan to Selene, in the garden. "And it's harder for him to come down the stairs. I know it is, though he won't own up to it."

Selene glances up at the large expanse of window on the third floor, with the sun shining on it like a spotlight.

"I'm so sorry, Nan. I do love Bernard. What can I do?"

"Come to see him, of course. He loves to look at pretty women."

"Then it's good he has you to look at all the time."

Nan stoops to inspect the patch of impatiens at their feet.

"I'm going to move him downstairs, to that room near the kitchen that Howard used as a study. There's a bathroom right next to it. It was the first bathroom installed in the house. Almost the first in the neighborhood, I'm told. In those days, all of the plumbing was on the ground floor, close to the kitchen. For convenience."

"Can you imagine living in this beautiful old house without a bathroom?" says Selene.

"Frankly, no. But Dad has talked about those days, although I'm not sure if it's his childhood or his father's he's remembering."

"He seems to enjoy his little attic apartment," says Selene, glancing up again, shading her eyes with her hand, as if she could see Bernard through the window.

"What he enjoys is his independence, from me and from everyone else. He doesn't want to impose on me. But it's either move downstairs where I can keep an eye on him or move into a 'home,' where he'll be taken care of."

"Is he that ill, Nan?"

Standing close to her, looking at her as she asks the question, Selene sees the answer in Nan's face.

Selene quickly adds, "I'm sure he'll choose to stay here, with you. And he'll be close to his garden, just a few steps away."

"I talked to his doctor recently," says Nan, as though she hasn't heard Selene. "Dad has probably been having little—strokes—for a while now. They're called TIAs. They last for just a few seconds. But they can be damaging. The next one might be—"

She stops, then says, "Do you remember when you were here a couple of Sundays ago, for breakfast, and Dad—?"

"He said he saw Anna. She was wearing a red dress. He said he smelled her perfume. Yes, I remember. Do you mean—?"

"Yes. That was probably a TIA. And his drinking doesn't help, of course."

"Does he—?"

"Yes. He thinks I don't know, don't notice, but of course I do."

"Can Alex and I help you with the move?"

"Of course. Thank you. We'll all pitch in. But first Griff is going to paint the room and put down carpeting." As if Selene's thoughts are written plainly on her face, which perhaps they are, Nan adds, "Yes. Griff offered to help, too. In fact, he's already helping. He's been clearing out the study. He's been here quite a lot, lately. I don't think he's very happy where he is."

"You mean with—?"

"Yes. Sue Smoller. I've never met her. He's never brought her here. But I think his staying with her is a—convenience. He doesn't want to stay here, with us."

"Why?"

Selene is trying to sound attentive, impersonal, but she came here, more than anything, to hear his name, perhaps to see him. Now, unexpectedly, he is a topic of conversation.

"I asked him to stay here, of course, when he first got here, but he refused. He hasn't spent one night under this roof. And now, with Dad moving out of the apartment ..."

"Have you asked him if he'd like to stay here, in the apartment?"

Nan shook her head, leading Selene slowly along the path, the wood chips warm under their feet. "I know better. The only way it will happen is if he asks me. And he won't. I'm almost certain of that."

Wanting desperately to continue the conversation, Selene says, casually, "Why won't he ask you?"

"When he left here," Nan says, slowly, "he told his father—he told Howard—he would never live in his house again."

"But that was so long ago and Howard is—"

"Dead. Yes. But Griff won't—he probably can't—forget having said it. If you knew him better, you'd know, you'd understand."

"I wish I did."

Selene looks away from Nan, arranging her face in what she hopes is polite attention rather than avid interest. When she is ready to speak again, she says, "Griff is—so different from Alex."

Nan hesitates for a moment, then says, "Yes. They circle around each other, but they seldom connect."

Feeling her hesitation, Selene searches for a question or a comment before Nan can turn the subject. "So Griff is here—a lot?"

"Lately, almost every day. But he's also painting Sue's house—so he tells me. I never know when he'll show up. Sometimes, he just looks around for a few minutes, then leaves. Takes a few measurements. That sort of thing."

Selene's stomach twists with sudden intensity. *So he's here every day. And he's painting that woman's house. When he could be with me. I hate him for that. The bastard!*

She says, politely, "Is Griff—trained—for anything?"

They have made the rounds of the garden. Nan draws Selene down beside her on the wrought iron patio swing, which sits in the shade of a large maple tree. They rock gently.

"He's good with his hands. He gets that from Bernard. But he couldn't stay the course in school, so he doesn't have a degree. I don't think it's important to him. He went to school, off and on, for two or three years. Oberlin. He would say to me, 'It's all a lot of bullshit, Mom.'"

Selene stiffens, a little shocked, as Nan intends her to be. Nan is careful, deliberate, in her choice of language.

"Finally, he stopped going altogether. Then he left. He left us. He left—me."

Selene says, almost in a whisper, "Why?"

"For letting him down, I suppose. He had this idea of me that I didn't live up to. That I couldn't live up to. I've made, oh, so many mistakes. Mostly in thinking that Howard, my husband, could take the place of—of Griff's father."

They rock gently on the swing, both absorbed in their thoughts. Gradually, the sounds around them fill up the silence. The swing, with its tiny creak, just there, at the edge of the backward motion. The maple leaves whispering. Birds twittering shyly, as if reluctant to break into the quiet. A squirrel, on a branch overhead, crunching rhythmically. A tapping sound—woodpecker?—from a neighboring yard.

Nippy, who appears every few minutes, to check on them, then disappears to continue his exploration of the garden, growls softly. This sound, like the others, reaches Selene's consciousness, for she has heard it before, recently—that growl between a warning and a welcome. Nippy is standing at attention some distance from them, pressing forward, on his toes, his head and tail up, his ears pricked. He is staring intently at the gate near the garage that edges Nan's property.

Selene hears the gate open. Nippy springs forward, barking, then yipping excitedly, uncertain whether to welcome or detain this almost-stranger. Griff appears, Nippy skirting around him, at a safe distance. Nan gets up from the swing and walks over to greet him.

"Griff, we were just talking about you."

She kisses him lightly on the cheek, puts her arm through his. They walk toward Selene, who is still on the swing.

"I was telling Selene about how you're redoing the study, for Gramps. Have you come to work, or to visit?"

Griff stops a few feet away from Selene. He nods.

"How's Gramps?" he says, to Nan.

"He's still upstairs. Let's all go up and see him. He'd like that."

"I can't, Nan," Selene says, suddenly.

"What?" Nan looks surprised. "But I thought—"

Selene gets up from the swing. She dressed carefully for this visit, in a new green and purple outfit, the top snug, sleeveless, the skirt long, graceful, a wraparound skirt, with honey-colored sandals, brightly painted pink toenails. She stands in front of Griff, so that he can see her, so that he can take her in.

"I'm sorry, Nan. I lost track of the time." She glances at her watch. "I'm expecting a call. From Kirby Woods. You know. I'm editing his book. I don't want to miss it. The call, I mean. Come on, Nippy."

She hugs Nan, briefly.

"I'll come by again. Give my love to Bernard."

She is close to Griff, but her eyes cannot quite travel up to his face.

"See you again," she says, gulping the words, almost swallowing them in her haste to get away.

CHAPTER 8

"*Griff, are you nuts?* You're painting the whole goddamn house the same color!"

"And?"

Sue, who had just returned from work, stood with her hands on her hips as Griff continued to sweep the paint roller up and down the wall with practiced strokes. They were in the living room. All of the furniture had been moved to the center of the room, where it was neatly covered with drop cloths. Drop cloths also lined the floor along the sides of the room, where Griff was just finishing up the first wall.

"And? And?" Sue was sputtering with disbelief. "Do you think I want to live in a *tan* house, with a *tan* bathroom and a *tan* bedroom and a *tan* living room? What about the kitchen? Does your color scheme include the kitchen?"

"Yep."

Griff dipped the roller in the paint pan, letting the excess drip off, again applying the roller to the wall, carefully working his way from the center to the top, then to the bottom. He had pressed masking tape against the molding and the baseboard.

"No fucking way. I want a yellow kitchen. I absolutely draw the line there. I won't have a *tan* puking kitchen."

"It's not a bad color," said Griff, pausing to survey his work. "More of a rosy tan. And—"

"And?"

"I got it on sale."

"So paint somebody else's fucking house with your bargain tan."

"I am. I'm painting a couple of rooms off Mom's kitchen—for Gramps."

"Well, maybe your gramps likes fucking tan, maybe he's color blind at his age, but I want color. Do I look like a tan person to you?"

"Nope. And you don't sound like one either."

"Great. Fantastic. Color me blue. Color me green. Color me orange. Just don't color me fucking *tan*."

Griff looked at her and grinned. For a moment, Sue was immobilized. He hadn't looked at her that way since—since—

She was searching her memory when the paint roller slid gently down her arm, leaving a tan stripe in its wake.

"What in the hell are you doing, you lunatic?"

"I'm coloring you fucking tan," said Griff.

As she stood frozen, examining her painted arm, he slid the roller down her other arm. Despite her shock and anger—she had used her Spangleman's discount to buy this blouse less than a week ago—she shivered with excitement.

"You have three seconds to take it off," he said, nodding toward her blouse.

"I'm not—"

"Three seconds."

"Or what?"

"Or I'll paint the rest of it fucking tan."

Sue put her hand on her blouse and released the top button. She looked at Griff, but he had turned his head to look out the front window. He was looking for Jimbo's motorcycle.

"He's not here," said Sue, releasing the next button down. "I looked when I came in."

Griff turned his head back to her and slowly, slowly, that grin returned to his face. Then Sue remembered. He had looked at her that way when he first saw her in the spring, walking downtown. He had leaned out the window of his truck, waving and grinning just like that, picking her up and picking up their life together just where they left off, right after high school, for God's sake, when they were an item for a few months, as though all those years in between—and Jimbo and his no-good father—had never happened.

Quickly, so that she wouldn't lose his attention, so that she wouldn't lose that grin, Sue unbuttoned her blouse and slid it off, pulling the sticky painted edges of the sleeves away from her skin. Griff looked at her breasts, nodding once. Sue reached behind her, unfastening her bra. It slid to the floor, and she stood before him in her snug-fitting skirt, and the comfortable sandals she wore to work in warm weather. He was still holding the paint roller. He cocked his head to one side, surveying her. Then, he took the roller and gently pressed it against one nipple, then the other. Sue winced with pleasure. He turned away from her, placed the roller in the paint pan, turned back again, and stepped close to her, so that she was forced to step back a few feet. With a little pressure, as though she were an almost-felled tree and he was releasing her last tenuous connection to her base, he pushed her backwards. She lost her balance for a fraction of a second, then felt the cushioned back of the couch against her thighs. It was facing the center of the room, where it huddled beneath drop cloths with the chairs, end tables, and lamps that furnished the living room.

As Griff pulled up her skirt and pulled off her panties, Sue watched his face, as if that grin might disappear if she looked away. He fumbled for the zipper of his jeans, reached into a back pocket for a condom, tore at the seal with his teeth.

So he keeps them there, too, Sue thought. *Always prepared. Like a fucking Boy Scout.* But then he entered her and she had no thoughts.

Sue pulled his face close to her and said, against his ear, "Fanfuckintastic."

The drop cloths rustled beneath them, like distant applause.

* * *

Bernard sat in the garden, in a comfortable lounge chair, an iced drink beside him, reading the Sunday papers, while Nan, Griff, Alex, and Selene moved his belongings downstairs, to his new quarters on the first floor. He had no real interest in the proceedings. The decision had been made that he was no longer capable of maintaining his residence on the third floor, just as, some years before, the decision had been made that he should sell the house he had shared with Anna and move into Nan's house.

He was consulted concerning these decisions, but they were not really his decisions. He had been made to see the wisdom of the choices that had already been made for him. So be it. He was an old man put out in the sun to "relax and enjoy the day," while his family scurried up and down the stairs, stripping his eyrie of his few remaining possessions and transposing them to the newly painted and carpeted first-floor room, which had been designated as his quarters until he completed the next stage of his dying.

The room still smelled of paint and the chemicals that were embedded in the carpeting material, but Nan and Griff assured him the smell would dissipate in a few days. Bernard had shrugged. "I'm an old man," he said. "My sense of smell is not what it used to be. Good smells or bad, it's all the same to me." Nan and Griff had looked at each other, but they had not contradicted him. He was less and less contradicted these days. So be it.

He snapped the pages of the newspaper and adjusted his reading glasses. So this is what was meant when they talked about a "second childhood." He had seen something about it in the newspaper only recently. It was this feeling of powerlessness, this nagging perception of incompetence.

I should have moved into a shack in the woods after Anna died, he thought, bitterly. *I should have lived in that shack until I died, alone, the way a sick animal goes off to die by itself, knowing there can be no companion on that last journey. I've been a sick animal ever since Anna left me.*

He turned his head, looking up at the third-story window, and saw Selene looking down at him. She waved to him from the open window. He raised his hand, saluted her. They gazed at each other for a moment, then Selene waved again as she moved away from the window.

* * *

When Selene and Alex had arrived that morning to help with the moving, she had come to Bernard as he sat in the garden, and kissed him.

I guess I'm not dead yet, he thought, fixing his eyes on the garden, thinking about Selene as she had looked then. Yes, she was quite beautiful, with her gray eyes and her hair a sort of muted blond—an almost silvery ash. Today, she was wearing her hair pulled away from her face, with a clasp high on the back of her head. She wore tennis shoes, and no socks. Her legs were bare. Her shorts looked as if they may have been jeans at one time, the pant legs carelessly ripped off well above the knees. She wore a skintight top, low in the back and almost as low in the front. The top was a pinkish beige, close to the color of her skin. For a moment, as she had approached him, he thought she might not be wearing anything at all on top. As it was, it wasn't that much of a disappointment, as the soft fabric was molded to her breasts. He could even see the outline of her nipples pressing against the skimpy lace of her bra.

This was apparently the latest fashion, showing off the contours of one's upper body while supposedly fully clothed. Bernard had no objection. He was gratified to see as much of her body as was allowed him. When she had stooped to kiss him, he could smell her clean hair and a faint, flowery scent. There was a gratifying sensation in his loins. *Not dead yet*, he had thought, looking up at her from his lounge chair.

"How are you?" she had said to him.

"Never better. I don't have to ask how you are. Just looking at you says it all."

She seemed bathed in light. It was almost painful for Bernard to look at her—at her youth, her beauty, her vibrant, tangible health.

All gone, he thought, even as he continued to look up at her. *She is lost and gone forever, oh, my darling Clementine.* The words and melody of the old song floated through his consciousness. His eyes glazed as his mind dragged him back to his past, to Anna sitting at the piano, playing that song, while he sat next to her on the piano bench, singing those words. *Lost and gone forever. Oh, my darling—*

* * *

"Bernard?"

He opened his eyes, not knowing that he had closed them. Anna's face was close to him, out of focus, but so lovely, so loving.

"Anna?"

"No, Bernard. It's me. Selene. Are you all right?"

"Of course I'm all right. Why wouldn't I be?"

"Are you sure?"

"Of course I'm sure."

He pulled himself up straighter on the lounge chair.

"Now I know what they mean by that expression, 'You're a knockout.' I think you knocked me out for a second there."

"It was more like a minute. Or it seemed so to me. Can I get you anything? Would you like to come in the house and rest?"

"I *am* resting," Bernard said, irritably. "That's all I do is rest." He laughed, a brief, grunting laugh. "I guess I'm resting up for the final rest."

"Don't say that, please. I can't bear to hear it."

She was stooping so that her face was level with his. She was holding his hand. When had she taken hold of his hand? How could he have missed that, the pleasure of it? He put his other hand on top of hers, so she wouldn't let go.

"You're good for me," he said. "You're like sunshine."

"Promise me you'll take care of yourself," she said, solemnly. "Promise me."

"I promise," Bernard said, not quite knowing what he was promising, not quite hearing what she was saying, but wanting to please her, wanting to feel the warmth of her hand. *Don't hover*, Anna used to say to him, when he was too attentive. *Give me some space.*

Selene slid her hand out from between his hands. She stood up. Her back was to the sun, and her face was suddenly dark, featureless. Was she Anna? But no, this young woman could not be Anna. Anna had never dressed like that. Anna was modest, to a fault.

Selene said something else to him, which he did not catch, kissed him lightly on the forehead, and walked away. He wished she had stayed longer, so that he could look at her, but no one had time anymore.

*   *   *

Bernard picked up the paper, which he had let fall on his lap. He reached into his shirt pocket for his reading glasses. Not finding them there, he felt around for them.

"Got 'em, Gramps." Alex stood in front of him, holding his glasses. "They fell in the grass."

"How are you, my boy?" Bernard said, taking the glasses.

"Never better. Give us a couple of hours and we'll have this whole move squared away. Need anything?"

"This iced tea could use a little kicker."

"I'll see what I can do about that," said Alex. "Anything else?"

How big he is, Bernard thought, shaking his head. *He and Griff both. Big men. Solid. Strong. Alex more like Howard, his father. A business man. Decisive. A take-charge type. Griff— maybe even taller than Alex. Probably stronger. Good with his hands. Bright and clever. But not stable. Not—knowable.*

Alex put a hand on Bernard's shoulder, squeezed it, then disappeared. *He's strong all right,* thought Bernard, rubbing his shoulder. *Doesn't know his own strength. Wonder if he'll remember to bring me the kicker?*

He settled the glasses on his nose, opened the newspaper, fixed his eyes on the page. A drop of moisture fell on the words; he looked up at the sky, expecting to see gray clouds overhead. But the sky was a clear, cloudless blue. He looked down again at the newspaper as another drop hit the page, creating a small pock mark. "What the—?"

Then he realized his eyes were watering. He leaned forward and reached into his back pocket for the clean handkerchief he always kept there. As he leaned forward, more drops fell on the newspaper, from his eyes, his nose. He took off his glasses and wiped at his face, looking around to make sure he wasn't observed. He heard voices coming from the first floor, the scrape of furniture, a muffled laugh.

"Old fool," he muttered, pushing the crumpled handkerchief back in his pocket. "Old fool."

He settled himself on the lounge chair, picking up the newspaper once again, but the words were blurred. He reached up to adjust his glasses, then realized he was not wearing them; they had slipped away—like his life, like the muscle and mass beneath his loose flesh, like time, like the delicious luxury of planning ahead. He felt around for the glasses. Not finding them, he rolled the newspaper and tossed it into the garden, where it fell with a clunk among the hydrangea. He leaned back, closing his eyes.

This is better, he thought, *better than words on a page. Reading is just a distraction. This is real, the sun on my face, my arms, my legs. That robin's liquid call, again and again, with a little pause in between, as if waiting for a response. The scent of grass growing, flowers blooming. The leaves quickening with the breeze, like the rustle of a woman's skirt.*

Let it last a little longer. Jesus God, if you're up there, let it last a little longer.

* * *

Selene was happy, happier than she had been for weeks, happier than she had been since the last time they were all together in this house, welcoming Griff home with a family dinner. They were all working together to get Bernard moved downstairs. There was a stirring, a planning, a camaraderie about it that pleased her, excited her.

Griff was everywhere, directing the move. Alex, wearing khakis and a white T-shirt—as casual as he ever was, away from home—seemed content to take orders. He saluted Griff periodically, followed his directions, winked at Selene when they passed each other in the hall, pinching the back of her shorts when he followed her up the stairs to the third floor.

"You look sexy today, my love," he said. "Hard physical labor becomes you."

"I don't know how you can tell how I look from that angle," she called back to him, racing ahead of him up the steps.

"Your cheeks are rosy," he said, stopping to catch his breath. "Both sets. I'll comment on the rest of the view later."

At the top of the steps, Griff stood waiting for Selene—or, at least for a joyful moment, he seemed to be waiting for her. As soon as she reached the top of the staircase, he picked up the rocking chair beside him, preparing to descend the stairs with it.

"Can I help?" she said.

"Not with this." Griff was already on the stairs. "Mom's sorting through the cupboards." He tilted his head toward Nan in the kitchen alcove. "You can give her a hand."

"Alex is on his way up."

"Good. He can help me with Gramps' armchair. I'll be right back."

I'll be right back, her mind echoed. *I'll be right back.*

She walked over to Nan, who was pulling plates, glasses, mugs out of the cupboard in the corner kitchen area.

"These were his and Mom's," she said, as Selene stacked them in a box, arranging crushed newspaper around them. "He'll miss them if I leave them up here. I hope I can find space for them in the kitchen." She glanced over at Selene. "You look especially lovely today, my dear," she said. "You have a glow about you."

Selene felt herself blushing slightly. *What would she think of me if she knew,* she thought, and then— *She does know.*

"I'll take them downstairs," Selene said, picking up the box. "Shall I put them away?"

"Just leave them on the kitchen table," said Nan. "I'll put them away later."

"I'm not the man I used to be," said Alex, from the top of the stairs. He came puffing into the apartment and sat down with a sigh on Bernard's armchair. "How many trips so far?"

"Who's counting?" Griff was just behind him on the stairs. "Hey, if this is too much for you, we'll put you outside on the lounge chair with a glass of iced tea, and I'll have Gramps move the furniture."

Alex groaned. "Jesus, that's tempting."

They laughed. Selene put her box down, pulling Alex out of the chair as Griff tipped it forward from the back. Alex got to his feet reluctantly. He took hold of the bottom of the chair.

"You go first," he said to Griff, who was lifting the chair from behind.

"No, you go first," said Griff.

"No, you. I insist," said Alex, turning the chair so that Griff was closest to the stairs.

"I wouldn't think of it," said Griff, mock polite, as he swung the chair so that Alex was wedged in the doorway at the top of the stairs.

"May I make a suggestion, you two oafs?" said Nan, walking over to them.

"Please," said Alex, setting his end of the chair on the floor, groaning as he straightened up.

"This chair is almost too wide for the stairs," said Nan. "I remember when the movers brought it up here. Now, you back it down the stairs, Griff. Gently. Watch out for the rails. You may have to lift it above the rails when you turn the corner. Alex, you tip it so the arms don't rub against the wall or the rails."

Alex gave her a sharp salute, bending down to lift the front of the chair again.

"And don't make Griff carry all the weight," she added, as Alex straightened up.

"It wouldn't be the first time," said Griff.

The huge old armchair, regal in its elevated position, began its descent, with the two men fore and aft. Their banter, obviously meant for the women watching them from the top of the stairs, floated up to Nan and Selene.

"Can you handle it, old man—emphasis on the *old?*"

"Nothing to it—emphasis on the *nothing.*"

"That's because I'm carrying all the weight, you jerk."

"Watch it. Slow down," said Alex. "Directional shift just ahead. Starboard side."

"So quit pushing," Griff growled. "Give me a chance to lift it. There. Now turn it sideways. Not that much!"

"You okay?"

"I will be, right after I get out of traction."

"We're almost there," Alex called up the stairs. "Just a few more steps."

"Easy for you to say. Lift it up a little!"

"How's that?"

"Jesus Christ, Alex, I'm pinned against the wall. Back up a little."

"Better?"

"Better than a chair in my gut. Keep it right about there."

"Steady as you go. Just one more flight before we drop anchor."

Their voices, punctuated by curses, faded as Nan and Selene stood listening at the top of the stairs.

"I haven't told them yet that the furniture in the study has to come up here," said Nan. "I'd like to make this apartment a study. A place for quiet contemplation. Now that Dad has stamped it with his presence."

"Oh, Nan, I love that idea. Perhaps you wouldn't mind my coming here now and then to contemplate."

"I would like that very much," said Nan. "We don't see enough of one another." She looked around the almost-empty room. "This apartment has always been special to me. I love the way the light comes through the window. It's almost like a—"

"A sanctuary," said Selene, finishing her thought.

"Yes, but not so solemn." Nan took a deep breath. "It's a place—a place—to be happy."

"Why, yes," said Selene, studying her face. "Bernard always called it his 'eyrie.'"

"So it is," Nan replied. "Removed from the world. Safe and quiet and—lofty." She laughed at her own joke, then added, "I'd almost rather live here than—down below." She laughed again, then shrugged.

A thought occurred to Selene. She asked, "Did you—spend time up here before Bernard—?"

Nan was still, her face turned toward the window. "Yes, I did," she said, slowly. "A long time ago. When we first lived here."

"Was it an apartment then?"

"Yes. It was. It was always an apartment."

"Did you—" began Selene, but Nan interrupted her.

"Maybe we'd better check on our moving men," she said. "They haven't a clue how to set up that room."

"Are you moving the bed downstairs?"

Nan turned away from the window and looked toward the open door of the bedroom. She said, firmly, "No. The bed stays where it is." Then she added, as if an explanation were needed, "It's too big for the study. I've ordered a hospital bed for Dad. It'll be delivered tomorrow."

Selene walked over to the bedroom door. "It's a great bed. A real old-fashioned four-poster. Has it always been here?"

"Always. Since we've been here."

Selene went into the bedroom. She walked around the bed, caressing the carved maple posters. Then she sat on the side of the bed and bounced, like a schoolgirl. She said, looking up at Nan, who was standing in the doorway with her arms crossed, "I can see why Bernard enjoyed living here."

"This will be his last night sleeping here," said Nan. "Tomorrow morning, I'll help him down these stairs for the last time. Thank God."

"You're worried about him," said Selene.

"Yes. Very. He's been having these episodes—" Nan turned away from the doorway. "What do you say we carry these boxes downstairs and start shifting the study furniture up here?"

"We should give the mighty movers a break first," said Selene, getting up from the bed. She followed Nan into the living area.

Nan picked up a box, lifting her chin to indicate another open box close by. "Let's take these down. We'll give the boys a beer, and five minutes to drink it."

*   *   *

Nan, Alex, and Bernard sat at the glass-topped table on the flagstone patio, lingering over their meal, talking quietly, citronella candles burning around them to discourage early-evening insects. Their voices floated into the kitchen, where Selene was brewing coffee and scooping ice cream into small bowls. She wondered if Griff would return before the ice cream melted.

Griff had taken a phone call and then left, abruptly, while they were sitting around the table, enjoying the beef casserole and summer salad Nan had prepared to top off the transition from downstairs study to bedroom, and from third-floor apartment to study.

"I think it works," said Nan, passing the casserole to Bernard. "Your bedroom looks like it has always been your bedroom, Dad, and there's just enough room on the third floor for the bookshelves and furniture that were in the study. You'll see when you go upstairs tonight."

"If that's the case, I may not want to move," said Bernard, helping himself to the still-warm casserole. "Maybe I'll just stay put."

Alex leaned back in his chair and clasped his hands behind his head. "After the workout we had today, it wouldn't take much for Griff and me to haul you downstairs. We'll just put you in a straight chair and tie you down. Griff will lift the back legs. I'll lift the front. Smooth as an elevator ride."

"I heard you crashing around and cursing earlier today," said Bernard. "I think I'd rather manage on my own steam. How'd you do with my big old easy chair?"

"Safely transitioned without a bruise or a scar," said Alex, then added, "No bruises or scars on the chair, that is."

"I wonder where Griff went off to," said Nan. "He took that phone call and left without a word."

"Was it Sue Smoller?" said Alex.

"I think it was," said Nan. "I answered the phone, but I didn't ask her name."

"Have you ever met Sue?" said Alex.

"Never," said Nan. "He's never brought her here."

"Isn't that a little strange?" said Alex. "After all, he's been living with her for a couple of months."

"He doesn't bring her here because he knows she wouldn't fit in," said Bernard.

"I never said or implied—" said Nan.

Bernard put down his fork with a sigh of satisfaction. "You don't need to," he said. "Griff is nobody's fool."

"What do you know about her?" said Nan.

"Enough," said Bernard, wiping at his mouth with his napkin. He looked toward the kitchen and called, "Selene, my beauty, how's that coffee coming?"

"It's coming," Selene called back. She picked up the tray of ice cream and carried it outside, stepping carefully down the steps off the back porch. She walked around the table, placing the bowls of ice cream at each place. "Will Griff be back in time?" she asked, to no one in particular.

"If he isn't, I'll eat his scoop," said Bernard.

They laughed, softly. Selene went back inside for the coffee. She walked through the house to the front door and looked outside, hoping to see Griff's truck in the driveway, or parked across the street. The quiet, tree-lined street was bumpy with parked cars, but there was no sign of Griff's pickup. She leaned her head against the door frame. What right had Sue Smoller to interrupt her perfect day and take Griff away from her? Griff— who had been almost natural, almost comfortable, almost relaxed with her, for the first time. How many weeks had she waited for just such a day?

An evening breeze blew through the screen door, lifting ten-drils of hair away from her face. She picked her way through the hours just behind her, thinking about Griff, standing close to her, talking to her, joking with her, not a stranger anymore—or so she thought—but a man frankly conscious of her, as she was of him. They had bumped against each other, back to back, at one point, each carrying a load, then had turned toward each other, laughing, bumping each other again. She had helped him carry a table upstairs, lightweight but long, narrow, awkward going around the corners. He had taken a box of books away from her when he saw her struggling to lift it.

They hadn't said much to each other, but they had encountered each other again and again. Selene felt that he was feeding off those encounters, as she was, gorging on the sight, the sound, the smell of her, as she was on him.

Now he was gone, called away by that woman, Sue. She hit the screen with the flat of her hand and felt it give under the pressure. She remembered, when she was in grade school, hitting a girl who had taunted her—the way it had felt to punch her in the stomach, to push in that soft, sensitive part of her; she remembered the way the girl had cried; the satisfaction she, Selene, had felt.

I hate her, she thought, turning away from the door, walking back to the kitchen for the coffee tray. *I hate her.*

*   *   *

"It's his leg, Griff. It's his leg. The motorcycle fell on his leg."

They were standing in the waiting room of the Emergency Care Unit at Clearview Hospital. Sue was gripping Griff's hand and wrist with both her hands, as though she were hanging from a cliff.

"How did it happen?" said Griff.

"He was out riding with a friend—maybe a group of friends. I don't know. They took off, the lousy bastards. They left him there, Griff. They—"

"Just tell me what happened," said Griff.

"It was across the street from a gas station. On Mill Road. Way out—halfway between Sylvan Springs and Clearview. The police said Jimbo skidded on something. There were tire marks. A car was coming from the opposite direction. It veered over to the side of the road, but then Jimbo's bike went out of control. He slid to the same side of the road. There was a fence—or, no, I think maybe it was a wall—a barrier of some kind."

"What happened then?" said Griff, his voice low, calm.

"I don't know, exactly." Sue's face was blotched, her dark hair tangled. She was dressed in the gray sweatpants and sweatshirt she had been wearing when she got the call. "I'm getting all this from the police, and they don't—they weren't—"

"Tell me," said Griff.

"Jimbo fell off his bike. The bike fell on his leg. The car—the car—hit the bike."

Her voice had dropped to a whisper, barely audible, as though she couldn't bear to hear the sound of the words. Griff held her quietly for a few moments, then sat her down in a chair and sat beside her. There was no one else in the small waiting room, populated only by chairs pushed against the wall, a few end tables, an overhead TV, its flashing images muted.

"It's his leg," she whispered. " He may lose— They may not— It was crushed so bad—"

Griff pulled her close to him, bringing her head down to his shoulder. He looked up at the flickering images on the TV screen, listening to her weeping, choking voice as she recounted the accident again and again, trying to put the pieces into place, as though she were working on a complicated puzzle that required all of her attention.

"It was by a gas station, you know the one, Griff. I think it's a Mobil. I've stopped there. They were tearing down the road, probably high on something, and Jimbo, he— You know he's a good driver, good with his bike, anyhow—but he hit a grease slick or something, and he just slid clear across the road, and the bike hit a bump, or something, and he came off, and the bike fell on top of him, and the car—the driver went off his side of the road, but Jimbo was right there and the car—hit the bike, and the doctor said, the doctor said—"

CHAPTER 9

"*I really don't* want to go," said Selene.

"What? Miss a trip to Chicago? Lake Shore Drive? Shopping on Michigan Avenue? Deep-dish pizza?"

"It's just business, Alex. It's just Kirby Woods trying to act like a writer when he's really just a good public speaker."

"Which is why you're doing what you're doing."

Selene watched the early-morning traffic flowing past them, headlight beams glaring in the half light. They were almost to the Cleveland airport. She wondered why she felt so reluctant to take this overnight trip. Alex was right. She usually took every opportunity to get out of town, especially to Chicago or New York or Boston. She loved the city streets, the contact with numberless strangers hurrying God knows where for God knows what purpose, but hurrying, hurrying. Sure that hurrying was the only way to get there—wherever "there" was. She always came back charged up, full of the city, brimming over with talk.

There was nothing she could do for Griff, who was caught up in the drama of Sue's life, Sue's catastrophe. Selene hadn't seen him since the day of Bernard's move. She didn't expect to see him any time soon. Yet, she wanted to be here, close to where he lived and breathed, just in case.

Her dislike for Sue, her resentment of her, was intensified now by her knowledge of Sue's unfortunate son and his unfortunate accident. Sue had reeled Griff in like a fish on a hook when that had happened. Selene could not forgive her for it. She knew she was being unreasonable and unsympathetic, but no one else knew this, so she nurtured it, let it grow.

"Don't try to park," said Selene, as they turned onto the airport drive. It's too much of a hassle. Just drop me off and go on to work. You'll miss the heavy traffic."

"I'll miss you more," said Alex.

"Will you—will you see Nan today?" said Selene, a little breathless.

"I promised I'd let her cook dinner for me and console me in your absence."

"Has she—has she—heard anything?"

"From Griff?" Alex slowed down as he approached the airline departure lane. "Not that I know of. Not since last night."

They had spoken casually of Griff that morning, while they were getting dressed, and again on the way to the airport, so Alex easily picked up on her reference.

Am I that transparent?

"I thought maybe—maybe you'd talked to her this morning."

"My dear girl, it's not even seven o'clock."

"Of course. I wasn't thinking."

You're not thinking You're not thinking! she chided herself, as Alex pulled up in front of the entrance.

"Please don't get out," she said, as he reached for the door handle. "Just pop the trunk and let me get my bag." She leaned toward him for his kiss. "Be good."

She pulled her overnight bag out of the trunk, then slammed the lid shut. Looking in at the window on the passenger side, she mouthed the words, "Love you," and turned away, walking quickly inside.

Before she glanced back, she knew that he had driven off. She wondered what he thought of her at that moment. *He knows me so well. Too well. Does he know anything? Everything? He is so smooth, and Griff is rough, like sandpaper. Even his voice is rough, rasping, and I haven't heard it for so long!*

She stopped inside the entrance, a rock in midstream, letting the human traffic flow around her. She was listening for his voice, the sound of his voice in her head, but it wouldn't come. She felt as though she had left something behind that was absolutely essential to her. She turned around, as if to retrace the few steps to the entrance, then shook her head impatiently.

I'll get on the plane, she thought, glancing up at the monitors, searching for her flight and her departure gate. *I'll find my seat, put away my bag in the overhead compartment. I'll sit down in my window seat. I'll fasten my seat belt. I'll think of him. I'll be alone with my thoughts and I'll think of him. He will be mine. I won't think of Alex, what he might know. I won't think of Sue, how she is binding him to her with her troubles. He will be mine, until we touch down.*

* * *

Somehow, in Chicago, Selene lost all hope. She wasn't sure why, or when. Her meeting with Kirby Woods had gone well. They had worked, in his comfortable suite at the Drake, from midmorning, when she arrived, until late last night. She had gone to her own small room exhausted, barely able to tear off her clothes and brush her teeth before she fell on the bed and into a deep sleep.

In the morning, she met Kirby for breakfast in the hotel dining room, tied up the loose strands of their marathon meeting, and left the Drake. She spent several hours shopping at Water Tower Place on Michigan Avenue before she picked up her luggage and took a cab to the airport. She had some pretty things for herself and a gift for Alex in the Marshall Field's shopping bag which she had crammed into the overhead bin. In a window seat next to the wing, she sat looking out at mist, trying to assess the sleepy, hopeless, downward-pulling haze of depression that seemed to surround her.

Perhaps it was the rain. Whenever she had taken a moment to look out of Kirby's window, it was drizzling. The people on the street far below, beneath umbrellas, or with bare heads exposed, hurried back and forth, like scurrying insects. She felt an urge to stamp on them, to stamp them out, to make them stop, even if to stop them was to crush them.

The spring rains at home had been so refreshing, like a cool drink in the sunshine. Here it was chilly and needling, even in the dry comfort of Kirby's suite. Kirby said it had been drizzling like that for days, that it was depressing the hell out of him.

*   *   *

"It's all in my head, Selene," he said to her, early in the day, pacing back and forth next to the conference table where she was keying in notes on her laptop. "The whole goddamned book." He stopped, grinning his impish grin. "I just need a muse."

She looked up at him, her expression pleasant, professional. "I know, Kirby. You need a muse who can write and edit."

"And I chose well, didn't I?" Kirby's dark brows arched triumphantly. "You inspire me. You capture my thoughts on your magic machine. I can rest my eyes on you with the greatest satisfaction."

"You can look all you like, Kirby. Just don't touch."

Early in their acquaintance, Kirby had flirted with her, blatantly. She had been gracious, although Kirby, small, quick, with intense, penetrating dark eyes, sensed her indifference. It was not by accident that Kirby Woods chose psychic phenomena as his next book topic. His new book, he felt in his bones, would be his opus. He was at home with his subject matter. He could think it out and talk it out, but he couldn't write it out.

And this little slip of a girl can, he thought, still looking down at her. *So don't step over the line, you horny bastard. You don't want to lose her, or her magic machine.*

"You're a little listless today, my pretty one," he said to her at one point. "Are you feeling all right?"

She nodded and smiled, as if making an effort. "I'm right as rain," she said, nodding toward the windows. "Do you like my ideas for section headings and pointers? Do you think they'll appeal to your readers—the Socratic-like dialogue between the reader and the writer, the questions they ask and you answer, the references to the phases of the moon?"

"I do, indeed. They are the stuff of inspiration. You've been doing your research."

They had worked amicably through the day, Selene skirting any reference to the personal, Kirby treading carefully, delighted with her insight, her ability to organize his zigzagging thoughts and make them into coherent chapters.

* * *

The seat next to Selene was empty. The aisle seat was occupied by a woman intently reading a book. The return flight was smooth, relatively silent, with many empty seats, and attendants who were content to huddle together and chat, after having offered a beverage to each passenger. The roar of the engine was muffled, as though the plane were wrapped in cotton instead of mist. Selene felt that she was hovering in space, suspended, between the lives she had chosen and the men she had chosen, without a will of her own.

The brief trip had made her look with revulsion at the Selene of this past spring, who had turned away from her husband, in spirit if not in fact, and given herself up to a man she did not know, could not know. She would never know Griff. He was an enigma, coming out of nowhere, his link with Alex, Bernard, even Nan, severed by time and distance. Even his return had been tentative. He had chosen to take up his residence with Sue Smoller instead of with his family; he had stayed with Sue throughout the spring, knowing Nan wanted him closer to her, that Bernard was alarmingly ill, that even she and Alex would have—

But that was absurd. Nan had the right and the space—and there was that steely distance between Alex and Griff, still so obvious. She thought about Griff living in her house, in the house where she had grown up, the house that held so many memories—of her mother and father, of her childhood, of sweet-smelling Christmas trees in the corner beneath the staircase where, from one of the highest steps, she could place the angel on the treetop ...

She quivered, feeling her skin flush with—what? Excitement? Shame? Regret? She had pictured him living there many times, had even, when Griff first arrived, discussed it with Alex, who had never considered it seriously.

*　*　*

"If he decides he doesn't want to stay with Sue Smoller," Alex had said to her soon after Griff arrived, "he'll find his own place, or he'll disappear again. I don't see him staying with Mom, and he sure as hell wouldn't stay with us."

"Why not?" she had asked, petulant.

"There's not much brotherly love lost between us," Alex had replied, "in case you haven't noticed."

"But still—"

"Griff doesn't want to owe anybody anything. And we're not just talking about money here."

"You mean—gratitude?"

"Gratitude. Affection. Love. You name it. He'll find a way to even the score in his favor and then he'll disappear, before you can shift the balance. The worst thing you can do—if you want the son of a bitch to hang around—is to give him more than he wants to give back."

"What about his—your—the money Howard left to you and Griff?"

"That's different. He can't give that back. Dad's dead, and Mom doesn't need it. It's such a little bit I'm not sure how he makes a go of it. I just reinvest my portion. But Griff can stretch a buck until it screams for mercy."

*　*　*

Selene sighed and shifted in her seat, peering out at the thick, impermeable mist. She thought about Alex and how much she missed him, even in this brief space of time. She loved him. He was her husband, and she had braved much to be with him. She had made him unhappy for a long time; she had made Carolyn unhappy; she had certainly made Kevin and Wendy, their children, unhappy. Now the scales had tipped back. Alex was happy, seemingly, although his grown children were almost lost to him. She would have given him a child, gladly, to even the scales, but she did not get pregnant. Alex, the doctors told them gravely, had a low sperm count.

Who was this Selene of the past few months? Had she given a moment's thought to what she was doing, or hoping to do? She shook her head, as if to clear it, then glanced obliquely at the woman in the aisle seat, who was still intent on her book. When she looked out the window again, the mist was thinning. She could see the sky. Then they were above the mist, thudding through blue, clouds beneath them, the plane making its own shadow.

She sat up straighter and thought, before she could suppress it, *I'll see him again soon. I'll find a way to see him.*

Other thoughts pushed their way into her consciousness. *This is who I've become. I can't change. I don't want to change. To change would be to lose what I'm feeling, and I can't. I can't lose it.*

I have to be careful not to scare him away.

But why bother? He'll go away when he's ready to go away. There's nothing I can do to change that.

There was a shift in the rumbling roar of the engine, as if it were catching its breath; then the plane began its long descent. The heaviness pressed down on Selene again. She leaned back in her seat, closed her eyes. She may have slept briefly. When she opened her eyes, they were surrounded by mist again. The midwestern twang of the flight attendant was painfully accentuated by the loudspeaker, as she instructed them to bring their seats upright and fasten their seat belts. They might encounter some turbulence during the descent.

I can never be upright again, she thought dully, tightening the belt she had never fully released. *I reclaimed my goodness when Alex and I made our life together, but now I've lost it again. Lost it for someone who cannot love me as Alex does. Who cannot love me at all. Who, perhaps, cannot love at all.*

The plane touched down with a bump and a series of prolonged hissing, skidding thuds. The airport was bathed in mist. She felt as though she were waking up from a dream into another dream, peopled with ghostly strangers. Then she heard the voice of the flight attendant, nasal, hurrying through her script, welcoming them to Cleveland, urging them not to do what they were already doing, as they released their seat belts and reached for their luggage in the still-moving cabin.

Selene sat motionless, looking out the window at the mist, ignoring the bustling movement around her. She would wait until the passengers pressing against each other on the aisle left the plane. She would pull down her luggage and her shopping bag, walk without hurry to the front of the plane, nod to the flight attendant, and leave. There would be no one to meet her, so she would walk back to the center of the terminal and find a cab.

At home, Nippy would greet her joyfully, as he always did when she returned from a journey. She would walk through the house, greeting it, as Nippy greeted her—the house she had shared with her parents and now shared with Alex. She would take up the life she and Alex had built on the remains of an earlier life, which had belonged to Alex, Carolyn, Kevin, and Wendy. It was now their life—hers and Alex's. This house was their nesting place, their shelter. But did it really belong to them—this life, this home? Would it ever belong to them, truly?

She lived in her parents' house because they had died too soon in her life, because she was unable to leave behind this tangible reminder of them. She had brought Alex to the house of her childhood because it seemed to guarantee their happiness, this house where she had been happy as a child.

But is it really his house as much as it is mine, or is he living there because he has no home, because I've deprived him of his home, destroyed it?

Perhaps Alex was living with her as Griff was living with Sue Smoller—for shelter. Temporary shelter.

Will I ever live with Alex without guilt? Will I ever think of Griff without hopelessness?

CHAPTER 10

"*I always liked* your breakfasts, Olyn," Alex said, as Carolyn poured more coffee into his cup.

"Thank you for the crumbs from your table."

"I'm trying to be complimentary here."

"'Trying' is the operative word."

Alex shook his head in mock disgust. "Women," he muttered. "Don't understand 'em. Can't please 'em."

"Which 'women' are you referring to?"

Alex lifted his hands as if she were pointing a gun at him. "Okay. Okay. I give up already."

Carolyn sat across from him, admiring his fresh-shaven face, his white shirt, dark blue suit, striped tie. She could have wept with satisfaction, or clapped her hands and laughed. How she had missed this. How she had missed him! She had accepted his hurried visits, the brief but affectionate sex, because it was all he could offer her, and she wanted him in her life. But this—this was what she yearned for. His face across the round oak table that had traveled from the sunny east-facing kitchen of their house at Twin Oaks to the "dining L" of her new condo.

He glanced at his watch; her eyes went to the round clock with the rooster face that hung above the counter.

"Are you late?" she asked.

"Not so very," he said, adding liberal amounts of cream and sugar to his coffee. "Meeting at ten."

"How is it going?"

He cocked his head to one side, squinting at her.

"Your work," she said. "How's it going?"

He still squinted at her, as if not quite seeing her.

"Did I say something wrong?" she asked.

"No. No." He relaxed, sipped his coffee. "No, of course not. I was just thinking."

"About what?"

He put the cup down. "About Selene, if you must know. It's just that—well, I just realized something."

Carolyn waited, not happy to hear Selene's name but sensing a revelation.

"Isn't it funny how this sort of thing comes to you? You go along, from day to day, thinking that everything is as it should be—or, no, not thinking, because, when everything is as it should be, there is no need to think about it. Then, someone says something, something ordinary, and you realize that everything is not as it should be. That something is out of whack. That's what happened just now."

"But I was just asking about your work—"

"That's just it."

"But why did that make you think of Selene?"

She didn't want Selene here at the breakfast table with them. She wanted to be his wife again—still—as long as he was here with her. Until he went back to Selene.

"Selene and I haven't talked about my work in a long time."

"And?"

"And that's not right. Not normal. You see, we always talk about my work. And about her work. It's—an important part of our relationship."

He glanced at her, looking uncomfortable, as though the word "relationship" suddenly made him aware of where he was, who he was with.

"She's changed, Olyn, in the last few weeks or—months. I didn't even notice. How fuckin' blind can I be?"

Carolyn opened her mouth as if about to speak, as if about to question, then closed it again, watching him. This was her Alex. Hers, she would always consider him. Hers. He was suddenly seeing Selene in a new light. The best thing she could do would be to let it happen. Let him see who she was, this woman who had taken her husband, her Alex, away from her. His words, when he spoke next, would be careful, deliberate, drawing her in, in the old way. The house at Twin Oaks was gone, but there was still this.

"I shouldn't be talking to you about this, but, hell, who else would I talk to? You're— Well, you're—"

She nodded, a barely perceptible nod.

"Selene hasn't—we haven't—" He paused, then said, "We haven't had sex—lately."

Carolyn turned her head away from him.

"I shouldn't have said that. I'm sorry. But, you see? That's another thing that has changed." He looked at her averted face. "Maybe I shouldn't talk about this—to you. Maybe this is a mistake."

With a great effort, she turned her head back, facing him directly. "No," she said. "No. Go on."

"Our relationship—Selene's and mine—our marriage—is built on those two pillars."

He stopped and thought about this.

"One pillar is our work, and our commitment to our work. The other is—" He hesitated, glancing at her, then quickly looking away. "The other is—"

She turned her head again, reaching up to touch her face, as if it were bruised, or flushed.

"We have—we had—a good sex life," he said, defiant, yet apologetic.

Like a naughty child, Carolyn thought, before she could stop the thought.

"For me, as you know, it was—compelling." He paused. "It changed my life." He paused again. "Our life."

He picked up his cup, gulped down the coffee. "But there was more than that." His cup clunked against the saucer. "Much more. More than our work, now I think of it. It was the satisfaction—the intellectual, the social, the almost physical satisfaction we got from our work. The book we wrote together—that got us together in the first place. It was— It was—"

Carolyn thought, *It was so long ago, when all of this happened, when he left me. How can it still hurt so much?*

"Anyways, that—and the sex—have always been there—until recently, that is."

"Recently—when?"

He shook his head. "That's what I have to figure out. You see—" He put his elbows on the table, leaned forward, clasping his hands. "There's been my work. It's been sucking me in more than ever lately. And there's been—you." His smile was intimate. Unwillingly, she smiled back at him. "When did we start—this?"

"You tell me," she said. Knowing the date. The day of the week. The hour. The minute.

"Don't worry. There will be no test around this. I don't remember either—exactly. It just seemed so natural. Coming to you. Being with you."

"You feel—?" She hesitated, wanting his words.

"I still feel married to you."

She marveled at the simplicity with which he said it.

"And what about Selene?"

"I feel—committed—to her." He expelled his breath, suddenly.

"Do you love her?" She forced herself to say this.

"Yes," he said, his voice low. "I love her."

"Oh, Alex," she said, wearily. "Go away."

"No. Not until you hear me out."

Carolyn clutched at her robe. She had bought it at Victoria's Secret, just for him. It was silky. Blue. A knee-length wrap with wide sleeves and a waist tie. She felt suddenly ashamed. She wondered if Selene had felt like this when she was the "other woman." She wondered if she were ashamed of herself, or ashamed for Alex.

"It's not as though there's nothing else between us," Alex continued. "You can't build a marriage on—that. But it's always been there, holding up the edifice."

He sat back in his chair and held out his hands, palms up, lifting one hand slightly, then the other. "The work. The sex." He shook his head slightly. "I'll be damned if somewhere in the last few months the whole structure of our marriage hasn't shifted."

"Maybe it's us," said Carolyn, without emphasis. "What we're doing."

Alex got up abruptly, grabbing his chair before it tipped over, pushing it squealing against the table. He paced the length of the living room.

Carolyn said nothing more, knowing he needed to be in motion to think this out. In motion and undisturbed. Even his preoccupation gave her a thrill of satisfaction. It was so familiar. And the object of this pacing—Selene—what was she up to?

Oh, I hope it's bad. I want it to be bad, she thought, watching him. *I want him to hurt as I hurt.*

"Quitting her job," said Alex. "That was a good thing, or so I thought. She wanted to get out from under the corporate shit. Work on her own. This book she's working on—she took it with her when she left Cotter Publishing. It could be her best opportunity yet."

"Are you picking her up at the airport this afternoon?"

"No." Alex paced. "But why now?"

"What do you mean?" said Carolyn, thinking of Selene in Chicago. Wishing she would stay in Chicago.

"What triggered her decision to go out on her own? I assumed it was just—she was fed up. I didn't think much of it at the time. Now, I wonder ..."

He stopped, close to the table. She put out her hand to touch him, but he was in motion again, frowning.

"She works at home now. Every day. She doesn't seem to mind. It's as if she's—waiting, preparing—for something." He stopped, turned, paced. "I wonder if she's—no. I would know. She would tell me."

That would be the end for us, Carolyn thought. *Those two pillars might be crumbling, but a child, their child, would fortify the whole structure.*

"There's something else. Something—" He looked at her, seeing her this time. "Olyn. I'm sorry. I've got to go."

He came to her swiftly, kissing the top of her head, pulling her against him. They were still for a few moments—she seated, leaning into him, he standing, holding her almost absently.

* * *

Selene kissed Alex with what she hoped was enthusiasm. "What a nice surprise," she said, linking her arm in his as he took her luggage. "I thought you were tied up with meetings all day."

"Cancelled them. Wanted to give my wife a lift from the airport. Wanted to meet you at the gate."

They pushed through the crowd of arriving passengers, the groups assembled to welcome arrivals, then started the long trek to the entrance.

"Miss me?" said Selene.

"Always," said Alex. "What's in the shopping bag?"

"Michigan Avenue plunder," she said, holding up for him to see the sleek white Lord & Taylor shopping bag with its calligraphic logo, then dropping it to her side again. "Including a little surprise for you."

"You know I don't like surprises," he said, somewhat irritably.

"You'll like this one. I promise." She squeezed his arm, leaned against him. "Even an old ogre like you can use a surprise now and then."

"Am I old?"

"Not so's you'd notice," she said, lightly. Then, "Hard day?"

He glanced at her, as though assessing the question, then replied, "Not particularly."

"Do you think Nippy can hold it in long enough for us to go to dinner?"

"Is there something you want to talk about?"

"Not particularly," she said, mimicking him. "Just thought it would be nice to have dinner out with my husband."

He nodded, absently. "I'm for it," he said. "Where do you want to go?"

"Surprise me," she said.

* * *

Near home, in a noisy bar called "Smiley's," a favorite of local residents from student age to old age, Alex and Selene ordered burgers, fries, and one of the local brews. It was late afternoon, before the hassle of the evening crowd. The patrons were mostly regulars, sampling the brew and the burgers, for which the place was known. A TV hung from above each end of the long bar. They sat at a small table as far away from the bar as they could get, their privacy ensured by the incessant electronic blare, along with the raised voices of those competing with it.

"So what's my surprise?" said Alex.

"Can't you wait?" said Selene.

She was feeling better, now that she was home, with her husband, and a part of this noisy scene. Her stomach rumbled in anticipation of the meal. They clinked beer mugs, sipped at the foamy liquid.

"No, damn it," he said, amicably. He had relaxed visibly since they arrived. Selene realized it had been a while since they had had a "date."

"Well, if you must know, it's a robe."

"I already have a robe."

"That robe is almost always on the floor. Nippy has laid claim to it."

"But I like that robe."

"It's old, and the nap is almost worn smooth. Now you'll have a new, smart, elegant robe. Nippy can enjoy the old one without guilt."

"Nippy feels guilty?"

"Well, I do. I—sort of encourage him to curl up in it. He loves it so, and he looks so cute."

"You got me a robe so you wouldn't feel guilty?"

"Something like that, you ungrateful oaf. Oh, good. Here comes our food!"

They ate and talked, enjoying each other's company, catching up on each other's work, the mild sexual undertone of their conversation heightening their pleasure. Selene found herself flirting with her husband, hoping to arouse him, wanting him in the old way, the way she had wanted him before—

"Remember when we wrote 'The Book'?" said Alex.

"Of course, I remember," she said. "It's still one of the premier corporate management titles at Cotter."

"I was thinking about it today—maybe because you were away in Chicago working on another book."

"I'll never work on another book the way I did on that one," she said. "Or enjoy it nearly as much."

"What about Kirby Woods?"

"What about him?"

Alex shrugged. "Has he—"

"Yes. Yes, he has. And I've said no." Selene paused. "But that was a long time ago. You seem to be talking about now."

"I guess I am."

Selene reached across the table, touched his hand. "Not to worry," she said. "'The Book' is still intact."

Oddly enough, Selene thought, this gesture—or perhaps her words—seemed to disturb him. His hand slid out from under hers. He raised it to the waiter, gesturing for their check. As he suveyed the room, now packed with the post-five o'clock crowd, he said, "There's Griff!"

Selene turned to follow the direction of his eyes, hoping she had turned away quickly enough so that the shiver of excitement, the sudden flush that heated her face, were not visible to her husband.

Alex waved to him. Griff pushed through the crowd and stood close to their table, grinning down at them.

"How the hell are you?" said Alex. "Have a seat."

He gestured toward an empty chair. Griff spun it around and sat, legs apart, arms across the back of the chair. He nodded to both of them, his eyes fixed on Selene for a few moments. She flushed again, grateful for the semidarkness of the room.

"What brings you two here?" he said, still looking at Selene.

"It's one of our favorite places," said Alex, leaning back in his chair and studying him—rather critically, Selene thought. "What about you?"

"I come here a lot," Griff said, easily. "Never saw you guys here before."

"We tend to come early," said Alex. "Before the crowd." His face changed, softened. "How's Sue's boy doing?"

"It was touch-and-go there for a while," said Griff, somber. "They weren't sure they could save his leg. It was pretty badly smashed."

Alex nodded. "Yes, we heard. From Mom. I'm sorry. How is he now?"

"Doing better. They saved the leg." He grinned at Alex. "Maybe I should have been a surgeon after all. They do good work."

"Maybe not. It would have been a serious strain on your lifestyle."

Griff continued to grin at Alex but now the grin was strained, sarcastic.

"I'm glad he's going to be all right," Selene said, quickly, leaning forward, wanting to soothe him, to distract him, wanting his eyes on her again. "What is his name?"

"Jimbo," said Griff, still focused on Alex. "Everybody calls him Jimbo."

"And—Sue. Is she all right?"

Griff dragged his eyes away from Alex, turned to Selene. Selene watched as, with an effort, he wiped his face clean of expression. "Yeah. She's all right. Do you know her?"

"No," said Selene. "Only by sight. I see her around town now and then."

The sounds of the noisy bar swelled around them.

"Will you have a beer with us?" said Selene.

Griff turned again to Alex, whose eyes were fixed thoughtfully on Selene. "No, thanks," he said. He gestured at the remnants of their meal, which had not yet been cleared away. "Looks like you're about to leave."

"Oh, but I'd like you to—"

Their waiter elbowed his way to their table, put the check in front of Alex, swept away the dinner plates in one swift movement, and disappeared into the crowd again. Alex reached for his wallet. Griff stood up, pushing the chair away from him. A man standing at the next table grabbed the chair and sat down, with a quick nod in their direction.

"See you around," said Griff, with a brief salute, forefinger glancing off brow.

"See you," Alex said, counting out cash.

Griff stared at Alex for a moment, his face tense, his anger barely repressed, before he pushed his way to the bar.

* * *

Why so quiet?" said Alex, breaking the silence of their ride home. The early evening sky was overcast, gray, with an almost invisible drizzle spotting the windows of the car.

"That was cruel, what you said to Griff."

Selene spoke carefully, but she could hear the tremble in her voice.

"It wasn't meant to be," said Alex.

"Well, it was," she shot back.

Alex drummed absently on the steering wheel. The sound infuriated her.

"Stop doing that," she said, then turned away from him, staring out the side window, wanting to scream, wanting to cry.

"Why are you so goddamned concerned about Griff, about whether or not I hurt his goddamned feelings?"

"Because you're *not* concerned. Because you don't care."

"And you do?"

"Yes," she said fiercely; then, with forced calm, "Of course I do. He's your brother. And he's having a hard time. He's—been through a lot."

"It's Sue Smoller who's been through a lot. And her kid. Griff is just hanging out there."

"How can you say that?"

Selene turned to him, her voice harsh. At the same time, she found herself hoping that what he said was true, that Griff had forged no unbreakable bond with Sue as a result of her son's crisis.

"Because that's what he does," said Alex, sounding disgusted, weary. "He just hangs out. No direction. No commitment. No goals. That's Griff. That's been Griff, all his life."

"So what?" Selene heard herself as Alex must be hearing her, defending Griff as though she were defending herself, but she couldn't stop. "We're not all hard-driving business executives. We don't all want—success—as you define it."

Alex kept his eyes on the road, his voice neutral. "As I define it?"

"Yes. It's a pretty narrow definition."

"How so?"

His voice was polite. Politely interested. Selene was familiar with this voice of calm reason, but she chose to ignore it. Knowing the danger of ignoring it.

"You only have one way of looking at things. Your way."

"And that is?"

"Make money. Make the grade. Work hard. Don't be a slacker."

"And Griff's way is—?"

Selene paused, trying to pull her thoughts together. Trying to curb the impulse to blurt out what she felt at the moment she felt it. Knowing that Alex was weighing and assessing every word, every inflection, every gesture.

"He's— He's—"

She paused again, searching for words.

"He's—heading somewhere else," she said, finally.

"Oh? I hadn't noticed he was 'heading' anywhere."

"That's because you only see what you want to see. You want to see Griff—"

"I want to see him—what?"

"Fail," she said.

There, she thought. She'd said it, what she wanted to say. Even though she didn't know it until she heard herself say it. She held her breath, waiting for him to respond—but there was no response. They drove along the gray streets in silence, as the sky darkened almost imperceptibly, until they reached their house. Alex pulled into the drive, turned off the ignition and sat, still gripping the steering wheel. After a long empty time, he spoke.

"Maybe you're right," he said.

CHAPTER 11

"Where's Jimbo?" says Griff.

"In his room."

Sue and Griff are standing in the kitchen.

"I don't hear his boom box."

"He's probably asleep. The medication makes him sleepy."

Griff opens the refrigerator. He takes out a can of Bud Light and pops the tab. Sue watches him as he drinks the beer, his Adam's apple bobbing up and down as he swallows. She is limp with fatigue; the sight of Griff gulping down the beer makes her feel angry, irritable.

He stops drinking, puts the can down on the counter, leaning back, crossing one ankle over the other. He crosses his arms and says, "Anything I can do?"

Sue looks at him, his arms crossed, his ankles crossed, as though fortifying himself against her. She shakes her head.

"Thanks, anyways," she says.

They have been polite to each other since the accident. Polite and distant. Sue reaches for the can, takes a long swallow. She smacks her lips in satisfaction.

"That tastes good," she says.

"I'll get you one." He turns toward the refrigerator.

"No." She puts her hand against his crossed arms. "No. That's all I want."

She looks at her nails as her hand rests against him—unfamiliar nails, the polish chipped, the nails cracked and broken, one nail carelessly pared down to where it had split close to the skin. She hasn't really looked at them in several weeks. Her manicure. The one thing about her appearance she always kept in perfect repair. She clenches her fists, then sits down at the kitchen table, feeling the strength in her legs give out.

"What's wrong?" says Griff.

Sue shakes her head. "Nothing. I'm tired." There's a pause; then she says, "Where were you?"

He looks away from her.

"Smiley's."

"Anybody there?" she says, with an effort.

"The usual crowd."

She starts talking. The words blot out the silence between them, her son's vicious anger and excruciating pain, the tiredness that drags at her, day after day.

"Haven't been to Smiley's for months and months. Saw a fight there once. Real knockdown drag-out fight. Chairs flying. Mirror smashing. Liquor bottles exploding. Like it was right out of a movie. Some guy got in a jealous rage over his girl. Went berserk. Beat the hell out of the other guy. Good thing he wasn't carrying a gun." She shook her head. "That was years ago. If it happened now, he probably would be carrying a gun, popping off anybody who stood in his way."

She reaches for the cigarettes and matches on the table, lights up.

"How do people get through the bad times without these things?" she says, holding the cigarette out to examine it. "I was down to half a pack a day but now I ..." She shrugs. "Who the fuck cares if I get cancer in thirty years? I can't think that far ahead. It's hard enough thinking about today. When are you moving out?"

He is staring at some spot on the wall above her head. He jerks back, as though she has pushed him off balance. "Who said anything about—"

She exhales, waves at the smoke hovering in the air. "Look. I don't have to be a psychic to see the signs. I've had a lot of practice."

He rests his hands on the counter behind him. "The kid—doesn't like me being here. Doesn't like me, period."

"He doesn't like anybody, much. He's not a real people person."

She grins impishly, looking up at him. "He calls you 'Shit-head.' 'Where's Shithead? he'll say to me. 'Out buying more tan paint?' I thought it was a good sign. Before the accident, you didn't even have a name. You were just 'he' or 'him.' 'Is he around?' 'What's up with him?' Now, it's like you're a member of the family."

She laughs, a brief, dry laugh.

"Well, distant relative, maybe. Where will you be going?"

Griff looks down, shakes his head.

If she were not so tired, Sue thinks, she would get up. She would walk over to him, she would put her arms around him, put her head against his neck, just beneath his chin. She would feel his warmth against her. Transfer his strength into her. But she can't make the effort. Bringing the cigarette up to her mouth and exhaling is as much as she can do.

"I can't figure you out," she says, "but then, I'm a knuckle-head when it comes to figuring anybody out, especially men. We had some good times, but I know the last few weeks have been hellish. Jimbo is the world's worst patient. I've missed a lot of work, been on edge. Shit, I've been over the edge and around the bend. I can't even think straight anymore."

Griff looks around for the can of beer, picks it up, takes a long swallow. He shifts uncomfortably but seems unable, unwilling, to sit down beside her.

"You never changed, Griff, from the time we were teenagers. You always kept yourself to yourself. You still do. I never know what the fuck's in your head, but I know you're an okay guy who doesn't like to get too close to anybody. You helped me through—this. I'm grateful. Real grateful."

"I'll still be around," says Griff.

"Yeah. I know."

Sue crushes out her cigarette. She crosses her arms on the table, rests her head on her arms.

"See ya around," she says, welcoming the heavy, sleepy, drugged feeling—hoping it will overwhelm her, so she won't have to think about Jimbo upstairs, in pain even in his sleep—won't have to think about Griff leaving her, how cold and empty her bed will be without him.

She is almost there, in the forgetfulness of sleep, when she feels Griff's arm across her back; his breath, faintly redolent of beer, is close to her face. Then, his other arm is under her legs. She is being lifted up, like a sleepy child, in his arms. She rests her head on his shoulder. He carries her into the living room and up the stairs. It is so comforting that she is almost asleep again before they reach her bedroom. He sets her down on the edge of the bed, pulls at her clothes. She doesn't help him. She is too tired. When she is naked, he grabs the old cotton night-gown at the foot of the bed and pulls it down over her head, lifting her arms one at a time to fit them into the sleeves. Then he lowers her gently down on the bed. She lies with her head against the pillow while he takes both her legs and slides them beneath the sheet, and the flowered comforter she bought just before the accident, to brighten up the "fucking tan" of the walls.

He tucks the sheet close around her neck, smoothes out the comforter. She wants to say something to him, but she can't find the words. Sleep is pulling her down and down. She sighs, turns her head, feeling the pillow against her cheek. She is almost asleep again when she feels Griff's hand against her forehead, smoothing her hair as he smoothed the folds in the comforter. She hears him leave the bedroom, closing the door softly behind him. She embraces sleep like a lover.

*   *   *

Selene looks around the enormous "Great Room," with its vaulted ceiling and numerous seating arrangements. She is searching for Alex, but he is circulating. The party, noisy, lavish, is for his friends and business associates, the people he sees all the time and she sees once or twice a year. She does not want to be here. She has come along as his wife, in a long, light blue, semi-sheer summer dress she pulled off the rack at Spangleman's, with what at the time was defiance and now seems like childish spite. The dress is drawing appreciative looks from the men, faint dismay from the women.

*   *   *

Earlier in the evening, Alex had groaned when she came down the stairs in her new dress, the deep V-cut top held up precariously with spaghetti straps.

"Are you going to wear that?"

"Yes," she had said. "Don't you like it?"

"What's not to like. You look—good enough to eat. But it means I'll have to spend the evening guarding you."

"Guarding me?"

"Against every man at the party."

"Oh." She had cocked her head. "You won't be— embarrassed?"

"Do you want me to be?"

"No. Well, yes—maybe—a little."

He had said, almost patiently, "Then I'll do my best to oblige you."

* * *

The West Hills house is crowded, with guests spilling out onto the deck, which is lit with lanterns and candles. It's dusk. Music from the stereo permeates the islands of conversation, lifting them into a rhythmic chant. Selene listens as Madonna, in one of her incarnations, sings "Ray of Light." She hears the conversation around her, but not the words.

"—don't you think?" says a voice at her elbow.

She turns toward the woman, who is slight, dressed conservatively in a knee-length gray dress with red trim and cap sleeves—obviously *not* pulled off the rack at Spangleman's. She knows her, has been introduced to her more than once, but can't remember her name. She belongs to Harry, one of the executives who is giving Selene and her dress furtive glances. Harry is standing nearby, talking to Alex, and Jan and Tyrone Themes, the couple who are hosting the party. Harry nods to her. She nods back, then turns away, self-conscious, as his eyes travel up and down the length of her dress. She sits down on a chair across from his wife, who is sitting on a couch with another woman Selene knows but can't identify.

"Molly and I were just saying how perceptive our pets are," says Harry's wife. "She says her cat, Rudolf, is waiting at the window whenever she comes home, no matter what hour of the day or night. And my dog, Crackers, is—"

"Yes, I do think they sense where we are and what we feel," says Selene, the woman's question having returned to her, even though she doesn't remember hearing it. "Our dog, Nippy, is acutely sensitive to me. In fact, I believe he's telepathic."

"Next thing you know, we'll be giving our dogs, cats, rabbits, and hamsters a soul," says Harry.

Harry is standing close to her, his eyes skiing up and down her dress.

"And why not?" she says, resenting him even as she acknowledges that she has invited his attention by wearing the damn dress. "Can you prove otherwise?"

"I don't have to," Harry says, sitting on the couch between his wife and Molly. He puts an arm across the back of the couch, grasping his wife's shoulders, crossing his legs. He is large, bulky, 40-something. His eyes, which protrude slightly, are still fastened on Selene. "We're rational creatures."

"Descended from apes," says Selene.

"So, you're saying animals do have a soul?" he responds.

"I'm saying this," says Selene, his complacent smile, his casual possessiveness of his wife, his wife's eager acceptance of it, rousing her animosity: "At what point in our evolution did we become infused with a soul, and rise above every other creature?"

"You mean at what precise historical moment?" Harry says, less complacently.

"Be careful how you answer that," says Alex, who has just joined them. He perches on the arm of her chair. "Selene is editing—more like ghostwriting—a book on psychic phenomena, and she's been doing her homework."

"How exciting," says Harry's wife, leaning forward. "Tell us about it."

"Well, we are planning on bringing in the human-animal connection, especially as it relates to household pets. Which is why I'm interested in what you were saying."

She nods kindly to Harry's wife, avoiding eye contact with Harry.

"We certainly don't behave much like rational creatures," says Molly, who has been sitting quietly, watching Harry watch Selene. "I think we're still about 95 percent instinct. Look at Clinton, our president and national role model. He can't keep his hands off other women."

"It's the Monica syndrome," says Alex easily, carefully not touching Selene as Harry is touching his wife. "We've put down our weapons. What's left is—passion."

"What do you mean?" says Harry's wife, shifting out of her husband's grasp.

"We can no longer have patriotic wars," says Alex. "Not in the 'free' world. Not with any sort of consensus. In that sense, we've lost our power, our brute force. So, we have scandals. The scandals are about money or sex because, after war, that's what's left—money and sex."

"Really?" says Selene, glancing up at him, grateful for his careful distance. "Is that all that's left?"

"Just about," says Alex. "We're hunters and gatherers. There sure as hell isn't much hunting going on anymore—at least if you're politically correct." He looks down at Selene, gives her a comradely wink. "So what's left? Scandals. Money scandals. Sex scandals. Public figure up against a wall. Fifty verbal guns aimed at his belly. Simultaneous blast. Guts splattered all over the television screen."

The laughter is spontaneous, genuine. Everyone relaxes, even Harry, who is no longer staring at Selene, having crossed gazes with Alex at some point in the conversation.

Selene gets up, bending over to smooth her dress. She sees Harry take a hasty, summary look at her. She smiles at him, a small, malicious smile, and moves off with Alex.

"Thanks for rescuing me," says Selene, taking his arm.

"He's an asshole," says Alex. "A turkey has more between his ears than that joker. And they made him a senior VP, for Christ's sake."

"Can we go home now?"

"Not yet. I'm just getting into this rescuing bit. Makes me feel like a he-man. That dress is bringing out the best in me."

"Or the worst."

"I'm in for the kill, good or bad."

He joins a small group standing politely around an elderly man. She recognizes as a board member.

"Say, Roger," he says, taking Selene by the elbow, guiding her through an opening in the group, moving up close to the board member. "I'd like you to meet my wife, Selene."

The old man turns a tired gaze on Selene. His eyes flicker and light up, almost comically, like an actor doing a double take. Selene laughs, suddenly sure of herself. She takes the freckled hand the old man holds out to her, giving it a long, warm squeeze.

"Hello, Roger," she says. "How are you?"

"About twenty years younger than I was a few seconds ago," says Roger, squeezing back. "Alex, where in the hell have you been hiding this delectable creature?"

"I keep her at home, usually locked up, mostly barefoot," says Alex.

"Well, you should be shot for that," says Roger. "This lovely woman is meant to be seen."

"You're seeing most of her right now," someone says. The group titters.

Selene flushes and looks at Alex, who is standing just behind her. She is suddenly aware of his anger. It has been there all evening, carefully masked by humor and courtesy, ever since she walked down the stairs in her new dress. A little *frisson*, which she recognizes as fear, makes her shiver involuntarily.

They move among the guests, Alex staying with her now, not possessively but casually, his presence shielding her from the long looks and the half-heard remarks. After a time, Selene realizes that he is systematically making the rounds of the guests, penetrating each small circle, so that, when they join their host and hostess less than an hour later, he can say goodnight to them with no possibility of anyone saying that Alex Price whisked his half-naked wife away because he was ashamed of her.

"That was very cool," she says as they walk out to the car in the clear night air. "You were very cool."

"Had to be," he says. "Shark water in there."

"I'm sorry I embarrassed you."

"Thought you wanted to," he says, opening the car door for her.

"Just a little, remember?"

He waits for her to curl in, then slams the door and walks around to his side. He gets in, starts the motor.

"Remember?" she says again.

He turns to back out of the drive, his arm across the top of the seat, so that he is facing her squarely. There is something in his expression that she can't quite fathom. It is not anger. The anger is gone now. It's certainly not shame. It is, she's almost certain, self-reproach, even guilt. But why would Alex—her Alex—feel guilty?

"I remember," he says.

*   *   *

"Mom, did I make a mistake?"

"By marrying her, you mean?"

"Yes. By marrying her. By perpetuating the affair."

Alex and Nan are sitting on Nan's porch, away from the direct rays of the sun. It's hot, humid. Their tall frosted iced tea glasses clink pleasantly with ice as they sip at them. It's early Sunday afternoon, the day after the party. Selene has taken Bernard for a ride—his first "outing" in several weeks.

Alex, somber, preoccupied, had been sitting in silence, answering her inquiries with monosyllables, until Nan, startled by the forcefulness of his response, said, "Is it your marriage? Is it you and Selene? Is that what's wrong?"

"Maybe it's better what you did," he says, after a while.

"What I did?"

"Yes. What you did."

He hesitates, then says, "You and Dad stayed married, even after— Maybe I should have stayed with Carolyn."

Nan looks at him, searching for something in his words, in his expression.

"Did you leave Carolyn because I didn't leave your dad? Because your dad didn't leave me?"

Alex looks out at the garden, glittering with color after a morning shower.

"That was part of it, I think. At some buried level. But at the time it just seemed—right."

"What makes it wrong now?"

He hesitates again, pulling back, almost visibly.

"Is it Carolyn?"

"Well, yes. There's Carolyn. And the kids."

"Kevin and Wendy are adults now," says Nan, "and I think they're doing all right—or at least Wendy is doing well. Although I rarely see Carolyn, she seems to be—"

She stops, conscious of his almost tangible uneasiness. Then, she says, quietly, reflectively, almost to herself, "We never stop paying, do we?"

He faces her, alert, questioning. "What do you mean?"

"For our—choices. What some might call our—mistakes. We never stop paying. If our choices are uncomfortable, upsetting, if they change the course of our life—the smooth, comfortable, acceptable tenor of our life—they are perceived as mistakes, even though—" She stops.

Alex says, "So, you have no regrets?"

Nan says, appealingly, "How can I regret Griff?"

They listen to the summer bird sounds surrounding them: chickadees calling each other with an insistent "chick-adee-dee-dee-dee"; the ticking sound of a bird hidden in the maple tree that shades the patio; the liquid, three-part harmony of a robin, repeated like a singer warming up for a concert. They watch as a hummingbird whirs gently, hovering at the feeder Nan has hung nearby. Its greenish gold body glistens in the sun. Its wings are a blurred halo. Beneath the table, Nippy sighs in his sleep, then emits a soft, dreaming growl.

Alex says, "Maybe if Selene and I had a child—"

Nan shakes her head. "A child isn't a fixative, or shouldn't be. What's the real problem?"

Alex shrugs. "I am. Selene is. We both are."

"You both are—what?"

"Guilty," he says.

Nan studies her son. She sees that he has come to her not out of his need for her but out of desperation, the urge to confess, to clear his conscience. And she knows, perhaps better than Alex, the compulsion that is driving Selene.

"Are you and Carolyn—?"

She stops, knowing already.

He turns his head away from her. He nods, once.

"Good God, Alex."

"I know, I know. It's all wrong, and yet—" Alex faces her. "It doesn't feel wrong. I still feel—"

"Married to her?"

"Yes."

THE SECOND MRS. PRICE

"Alex, you're a fool. You're a fool to think you can have it both ways. You're worse than a fool. And Carolyn is—well, never mind her for now. You made a choice, years ago. You hurt Kevin and Wendy, you broke something in Kevin, something that he can't seem to repair. Now you're *undoing* your choice, you're *undoing* your life with Selene—"

Alex gets up, walks away from her. He stands with his back to her, one hand pushed into the pocket of his pants. Beneath his polo shirt, his shoulders are broad and slightly hunched.

She says, "Alex, I'm sorry."

"Don't be sorry," he says. "I know you're telling me the truth, from your heart. It's just—hard. Going down."

"Did you think I'd be sympathetic?"

"I thought you'd be honest. You're the most honest person I know."

"Honest, perhaps, but not good. Not always having been good. And, therefore, sympathetic."

He shrugs his shoulders under the white polo shirt, which is gleaming in the sun. She feels a sudden surge of love for him. He is her son, after all, not a middle-aged man who is separate and apart from her.

She stands up, walks over to him, puts her hands on his broad shoulders, looking up at him. She pulls him close and hugs him, as she did when he was a child, small enough to look up at *her*. She feels the tenseness in him give way, the muscles soften.

She releases him and steps back, her hands still on his shoulders. Then she puts her arm through his, saying, "Let's walk in the garden."

*　*　*

Nan and Alex are sitting on the porch again, fresh iced tea in their glasses, when Selene and Bernard return from their ride.

Nippy rushes to Selene, frisking about her, but Selene barely acknowledges him. Nan looks at Bernard; then, alarm in her face, she looks at Selene.

"He's all right," Selene says hastily, to Nan, while Alex helps Bernard to a chair, and a glass of iced tea. "He's just a little—drunk."

"But how—?"

"We ended up at our house. Bernard hadn't been there for such a long time that I— He asked for a drink, and then another one. He seemed okay, so I—"

"How much did he drink?"

Nan is calm now, looking at Bernard, listening to Selene.

"I'm not sure. I left him alone for a few minutes while I went upstairs." She shakes her head. "The liquor is in plain sight. I'm not sure."

"It's okay," says Nan. "He'll be okay. I can tell."

"I'm so sorry," says Selene. "It's just that he—"

"I know," says Nan. "He can be very—persuasive. He has his own little stash here, which he thinks Alex or Griff restocks."

"Do you mean you—?"

"Yes. He gets so depressed. I've talked to his doctor about it. It helps him. Sometimes more than I can help him."

Selene looks at Bernard, who is relaxing in his lounge chair, his iced tea on a side table close to him, listening to Alex, nodding his head while he surveys the garden.

"It's just that—he's so fragile, Nan. It's frightening. When he talks about Anna, about his life with her, I can feel him—crumble, somehow."

"It's the loss," says Nan slowly, "and the guilt."

"The guilt?"

Nan considers, then says, "He hurt her once, badly. She forgave him, but he's never forgiven himself."

"Was it—?"

"Yes. It was a woman. Something—passing. Never meant to last. Maybe just an attraction that went too far. Dad has always been an admirer of beautiful women."

Nan looks at Selene, who flushes and looks down. "But Mom found out about it, somehow, or perhaps she just sensed it. She was very intuitive."

"So are you," says Selene.

"Perhaps. A little. Maybe we all are, a little."

"I believe that," says Selene.

"You must. You're writing a whole book about it."

"Editing. I'm editing a book about it. But you're right. My ideas are getting infused in the manuscript. I'm changing the texture and the weave by putting my hands on it. On the words."

"Thereby making it better, I'm sure," says Nan.

"Better, I hope, and—more mine."

"Nan? Selene? Come on over and join us," Bernard calls from his lounge chair. "We're talking about you, so you may as well hear."

"Don't worry, dear," Nan says to Selene. "He's in a state of mild bliss. Momentary, but very pleasant while it lasts. And we're here to see no harm comes to him."

Nan walks over to him, puts her hand on his shoulder, kisses him lightly on the top of his head.

"Was there ever an afternoon so beautiful?" says Bernard, putting his hand over hers. "I'm in love with this day."

He looks up at Nan, then at Selene, who is standing close to Alex, as though needing his support. "I'm in love with beauty."

"You always have been, Dad," says Nan.

"Not a bad thing to be," says Alex, playfully. "At least, it shows some discrimination."

"You chose well," says Bernard to Alex. "Both times."

He seems unaware of the uneasiness caused by this remark.

"But this one." He beckons toward Selene. "This one is extraordinary."

Selene's knees give way beneath her. She kneels beside the lounge chair and puts her head down, resting it against Bernard's thigh, facing away from him. He is surprised, but he pats her hair tentatively, then more confidently, smoothing it with his hand.

"Anna had hair like this," he says. "Fine and pale. It catches the light and reflects it, like the moon."

Selene is still, her eyes closed. Alex starts toward them, but Nan stops him, grasping his forearm, shaking her head at him.

"Like the moon," Bernard repeats. He leans back in the chair, his eyes closed, his hand still on Selene's hair. "Remember?"

He sighs, relaxing, the sun on his face.

"Remember the moon that night? We thought we could reach up and touch it. Maybe we did. We were so young then. Maybe we can touch the moon when we're young. Before it goes away. Before it all goes away."

His head falls to one side. He sleeps, snoring softly. .

Selene opens her eyes, lifts her head. "I'm sorry," she says to Nan, getting up. "I was afraid—"

"It's so close now," says Nan, rubbing her arms, as if she were chilled, although they are standing in the sun.

"What is?" says Alex.

"What's frightening her," says Nan, nodding toward Selene. "So natural and yet—so unnatural, somehow. Because we're never ready, no matter how much time we have, no matter how many years we're given."

CHAPTER 12

The summer settled in, hot and humid. Selene tried to remember the fresh days of spring, but it was as if they had never been. It had been so long since she had seen Griff, or even heard his name, that she wondered if he were gone, if he had disappeared as abruptly, as completely, as the yellow blossoms of early spring.

She huddled in her office, the window air conditioner noisy and intrusive, and tried to work on Kirby Woods' manuscript on extrasensory perception, wishing she were in the cool, temperature-controlled offices of Cotter Publishing, with Jeff tapping at her cubicle, pushing her to work ahead of schedule, admonishing her with a cascade of curses if she fell into a slump. At home, she worked in spurts, thinking she was working well, then stopped, realizing that she was picking at Kirby's lumpy words when what she really needed to do was to pick up the whole mass of it, thump it and pound it into a new shape.

She called Jeff, who obligingly cursed her out, but it didn't help, so she went to see him.

"You were a goddamned fool to quit Cotter," said Jeff, raking his hands through his thick, graying hair. "I should have made you stay until you—got through whatever the hell it was you were going through."

"I'm still going through it, Jeff, but thanks. It's nice to be missed."

"You're a good editor. You don't need to be sitting in a goddamned cubicle to do your work. But, dammit, where's the manuscript?"

"Some of it's still in Kirby's head. The rest is residing in my computer, like a message from an alien, waiting to be translated."

Jeff guffawed. "Kirby Woods is the most illiterate Ph.D. I've come across but, the hell of it is, he has something to say. Something people want to hear—and read about."

"I miss you," said Selene.

"It's your own damned fault."

"I know."

He spent an hour with her, questioning, prodding, drawing from her Kirby's vision and her interpretation of Kirby's voice, forcing her to rethink, reinterpret, until he was called away to a meeting. Selene was left staring out of the window of his office.

As she was leaving, a few minutes later, she stopped to visit several former coworkers, who were polite but preoccupied. Selene had quit the company. They feigned envy but were really, she saw, indifferent, having moved on easily without her. Indifference, she was reminded, is one of the primary corporate qualities, as everyone is replaceable and interchangeable. Hadn't she and Alex written about this in their corporate management book?

She pulled out of the parking lot after a chat with the parking attendant, who remembered her, obviously enjoyed looking at her, and was not indifferent. She pointed her car toward home, turning the air conditioning on high, waiting for the interior to cool, rubbing at her eyes, which had suddenly welled up. Self-pity, she thought, shaking her head angrily. She had chosen to leave; she no longer belonged there. Her place had been filled by an eager young woman who gushed with satisfaction at occupying Selene's position, Selene's cubicle. Her presence and tenure at Cotter Publishing were wiped out like footprints in the sand.

Beware your heart's desire, she thought, *for you will surely have it.*

She pulled out onto the freeway and let her thoughts roam. Was she really working better now? Was she really more free? She thought about her decision to quit Cotter Publishing, to make herself more available to Griff, to put herself in the same relative space he inhabited. How foolish it was, how ineffective.

Our decisions are so impulsive, so immutable, she thought, skimming in and out of the passing lane. *We never know for sure if they're the right decisions, the best decisions. We only know by what evolves from our decisions—whether what evolves is good or bad—and, for me, nothing has evolved as yet. I have no book, and I am no closer to Griff. Why can't I accept that and go home to my husband?*

An angry flash of headlights behind her brought her to attention. She pressed down on the accelerator, passed the moving van beside her, then swerved over to the right lane, allowing the impatient commuter to pass her. She shook her head to discharge the waking dream state she was in, but it washed over her again. She stayed in the right lane.

It's not too late. I can retrieve my life—my former life—go forward as though nothing has happened. As though Griff has not happened. But even as the thought occurred she dismissed it. I am changed, she thought. *I can't go back. My decision to leave Cotter Publishing was only one of many decisions I made that have already changed my life. I can no more go back than I could turn around in this traffic, on this freeway. I can only continue, passing slow-moving vehicles, avoiding obstacles in my path, watching for my exit ...*

She pulled off the freeway and made her way through the downtown streets of Sylvan Springs, bustling importantly with midday crowds. She glanced longingly at the shops, picturing herself turning over books at the out-of-print bookstore; trying on a crisp, cool summer outfit; pawing through the sidewalk shoe sale; sipping a cappuccino.

If a parking spot opens up on the street, I will stay. I will shop. I will ease the soreness of my heart's desire with a book, a scarf, a pair of sandals.

She cruised slowly down the main street, opening her window to let in the warm, soothing sounds of many people gathering outside on a summer's day to eat at a street-side café, to walk from one shop window to the next eager to be tempted inside, to look at one another and invite others to look at them. At the far end of the street, as she prepared herself to turn right and head home, a car turned on its blinkers, pulled out. Selene slipped easily into the space, then turned off the ignition. She sat for a few moments.

How easy it is, she thought, *to change the course of one's day, to change the course of one's life. We do it all the time. We just don't recognize it. We simply don't acknowledge it.*

She reached for her handbag, pushed open the door, and got out, slamming the door. She looked around, feeling the humid air settle on her, but pleasantly this time, sticky and real after the refrigerated air of the car. She walked to the meter and fished in her handbag for change, enjoying the clink of the coins in the metal slot, the churning sound of the meter as she pulled on the lever.

I can do this, she thought. *I have time. The meter says so. Cotter Publishing doesn't need me. Griff doesn't want me. Alex is distant and preoccupied. Kirby's manuscript is resting after being thumped into a semblance of a shape by Jeff's comments and curses.*

She turned away from the meter, smiling, pleased with herself, thinking only of the delicious freedom of the moment, and saw Griff, a few feet away, smiling back at her.

* * *

Selene has never, except for the time he stood in her kitchen, silent and uneasy, gulping down a soda, been alone with Griff. She sits across from him now, at a sidewalk café, a cappuccino in front of her, a soda in front of him, the round white table so small their knees almost touch underneath it, thinking that she would have missed this, would have missed him, if the parking space hadn't opened up at the moment she approached it, wondering at the timing, the luck, the good fortune of it, opening her mouth to tell him, then shaking her head and sipping at the frothy coffee instead, knowing he wouldn't see it as she does, not having restructured his life as she has, to allow it to happen.

The smile, the surprise, the gladness he must have seen in her face as she turned away from the parking meter and saw him, has put him at his ease. He is more comfortable with her than she has ever seen him—more so than on the Sunday they moved Bernard's things down from the third floor into the first-floor bedroom. They talk about Bernard now. Selene tells Griff about Bernard's ride with her the Sunday before, how frightened she had been, how alarmed by his fragility.

"When we stopped at my house afterwards, when he—when I left him alone and then realized he'd been drinking our liquor, I—I felt so guilty ..."

"When it comes to booze, Gramps is an opportunist," says Griff.

"I do love him, Griff," she says, wishing she could add, *as I love Alex, as I love Nan, as I want to love you.*

"He's a big part of the reason I came back," says Griff. "I wanted to spend some time with him before—"

"Before—?"

Griff shrugs and looks away from her, squinting into the sun. She looks at him, grateful for the opportunity to see him clearly—his eyes blue slits in the sun, pale lashes slightly curling at the ends, his mouth open a little, the etching of his upper lip, as he sits tentatively, shoulders hunched, on the undersized plastic chair. She cannot look at him enough. He seems to sense this. He picks up his soda, glances at her, then puts it down again, as though he has forgotten to drink it.

"We're always alone," he says, hesitating, "but Gramps is—he's—"

He stops, and Selene waits, silent.

"I went to see him a few days ago," says Griff.

Selene nods, signaling her complete attention.

"He was sitting in the living room, in that big chair by the window. He was alone. He was just sitting there, looking out the window. I said, 'Hey, Gramps, what are you up to?' He didn't answer me right away, didn't even look at me, so I sat down and I waited. After a while, he said, 'I'm emptying myself out.' I said, 'Emptying yourself out? Of what?' He didn't say anything for a long time; then, he said, 'Of life. Of the desire for life.'"

Selene sucks in her breath. "Did he—did he say anything else?"

Griff shakes his head, drinks some of his soda. "We talked some more, but I don't remember anything special about what we said. Then Mom came back from wherever she was, and that was the end of that."

Selene nods, afraid to look away from him, afraid to speak, almost afraid to breathe. She has never felt so close to him, as though she is adhering to him, to his thoughts. She wants only to keep him here, teetering precariously on the plastic chair that is much too small for his large frame, looking at her, talking to her. She wants only to be here with him, feeling the perspiration creep beneath her linen dress, making it cling to her, making her hair cling in tendrils to her neck and face, making her thighs adhere to each other, making her squirm in the heat.

"I'm thinking of staying there for a while," he says.

She thinks, *Where?* before she recalls that they are still talking about Bernard.

"I don't think Mom should do all of it—alone."

"We can help," she says. "I can help."

"You do help," he says. "You and Alex. Both of you. What I mean is, being there—right on top of it. Day to day."

"What about—?"

She can't bring herself to say Sue's name.

Griff shrugs. "She'll be all right. The place is crowded now, with Jimbo there all the time. Sue is—" He stops, as if to form the thought. "It's a damned hard way to go about it, but they're— getting reacquainted. They haven't really spent much time with each other the past few years. They're having sort of a—family reunion." He pauses before adding, "And I'm not family."

He picks up his soda, takes a long swallow, watching Selene as he drinks.

My God, she thinks. *My God. My God.*

She says to him, "So you're coming home." Hearing the vibration in her voice.

He puts the soda down, turns the paper container back and forth, back and forth.

"I have no home. This table and chair, my truck, a furnished room, that's as much my home as this town, as Mom's house."

"But why?"

"I don't belong anywhere. I don't have—I never expect to have—a home."

"But Nan loves you so," she says, her voice almost pleading.

He nods and says, "I know."

"Tell me." She says this before she can think about what she is saying. "Tell me."

Griff shrugs again, Selene knowing now—like fitting a piece into a complicated puzzle—that he isn't dismissing her question, he isn't dismissing her. She waits, the cappuccino cooling, the sounds around them—the buzz of people, the noise of traffic on the street just a few feet from where they sit—as if muffled.

"For a long time, I looked for a home," he says.

The words are as magical to Selene as if she were a child, and he had begun, "Once upon a time." She sits forward a little, to catch his words.

"I thought that was what was—missing—in my life. A place to be. Someone to be—with."

Selene nods, almost imperceptibly.

"I've lived—all over the country, and out of the country. I even went to India once." He shakes his head. "It's the American way, you know? If you don't find what you want where you are, you must be in the wrong place. So move on. So I moved on. And on. And on. Meantime, my family more or less gave up on me. Assumed I was just a bum. No direction. No goals. Nothing finished, not even my education."

"Nan didn't give up on you," says Selene.

"Maybe not," he says. "She's a lot more tolerant than—" He stops. "And she told me about—"

"Your father."

"So you know," he says.

Selene nods.

"Alex, he's—like Howard—like his father," says Griff. "They believe in work, in goals, in—stability."

Selene shifts uncomfortably. Griff turns his head away, amused by her reaction.

"Okay. Granted. He made an exception with you. I admit I was floored when I found out Alex had walked out on Carolyn and his kids. I thought he'd stay the course with her."

Selene can feel herself flushing. She opens her mouth to say something, then shuts it again, swallowing the words.

I won't distract him, she thinks. *I won't*.

"What I didn't consider," says Griff, "is that Alex isn't just his father. He's—"

"He's Nan, too," says Selene, again finishing his thought.

"Yeah. Who knows better than you?"

Selene flushes again. She rests her hands on the table, which hovers like a round white wafer between them.

"The thing is," he says, "while I was moving around, I was finding my home—brick by brick, you might say. I got that truck in Oklahoma City." He nods toward the street. "Put a bed cover on it in Denver. Picked up things here and there." He leaned forward. "That Chevy is my home. The closest thing I'll ever have to a home."

"It's a truck," says Selene, almost indignantly. "It's not a—"

She stops, confused.

"It's my home. It goes where I go. I don't need a bedroom, a bathroom, a kitchen."

He is looking at her, studying her. Selene softens under his gaze, feeling the heat rise inside her.

"I want you—to stay," she says, hearing the words before she has formed the thought.

Griff lifts his eyebrows. They are silvery in the sun.

"You're—part of my family," she says. "I don't have any other family."

She shakes her head, as if to correct, to clarify.

"You're my family now. You're—" She stops, then plunges ahead. "Don't you see? You're all the—family—I want."

He grips the edge of the table, pushing himself back a little, as though he is too close to her.

I can still take it back, she thinks. *I can make it go away. I can make it simple, innocent. After all, he is Alex's half-brother, Nan's son, Bernard's grandson.*

"I shouldn't have said that," she says at last. "I mean, I shouldn't have said it like that."

She draws in her breath, exhales, wishing she hadn't spoken, wishing she had listened. Just listened. But it's too late. The words are out there, pushing him away from the magic circle of the table. She opens her mouth to say, *Come back.* Instead, she says, "You and Alex and Nan and Bernard—you're all the family I have."

Griff relaxes perceptibly. He releases his grip on the table. He sits back, distancing himself from the table, from Selene. He crosses his right ankle over his left knee, clasps his arms across his chest.

"Won't you—won't you—have dinner with us? With Alex and me?"

She wants to weep as she says the words, the trite, polite words that push him away even further.

He shrugs. He is impatient with her, annoyed.

"I'm sorry," she says, sorry beyond words.

He is gone from her now, even though he is still sitting across from her.

"You're going through so much. With Sue's boy, and Bernard."

And with me, she wants to say. *Now I've added to the confusion, the tumult, and I can't make it better. Nothing I say will make it better.*

"Is there anything I can do?—we can do?"

She has circled back to the beginning of their conversation. All that followed that beginning, all the magic, is gone.

"Ask Nan," he says at last. "She's carrying most of the load."

Selene says, "I'm asking you."

For an instant, they connect again, looking directly at each other. Then he turns away. Although he still sits across from her, she is alone at the round white table, waiting for him to get up, waiting for his nod, his, "See you around."

Watching him walk away.

Watching until he disappears in the crowded, noisy, sunny street.

* * *

After her unexpected meeting with Griff, Selene made preparations—as though she were leaving—as though she were dying.

Perhaps I will die, she thought, and then, *Perhaps I will just disappear.*

She could no longer pretend that everything was just as it was before that afternoon at the sidewalk café.

He knows, she told herself, over and over. She had exposed herself, utterly, and he had walked away. *We never finish anything. He always walks away from me. Even knowing, he walked away from me.*

She stacked the pages of Kirby Woods' manuscript in neat piles; she made notes, but she could not work. She tidied the office, paid bills, paced the rooms of her house, touching the living room chair, the mirror, the landscape painting that she remembered from her childhood, standing at the foot of the bed where she and Alex had made love a thousand times.

This is where I live and have my being, she thought. *If all of this were to go away, would I still exist?* And then, *If I were to go away, would all of this still exist?*

At first, Alex seemed not to notice. He was preoccupied, he said, with work. The days following her meeting with Jeff at Cotter Publishing and her meeting with Griff downtown folded one into the other, with no perceptible variation. It was as though the structure of her life had crumbled from within. The supports were no longer intact. Her childhood in this house, her relationship with words and language, her marriage to Alex, were no longer enough for her. She was teetering, oh, so slightly, but enough for her to feel a dizzying shift.

"It's still summer," said Alex, teasing her, as she brought in stores of food, cleaned the house, sorted through the papers and magazines that cluttered their living room. "You're like a squirrel that gets a whiff of fall in the middle of July and goes into a frenzy. What are you getting ready for?"

"I'm not sure," said Selene, truthfully. "I just feel the need to put things in order, fill our little nest with food and supplies."

"Is the world coming to an end? Are we at war? Have I missed the news?"

He rustled the pages of his newspaper, peering at her over the top of his reading glasses.

Selene got up from the couch, where she was sorting through magazines, newspapers, unopened mail. She walked over to Alex, who was sitting in his favorite easy chair, kissed him on the top of his head.

"I don't think it's happening to the world." She wrapped her arm around his neck and rested her head against his. "It's just happening to me."

"Anything I can do?" said Alex.

"Not yet," she replied.

*　*　*

"You know him best, Nan. What sort of person—what sort of man—is Griff?"

It was a Saturday. Selene and Nan were preparing a late lunch for themselves and Bernard in Nan's kitchen. Bernard was sitting at the table, shirt sleeves rolled up, shucking peas—a task he enjoyed—while Nan boned and sliced chicken breasts for the sauté pan. Selene stood beside her at the counter, breaking lettuce into a bowl, slicing tomatoes, cucumbers. They had met earlier, by appointment, at the local farmers' market, with lunch and a visit with Bernard to follow.

Bernard hadn't left the house for several weeks, so Selene visited him at Nan's whenever she could. She didn't deny to herself that she hoped to see Griff there, but so far they had not met—not since the afternoon at the downtown café.

Nan paused, the boning knife in her hand. She looked out the window at the garden shining in the sun. "I did know him best, for many years, but now—"

"Now?" said Selene.

Nan shook her head as she severed the breast bone from the meat. "I'm not sure."

"Not sure you know him best?"

Nan began cutting the meat into thin narrow slices. "I'm not sure I know him at all."

Selene waited, gently mixing the vegetables in the bowl with her fingers, watching Nan as she cut the chicken breasts, sprinkled the slices with salt and pepper, dredged them lightly in flour, and placed them carefully in the pan, where they sizzled in the hot oil. She listened to the plunk of the peas as they fell into the bowl, glancing at Bernard, who seemed intent on his task. He was much quieter recently. Selene could not always tell if he were listening to them or to his own thoughts.

Bernard had asked for Griff, rather peremptorily, a few minutes earlier. Nan had admitted she didn't know where he was or how to contact him.

"I want to talk to him," Bernard had said.

Nan had looked at Selene helplessly.

"He'll come by soon, Dad. He said he'd be back in a day or two."

Bernard had said nothing more. They were silent until Selene worked up the courage to question Nan directly about Griff.

"Anybody who says he knows anybody else is a damn fool," said Bernard.

He held up the bowl for the two women standing at the counter. Selene reached for the bowl. She put it in the sink, running water over the plump green peas, lifting and moving them with her fingers, enjoying the feel of them as they moved and regrouped in the water. Then she drained them, pouring the peas into the saucepan on the stove, where they bubbled and frothed in the boiling water.

"Shouldn't we know those who are closest to us?" said Selene, lowering the heat under the saucepan, settling the lid in place. "Shouldn't Nan know her own son?"

"No, to both questions," said Bernard.

There was a note of impatience in his voice that Selene had often heard in recent weeks. It was as though he were pacing himself and had no tolerance for evasion or pretense. He sat glaring at the two women at the counter, his head cocked to one side, looking like the old, vigorous Bernard, not withdrawn now, as he was more and more of late.

"So I don't know you, or Alex, or Nan—and you don't know us?"

"Damned straight," said Bernard.

Selene turned to him with delight.

"But I *want* to know you," said Selene, leaning against the counter, smiling at him, looking up at Nan, who was turning and browning the chicken, her back to Bernard. Selene saw her swipe quickly at her cheek with the knuckle of her free hand.

"Griff understands," said Bernard, ignoring her words. "There's nothing phony about Griff."

"Am I—phony?" said Selene.

"It's not about you or Griff or me or anybody," said Bernard, fiercely. "It's just the way it is."

He hit the table with the side of his hand. Selene jerked her head back, as though he had struck her.

"Why does it take us a whole lifetime to figure out what's right under our noses? Why can't I just say to you what I'm saying to you so you accept it and live with it—instead of deluding yourself for another fifty years or so."

"Dad—"

"Don't interrupt. I've got something to say and I'll be goddamned if I'm gonna be shut up like a doddering old fool."

"I'm not—"

"It's the people closest to us, the ones we think we know the best, who deceive us, whom we deceive. We deceive them because we *don't* want them to know us. Because if they did—if they knew us—we'd lose them."

"Why?" said Selene. "Why would we lose them?"

"Because we're not, any of us, who we claim to be. We're all living a lie. If we didn't lie to ourselves, if we didn't lie to others, we couldn't put up with it."

"Put up with—what?"

"Our lives," said Bernard.

"I don't understand," said Selene.

"That's because you're young—and deluded."

"Griff is young," said Selene, stubbornly.

Bernard shook his head. "But not deluded. Griff *refuses* to be—deluded."

He sighed heavily, then said to Nan, "Pour me a shot of whiskey, my girl, and don't make me beg for it."

Nan looked at him for a long moment, then nodded. She took down a glass tumbler, went into the pantry off the kitchen. They heard her rustling cans and packaged goods in the high, built-in cupboards.

"She tries to keep it hidden away," said Bernard. "Thinks I'm going to drink myself to death." He shook his head. "Now *that's* deluded."

"I want you to explain," said Selene, wanting to stomp her foot in vexation.

Bernard shook his head again. "You have to take your own blinders off. I can't do it for you."

Nan returned from the pantry, reached into the freezer for a handful of ice cubes, and placed the iced amber liquid in front of Bernard. He picked up the glass, saluted both women, drank. When he put the glass down, half empty, he sighed and said, "Ah. That's better." He looked at Selene, who stood at the counter facing him, frowning at him. When he spoke, his voice was mild, courtly.

"Do you think I miss Anna because we were so happy together? Because we never spent a day apart from each other? Because we somehow 'completed' each other?"

"But, of course, that's all true," said Nan, turning away from the stove to glance at them.

"Maybe," said Bernard. "Maybe. But that's not why I miss her so much."

He lifted his glass to his lips. The ice cubes clinked as he drained the glass. It was the only sound in the kitchen except for the sizzling chicken and the bubbling peas.

"I miss her because we left so much unfinished, unsaid. And now it can't be finished. It can't be said."

He drew in a ragged breath.

"I was never honest with her. Phony Boy Scout word," he mumbled, rubbing the back of his hand across his mouth as if to erase the word. "I mean, toward the end, I never shared a single complete true and honest thought with her. We drifted into—politeness."

He shook his head.

"We lied to ourselves and to each other. We deluded our-selves and each other. We were—polite. Right to the end, when she was being crushed and pulverized by—by pain—when being with her was like watching her being—violated—we were—polite."

His words were slow and halting, as though they were becoming too heavy for him. Nan put down the knife she was using to chop cilantro to sprinkle over the chicken. She went to him, sat beside him, took his hand.

"Griff understands," he said, not looking at Nan. "He's the only one who won't let me—won't let anyone—get away with a lie. Where is Griff? Why isn't he here?"

Selene said, unable to stop herself, "What is it he under-stands, Bernard? What is it he knows that we don't know?"

Bernard shook his head impatiently.

"He doesn't know anything we don't know. That's not the point."

"What is the point?" said Selene.

Bernard sighed, looked down at his empty glass, clinking the ice, glancing at Nan ruefully. "The point is—Nan, just a finger more, if you please—the point is, Griff sees things most of us don't see, most of us miss."

"Do you mean—?"

"Not exactly. Not exactly a sixth sense. But close. He has somehow managed to push back the blinders most of us wear. He sees—all around things." He held up his glass. "Nan, how about it?"

Nan took the glass, reluctantly, and disappeared into the pantry again.

"Do you see this?" he said to Selene, nodding toward the pantry. "It's a game. It has certain rules. You can only play it if you have your blinders on. Take them off and you can't play. It hurts. It hurts bad."

Nan came back, put the glass in front of him. Bernard picked it up, drank down the liquid in one gulp.

"So, we play the game."

He sighed and put down the glass, nodding his thanks to Nan. "Griff won't play the game. He won't—knuckle under. So he won't be around long. He'll leave, just like me. Only he might come back someday. I won't be coming back."

Selene looked at Nan. She saw that Nan was struggling to compose herself.

"Say, Nan, my girl. You know, that chicken smells good. I can almost taste it. But not quite. Any chance of transferring a slice or two to my plate?"

Nan put her hands up to her face. When she took them away, her face was wiped clean of expression. She said, with a little quake in her voice, "Yes, indeed. Everything is ready. Selene? Please sit down. I'll serve us right from the stove."

Selene sat down across from Bernard, who winked at her.

"You're looking especially pretty today, my dear. And you smell good, too. Almost as good as the chicken. What's that scent you're wearing?"

"Soap. Shampoo."

"Ambrosia. Everything smells so goddamn good. Let's go out in the garden after lunch. I want to smell the roses."

"You're always smelling the roses, Dad," said Nan, putting a plate with chicken, peas, and salad in front of him. "That's your gift."

"So it is," he said. He chuckled, then blandly looked up at Nan.

"You know, a glass of white wine would turn this simple little meal into a feast. What do you say, my girl?"

CHAPTER 13

Griff left so quietly, so completely, that Sue wondered if he had ever been there at all, if she had only imagined him. She didn't know, would never know, if he had come into town looking for her, or if he had just happened to see her on the street. He never seemed surprised by anything, so maybe— But it didn't make any difference. He always meant to leave her.

Jimbo was better now. It wasn't just his poor shattered leg that was on the mend. In the long moment when his motorcycle skidded off the road, and he fell off the bike, and the bike fell on his leg, and the car hit the bike, something in him that had been hard, unyielding, gave way.

At first, it had been just the pain, the fear that he would never be whole again, that they would take away his leg while he slept that endless, helpless, drug-induced sleep. And the fear in his mother's eyes, above her crooked, pasted-on smile. But then he remembered the giving way. Griff, watching him, his face wiped clean of expression, his blue eyes intense, said, "Don't lose it. Don't let it go." Jimbo knew he was not just talking about his leg.

Even when words came back to him, when he could talk, he and Griff said little to each other; they never went beyond the mundane. But Jimbo waited for his return, even asked for him now and then. When he was stronger, when he was home again, he became more awkward with Griff, even shy—which for Jimbo meant surly. But Griff didn't seem to mind. He watched him, as he had earlier in Jimbo's recovery. He seemed satisfied. Somehow, that soothed Jimbo as nothing else could do.

"You'll be okay," Griff said to him.

Jimbo took the words to himself, repeating them like a mantra. "I'll be okay," he said, silently and out loud, sometimes telling the phrase on his fingers, like rosary beads. "I'll be okay."

When Jimbo came home, when Sue saw that he was getting better, when she recognized that he was somehow a different Jimbo, she began to talk to him as she had before the accident, moving farther and farther away from self-consciousness as she became more comfortable with him. Like Griff, Jimbo had few words, and he doled them out like a miser. But Sue had enough words for both of them—for all three of them.

"The doc says there's no need to pamper you, that it might even—what's the word he used?—oh, yeah, it might even 'hinder' your recovery, but I says to him, I says, Doc, I don't know how many kids you got growing up around you, but I only got this one, and he's no prize, but he's my only kid. If I want to pamper him a little, I figure it's my call. He sort of chortles, kind of like a horse, and I says, see ya around, Doc. I gotta get my kid some hot dogs and some Rocky Road ice cream, and he says—"

"I'm not hungry," said Jimbo, the thought of the rich food making him nauseous. The drugs buried his appetite so deep—he wondered if he would ever be hungry again.

"Not to worry. It'll keep. Maybe tomorrow when the home nurse comes—"

"I hate her," he said, thinking of the long hours when Sue was at work, thinking of the round, cheerful home nursing aide, not much older than he was. He and his friends would have scorned her if they saw her at school or at one of their hangouts. She was timid with him, but insistent. Jimbo had to submit to her care, like a child.

The pasted-on smile was back on Sue's face. The worried squint in her eyes made her look as though the two parts of her face didn't go together.

"All right already. I get the picture. You got no use for the dinner menu, and the hired help sucks. When your leg doesn't hurt, it itches. Your doc is a pain in the ass. Your room smells like dirty jockey shorts. Your so-called buddies haven't come around to see you since you left the hospital. Your girlfriend has decided to move on. Your hormones are in overdrive. Your pimples are blossoming again. Your mom doesn't have a clue, and her man has taken a walk just when you were beginning to like the bastard. There's nothing much to do except watch the goddamn TV and listen to your boom box. You can barely make it to the bathroom, let alone go downstairs or get outside. Most of the time you feel like that fly over there on your window, caught between the screen and the windowpane, buzzing like crazy because it can't get out and it can't get back in. You're stuck in limbo. Even school in September is beginning to look good. You wonder if you'll ever feel normal again, if you'll ever be able to strut down the street with your pals, hang out at the mall, dance with some hot chick, ride a motorcycle, peel off your clothes and run into the lake. You wonder if you'll feel like some gimpy freak for the rest of your life." She took a breath. "Have I missed anything?"

Jimbo looked away so she wouldn't see his slow grin. He shook his head.

"Well, let me know if you think of anything else. Just make sure you tell me in three words or less. The doc says you should take it easy. I wouldn't want you to overdo it."

Jimbo thought, so this is why they stayed—Griff and the guys that came before him—and his 'no-good Dad.' They didn't stay long, but they stayed, because Sue Smoller let them see what a rotten, fucked-up world they lived in, then made them laugh about it. It came to him—but only as a passing thought, not to be shared with his mother—that he was getting better. He rested his head on his roped-up pillows and glanced at his mother, who stood with her arms crossed, her head tilted to one side.

"Maybe I am hungry," he said.

He turned his head toward the sunny window to watch the angry buzzing fly.

"Like I said to the doc, you're no prize, but you're all I got. If I could pick another Dad for you, I'd pick one that would stay longer than five minutes. But you're his kid all right. You got his eyes. You got his mean streak. You got his hairline, too, so don't be surprised if you're bald as a baby by the time you're my age. Serves him right, the bastard. Thinks he's God's gift to women. Well, they're welcome to him. I just wish he'd send us what he saves on haircuts. Even that would help. By the way, the doc says you'll be going to school in the fall, but don't expect to try out for the running team. Not unless it's a three-legged race."

She turned toward the door, her words shifting gears with the movement.

"Back in a flash with your fast-food order. Even got those chips you like, the ones that fit in a tube and taste like yesterday's mashed potatoes. If you're not up for the Rocky Road, I'll eat it for you. We can watch 'The Simpsons,' or 'Who Wants to Be a Millionaire.' We'll have a blast, one of those mother-son bonding things."

She was gone, closing the door behind her, although there was no one else in the house. Jimbo turned his head and looked up at the ceiling, his eyes following the puffy discolored crack that traveled across the room, dipping down to the frame above the door. He looked at it for a long time. Slowly, very slowly, his mouth began to twitch, his body twitched, even his shattered leg inside its plaster cast began to twitch. He succumbed to a few moments of silent laughter.

* * *

When Selene tries to trace back to the beginning the quarrels she and Alex are having more and more frequently, she always stops with her trip to Chicago. Before that, Alex seemed unaware of or unconcerned with the transformation that began, for her, the day she met Griff. After that, he seemed to back away from her, as though he needed to assess her from a critical distance.

It is his cold objectivity that infuriates her most. It is as though she is a key employee who has disappointed him, whose rise in the company is up for review. The revealing dress she wore to the company party, her defense of Griff, her inability to progress with her book, her tepid response the few times he turned to her in bed, innumerable minor offenses that revealed her inattention or her indifference—all are noted, she knows, in the mental file Alex labels: *Selene Fugate Price, Second Wife, promising but still immature (may not make the grade).*

The edifice she built so carefully—the home within the house where she has stored her earliest memories—seems to be crumbling. Selene is uncertain whether to flee or to let the dust and debris settle around her. But she has nowhere else to go. Even for Griff, she would find it hard to leave the solace of this house, with its creaky floors, its faded wallpaper, the warm nesting quality of its rooms. She has resisted all of Alex's efforts to convince her that they should move, or gut the house and remodel, room by room. His arguments are, as always, logical, but she can only shake her head stubbornly and say, "No, I can't do it. I can't—hurt it. It's meant to be this way." Knowing that she's not ready to move, and that she can't change the house while they're living in it. It would be—a desecration.

As always, he gives in, not because he's convinced but because it's her house. Alex wants a house that reflects his position and status, a house suitable for his business associates, a house that will showcase his beautiful second wife. Selene entertains occasionally but reluctantly, preferring the company of Nan and

Bernard, or their few mutual friends, to Alex's executive 'peers' and their spouses, who remind her of the corporate schemata she left behind at Cotter Publishing, the game of chess that ends only with banishment or total disengagement.

"Think about doing something in the early fall, late September, early October," says Alex now. "That gives you plenty of time to plan."

"I couldn't stand thinking about it for that long," says Selene, crossing her legs tailor-style on the couch, scanning television channels with her remote, looking for late-night news analyses. "That's months away."

"That's the idea. I want it to be elaborate. I want you to spend time and thought and money on it."

"Why? What's the occasion?"

"I just haven't done it yet. Not in a big way. Not since—"

"Not since you were married to Carolyn."

"And even then—"

"It wasn't as grand as the last one or two we've attended."

"Since you're completing my thoughts and sentences, I guess you already know what I have in mind."

Selene recites: "A dazzling array of food. Things I couldn't possibly prepare in my own kitchen. Brand-name wine. Plenty of booze. Low lights and candles to lessen the shock of being in this old house. A couple of caterers and a waitstaff. Valet parking. Nippy at a kennel. The executive's wife in a modest—but expensive—gown. Have I forgotten anything?"

"Shots," he says.

"Shots?"

"For Nippy. Before we banish him to the kennel."

He scratches Nippy's ear. Nippy, comfortably wedged beside him in the armchair, sighs and stretches himself along the length of Alex's thigh.

"He hates the kennel," says Selene.

"You hate leaving him in the kennel. From all accounts, he has a hell of a good time there, especially when he gets to chase around with his fellow boarders."

Selene shrugs her shoulders. "I'll plan your party. I'll impress your fellow executives. I'll look the way you want me to look, say the things you expect me to say. But I won't like it."

"If you don't like it, everybody will know it."

"No, they won't," says Selene. "No one knows what I think and feel, not even—"

"Not even me?"

Selene hesitates. "Now you're finishing *my* sentences."

"Am I right?"

"Yes," she says, tossing him the remote. "You're right."

He catches the device easily, without looking at it; then he turns down the volume. The news analysts seated at a table murmur importantly to each other, just beneath audible sound.

"What do you want, Selene?" he says, not raising his voice.

"To be—to be—" Selene stops, searching for the word. "Whole. To be whole."

"And what will make you—whole?"

But Selene is already there, beyond his question, intent on the image of Griff that is always just beneath the surface, more real than Alex sitting in his easy chair, watching her. She pushes it back, pushes it down, afraid he will somehow see into her mind, listen to her thoughts. She cannot speak because any words right now will give her away, but her silence is painful.

Alex gets up, dislodging Nippy, who lands on the floor at full alert, then sits back on his haunches, watching as Alex paces back and forth in front of the TV, then tosses the remote on the couch, beside Selene.

"I'm going out," he says. "Don't worry if I don't come back tonight."

"Where are you going?" says Selene, relieved by his words, which have enabled her to speak again.

"Does it matter?" he says.

Selene opens her mouth to respond, but he is already gone. She sits perfectly still, fighting the impulse to follow him, to give him the words he needs in order to stay. When the door shuts behind him, when she is in full possession of the house, Nippy already repositioned beside her, she relaxes. She picks up the remote, turns up the volume. The dickering of the news analysts soothes her. *They* have words, *lots* of words; they want only to make themselves heard in the waves of words rising all around them.

Then, suddenly irritated by the rising excitement in the voices of the new analysts, she presses the mute button on the remote.

* * *

"Is Selene out of town again?" says Carolyn, closing the door behind Alex.

"No."

"She's—away from home?"

"No."

"You were just—passing by?"

"No."

Carolyn laughs and gives him a little push, so that he steps backwards.

"Well, come in, anyways."

She leads him into the living room. He sits down on the couch, looks at the television set. She picks up the remote and hands it to him.

"Beer?" she says.

He nods.

In the small kitchen, she reaches into the refrigerator for a beer, snaps off the cap, listening to Alex methodically scan the channels. For the first time, she considers the possibility of his being free again, of his being without Selene. She thinks, *Do I want him back?* The question is so unexpected that she puts the beer down on the counter, resting her hands against it for support, feeling unsteady, a little dizzy.

"Are you all right?" she says, when she goes back into the living room, handing Alex the bottle of Michelob, his favorite, always chilled and ready for him.

He nods, an all-encompassing nod which answers her question, thanks her for the beer, and puts off any further explanation.

She sits down beside him on the couch. They gaze at the television set as Alex changes channels again and again. At last, after he has finished most of the beer, Carolyn takes the remote from him, turns off the set. She pulls his head toward her lap. He sighs and stretches his long length on the couch, his feet still on the floor.

"Thanks," he says, looking up at her, then closing his eyes.

She is struck by the pure sexual appeal of his glance, a look meant only to acknowledge the comfort she is giving him. Again, she thinks, *Do I want him back?* Again, she is stunned by the possibility that she may have a choice, that she might not choose Alex.

When did this happen? she thinks. *When did I release him? When did I release myself?*

She can't answer the question, but she makes a mental note to call Wendy in the morning, to try again to track down Kevin. She wants her children around her, the children that she and Alex created and raised, while she examines this newfound option.

* * *

Alex breathes quietly, in what he hopes will convince Carolyn is a light sleep, while his mind skips from one thought to another. If she is looking at his eyes, she may see them move beneath his lids, as he follows his thoughts. But he senses that she is resting her head on the back of the couch, that she may have fallen asleep herself. She is very still, as only Carolyn can be still when she's giving him her full attention. He slowly relaxes, feeling his head rise and fall gently with her breathing.

I miss my kids, he thinks.

Then, *Selene is plotting something, something that doesn't include me, something that shuts me out. Or maybe she's not plotting it out, maybe she's just waiting for it to happen, and it's taking all of her energy, all of her focus, just to be ready.*

Then, *My kids came from this woman, from Carolyn. I lost them because I let go of this woman. Was it worth it?*

Then, *Who am I doing all of this for? What am I doing all of this for? My kids are gone. My second wife may not want me. My first wife may not have me. I have no deep religious conviction. I don't race cars or fly hot air balloons in my spare time. Can work be all? Even if it's good?*

There is a soft buzzing noise; Alex, listening hard, realizes it's the refrigerator in its defrost mode. Down the street, two or three blocks away, a siren rises and falls monotonously, then is silenced. The condo, clean, efficient, compact—like Carolyn—is restful in its newness. Like the house at Twin Oaks, it has none of the quirkiness of the house he shares with Selene, because it has no history. Sometimes, he feels burdened by Selene's past—even though it is much briefer than his past—because it is compacted in the house they live in, the house her parents lived in.

They never seem to be totally alone. He cannot persuade her to leave the house, or stay in the house and make it different, make it theirs. "I come with a house," she said, early in their relationship. They laughed about it, about her "dowry." But he doesn't laugh about it now. He worries about it. He worries about his increasing reluctance to call her house his home, about her inability to leave it.

What does she want, my young, lovely, intelligent wife, tied so literally to her past? Who does she want? Is it still me? Or is it—?

Inevitably, if he clicks through enough thought channels, he comes to Griff. Even in his sudden absence, he is disturbing. His absence is as unsettling as his presence because it is—like everything else about Griff—unfinished, incomplete. He played around the edges of their lives, as he had even as a child, never fully participating, aloof even when he seemed to be most attentive. Their father—Howard—had been kind to Griff, but impatient with him, as is Alex. The small annuity he carefully divided between them seemed almost by way of apology for his disproportionate love for and pride in his eldest son.

That small annuity pleased Griff beyond words. Unlike Alex, he didn't look on it as a modest investment fund to add to his portfolio. For Griff, it was freedom, choice, direction. He dropped out of his third year of school at Oberlin, bought a motorcycle, and disappeared for two years. Nan was devastated. She loved Alex. She had, in her way, loved Howard, and she was grateful to him for accepting Griff as his son. But it was Griff who made her face light up. It was Griff she followed with her eyes. Griff came back for a few months, then disappeared again; that had been his pattern ever since. Nan had long since accepted this, but Alex resented his unannounced visits, his sudden departures.

Who in the hell does he think he is? What does he think he's doing with his life—with our lives? Squeezing and letting go, again and again. Why doesn't he just go and not come back?

*   *   *

With a sudden start, Carolyn raises her head from the back of the couch.

"I dozed off," she says.

Alex opens his eyes and looks up at her.

"Why are you here?" she says. "At this hour?"

"Felt like it."

"Everything all right?"

"I miss my kids," he says.

"They're not here."

He closes his eyes. "I know."

Carolyn sits quietly, liking the feel of his head on her lap. She can't resist the urge to smooth his hair away from his forehead.

"I can't sleep lately," he says.

Carolyn says nothing. After a while, he opens his eyes wide, startling her.

"Do you have any idea how it felt to do what I did, to amputate our lives together, yours and mine and the kids?"

"I guess I do," she says.

"Maybe," he says, sighing, pulling himself up to a sitting position. He sits beside her, leaning forward, his head in his hands. "But this is worse."

"What is?"

He lifts his head, looking around the living room of Carolyn's neat, modern condo, as if searching for the answer. Carolyn has almost resigned herself to his silence when he says, "Knowing I may have been wrong."

*   *   *

Selene picks up the wall phone on the second ring.

"Hello?"

"Hi. This is Griff."

Her hand goes to her throat, as if to hold back her joy, her relief.

"Is Alex around?"

"No," says Selene. "No, he's not." There's a silence. Selene adds, "I don't know where he is, Griff."

"Have you seen Gramps lately?"

Selene takes a breath.

"Yes," she says. "I saw him earlier today. He keeps asking for you." She waits, then says, "Have you talked to him? Have you talked to Nan?"

"Not yet."

She says, her voice almost a whisper, "Talk to me, Griff."

Selene hears a small brushing sound, followed by an exhalation, and knows he's lighting a cigarette. She has never seen him smoke.

She thinks, *How is it I know so little about you?*

"I'm not sure I can watch him die," he says.

"It's hard, I know. I've only known him a few years and it's hard for me." She looks around for her next words. "Nan does it well," she says at last.

"Mom knows how to say goodbye. I only know how to disappear."

"Are you close by?"

"Yes. Close enough."

I want you closer, she thinks. *Closer. Close enough to put my mouth on that cigarette you're holding, to draw in the same hot smoke.*

"I'd better go," he says.

"No." Selene grips the phone, as if to hold him back. "No, don't."

But he has already hung up. She looks at the white plastic phone as it signals the disconnection with a single detached wail.

"You bastard," she says, softly, into the mouthpiece.

CHAPTER 14

Selene's anger—toward Griff, toward Alex, toward herself—fueled her work. For several weeks, she worked steadily on Kirby Woods' rough, uneven manuscript, planing it, smoothing its edges, assembling and fixing its parts with solid, all-but-invisible pegs. Kirby is astonished and delighted as he sees the book becoming better than he thought it could be.

Jeff Wolinski, her managing editor, is quietly encouraging.

"You should ask for and get a full cover credit as co-author," he said, at one of their meetings at Cotter Publishing. "This is as much your book as Kirby's."

Selene laughed at this, knowing how disturbing it would be to Kirby's monumental ego. But she allowed herself to think about it; it enabled her to keep going.

"I think the centerpiece of the book should be a dialogue," she said to Jeff. "Between a believer and a skeptic. Someone who is sure psychic phenomena is real, and someone who is convinced it's a hoax."

"And where will you place the reader?" said Jeff.

"Where he or she belongs," said Selene. "Somewhere in the middle, but leaning toward possibility."

"Have you discussed it with Kirby?" said Jeff.

"No," said Selene, slowly. "We'll probably have to sell him on the idea, since it's not his."

"What about doing it right now?"

Jeff called Kirby in California, at his Berkeley hotel. Kirby, on speaker phone, leapt at the idea.

"I think it might work," Kirby said. "Go for it."

"What about the title?" Selene said. Do you like *New Moon Dialogue: A Conversation about Possibilities?*"

"Sexy," he said. "I'm always open to possibilities—especially where you're concerned."

"Is that what it means to you, Kirby?" said Jeff.

"What the fuck does it matter what it means to me?" Kirby shouted into the phone. "I want to sell books. I want to create a buzz around this book so my other books pick up sales, and I get moving again on the lecture circuit. If we have to make psychic phenomena sexy to do it, let's do it."

"You're a toad, Kirby," said Jeff. "But you've got a point."

"I always have a goddamn point," said Kirby. "That's why I make money for you bozos." There was a pause, then he said, "And another thing, just for the record. Don't try to take this book away from me, you and the moon goddess. This is my book. The premise is mine. The words are mine. The credit is mine. Per our agreement. Got it?"

Selene nodded and Jeff said, for both of them, "Got it, you son of a bitch."

"Maybe you should cut your ties with Kirby, write your own book," said Jeff, after they hung up.

"We need his name, and he knows it. Besides, there's the agreement."

"Okay," said Jeff, resigned. "Have it his way."

"It's good for me, too," said Selene. "Even without the credit. I am building a reputation—as an editor."

Jeff nodded slowly. "Okay. Kirby wins this round. But let's not concede the fight just yet."

* * *

"Where are you, Alex?" said Selene, cradling the phone with her chin while she emptied grocery bags on the kitchen table. "The pizza's getting cold."

"Working late."

"How late?"

"Don't know."

"But you said—"

"Sorry."

A few minutes later, Selene called his office number. There was, of course, no answer. If she questioned him about this, he would say he only answered his cell phone at night, and confront her with her own suspicions, which were so imprecise as to be almost nonexistent.

Selene missed her husband. Her passion for Griff, crystallized in the first moment of their meeting, was unchanged, but she missed Alex—his humor, his companionship, his large, reassuring presence. Lately, even when he was with her, he was absent, as though he had slipped out of his body and disappeared.

She opened the pizza box, pulled out a still-warm pepperoni slice, ate it standing at the kitchen table as she put away groceries. Nippy followed her every move, looking up at her appealingly.

"Okay," she said, breaking off a piece of the crust, "but don't let Alex know I did this. I keep telling him not to feed you from the table."

She held the piece of crust close to his head. Nippy took it with a delicate lift of his mouth, chewing it solemnly. He looked up at her again. Selene shook her head at him.

"Just like me," she said. "You should be satisfied with what you've got, but are you?"

Nippy wagged his tail, then stopped mid-wag, as if unsure of his response.

The phone rang. Selene picked it up, tucking it under her chin.

"Is that you, Selene?" said Nan.

"It's me eating pizza, trying to talk at the same time. How are you, Nan? How's Bernard?"

"I'm well. Bernard is—the same. And you?"

"Just got home a few minutes ago, with groceries and a pizza. Alex is working late again, so Nippy and I are scarfing down the pizza."

"Selene, I'm—I'm afraid."

Selene was startled. She sat down at the kitchen table, unable to make the transition from the Nan she knew to this Nan, who was afraid.

"Is it—Bernard?"

"Yes. He's—"

"But you said he was—"

"He is. He's the same, physically. Weak, but able to get around, with some help. But he's—he's given up, Selene."

"Given up?"

"He doesn't want to—go on."

"Oh, Nan." Selene took a breath. "I'll call Alex. We'll come over."

"I know it's late but—"

"That doesn't matter."

"The evenings are so long—"

"Have you heard from Griff?"

Selene made herself ask the question before she lost her courage.

"No. Not for almost three weeks. Bernard keeps asking for him."

The bastard, Selene thought. *Leaving just when Bernard needs him most. Leaving Nan. Leaving all of us.*

"We'll be there soon."

"Bring Nippy. He always makes Dad laugh."

When Selene called Alex on his cell phone, he sounded sleepy and preoccupied, as though he were somewhere far away, struggling to come back.

"Where are you, Alex?"

"I'm at work," he said. "I told you."

She told him about Bernard, about Nan's concern. He said he would meet her at Nan's.

"When will you be there?" she said.

"You know how long it takes," he said, irritably. "I'll see you there."

* * *

When she saw Griff's red pickup truck parked in front of the house, quick tears filled her eyes. *Now Bernard will be better.* Then, more honestly, she thought, *How I'm aching to see him, to hear his voice.*

Nan opened the door, wrapping Selene in a warm hug. In the living room, Bernard sat in his easy chair, with Griff beside him. Griff looked up and nodded when she came in with the box of pizza. Nippy bounded joyfully ahead of her. Bernard held out his hands.

"What is this?" he said. "Are we having a party?"

"If that's what you want," said Selene. She took his hands and leaned over to kiss him. "Alex will be here soon."

"Did you sound the alarm?" Bernard said, looking at Nan.

"Selene and Alex were planning to stop by," said Nan, lying smoothly. "But I had no idea Griff would be here."

Selene looked at Griff, hoping for a response, but he said nothing.

"I'm making coffee," said Nan. "I'll be right back."

She left the room. Bernard leaned his head back, closing his eyes, as if exhausted.

"Are you all right?" said Selene, putting her hand on top of his. It felt dry, parchment thin.

Bernard opened his eyes and said, kindly, as though she were a not-so-bright child. "No, my dear. I'm not all right. I'm an old man, and I'm dying."

"Oh, please don't," said Selene. "Please don't leave us."

"I'll stay as long as I can," he said, patting her hand. "You can bet on it."

She sat down at a little distance, close to Griff.

"Is he in pain?" she said to him, in a low voice. "Should we—"

Griff shook his head. "He says he's just very tired." There was a long pause, then he added, "I believe him."

"How did you know—" she began, but he shook his head again.

"I didn't. It was just a feeling."

Where were you? Selene thought. *Why did you stay away so long? Why did you wait until Bernard was dying to come back?*

"He's been dying for a long time," said Griff.

Selene jumped, startled by his response to her thoughts. She shivered as she sat looking at him, wondering if the book she was immersed in was playing tricks on her mind. After a time, he turned deliberately toward her.

"I'm what they call—sensitive," he said, grinning at her for a moment, before he turned to Bernard.

Selene stared at his back. After a long pause, he turned to her and added, "I've heard about the book you're writing."

"Editing," she said, automatically. "From Nan?"

Griff nodded. "It's not a trick," he said, "or a gift." He shrugged his broad shoulders. "It's just a matter of listening." He nodded toward the kitchen. "She taught me that." There was a pause, then he added, "We're both—good listeners."

"Damned straight," said Bernard.

Bernard was looking at them with complete clarity. Selene and Griff were laughing when Nan came in with the coffee.

"What did I miss?" she said.

"Just Bernard being—Bernard," said Selene.

Nan poured coffee for him, added cream and sugar, handed him the mug.

"Ah," he said, sipping the coffee, "just the way I like it." He looked around the room. "Where's Alex?"

"He's coming," said Selene. "He'll be here soon."

"That's good," said Bernard. "Since Nan sounded the alarm, we might as well all be together."

"I didn't—"

Bernard waved his hand. "What does it matter?" he said. "You're the people who mean the most to me. I'm glad you're here." He put the coffee mug down on the table next to him. "I've always wanted to go to my own wake. Why so goddamned solemn? Let's have a party. Hand me a piece of that pizza."

*　*　*

When Alex arrived, a few minutes later, he kissed Selene lightly, nodding toward the others. "What's going on? You said—"

"We're having a party," said Selene.

"Are you okay, Gramps?"

"Never better, my boy," said Bernard. "I may have to stay around a little longer."

Alex shook his head and grinned. "What are you drinking? Whatever it is, I'll have some."

"Nan was just about to offer us something a little more conducive to partying," said Bernard. "Weren't you, Nan?"

"I guess I was," she said.

"I'll help you," said Selene.

In the kitchen, Nan arranged whiskey, a bottle of water, ice bucket, and tumblers on a tray.

She said, "Dad is a different person since Griff came back."

"Did Griff say where he has—been?" said Selene. Nan shook her head. "All he said was that he knew Gramps needed him tonight."

"How do you suppose—"

"Dad and Griff have a special connection. He loves Alex, of course, but Griff—"

She looked around the kitchen, as if searching for the words. "Maybe it's because Griff was—because he didn't have—because—"

She stopped, took a deep breath, gripped the edge of the table, bending her head down.

Selene put her hand lightly on Nan's arm. "I'm sorry," she said. "I've upset you."

"It's not you," said Nan. "It's Dad. It's watching him—die."

* * *

It was the whiskey—that and the late hour, and Bernard's complete presence, his complete clarity. For a brief space of time he came back to them, solid, joyful, talkative, inhabiting the moment. They came together—Nan, Bernard, Griff, Alex, Selene—not smoothly, but intently, as they had at Nan's dinner party in the spring, right after Griff came into Selene's life for the first time.

"Keep an eye on him," said Bernard now, nodding toward Griff. "He may disappear if we let him out of our sight."

"I could say the same about you," said Griff.

They laughed at this, in a way that would have been impossible before the whiskey. Everyone seemed to accept that there was a finality in their impromptu party, an implication in even the most casual remark. The whiskey made them easy. Their usual caution and wariness dissolved with each sip.

"Tell us about your book," said Nan, turning to Selene during a lull, as they watched Nippy frisking from one of them to another, finally settling on Bernard's lap.

Selene hesitated.

"It's not really my book. You'll never see my name on the cover."

She stopped, looking around at them, at Bernard, so keen and relaxed; at Alex and Griff, sitting at a careful distance from each other; at Nan, nodding, encouraging her.

"Oh, what the hell," she said. "It *is* my book. Kirby Woods is just the traffic director. He lets some of my ideas in and redirects others."

"That's my girl," said Alex. "Give him the what for."

"It's a debate—a dialogue—a conversation, about extrasensory perception. Whether it exists and, if it does, what does it mean, what do we do with it?"

"You're up against a crapperful of books on the same subject," said Alex, sipping his whiskey.

Pausing before she answered, Selene wondered again where he had been tonight when she called him on his cell phone.

"Same subject, different approach," said Selene. "We're taking sides—well, both sides, to some extent. It's not about being objective. It's about being passionately convinced."

"So—who wins?" said Alex.

Selene glanced at Griff, then looked away, fearful the whiskey would betray her.

"Nobody wins," she said to Alex. "It's not about winning."

She gulped down the whiskey in the bottom of her tumbler, then said, defiantly, "Genuine passion isn't about winning. It's about—about—transformation."

Bernard held his tumbler up to her, the ice clinking like applause, "Well said, my child. Look at the passion of Christ."

He drank down his whiskey, giving the tumbler to Nan, who shook her head at him. But she filled it again with ice and the amber liquor.

"Can you withstand the comparison?" said Alex, mock-serious, watching Selene.

"His passion wasn't godlike. His suffering, his death, was *human*," said Selene, grateful for Bernard's encouragement. "Passion is the most human of our emotions. It's what makes us human. It's what makes us—"

"Whole," said Nan.

"Yes," said Selene.

"Hogwash," said Alex. "Everything's about winning."

"Only if you give a shit about the race," said Griff.

They all looked at him. Griff hadn't talked much, and he didn't usually challenge Alex unless he was cornered.

"The 'race,' as you call it, is what fuels the passion," said Alex. "Without the race, there would be no finish line. Without the finish line up ahead, there would be no passion."

"There's no way I could feel passionate about a finish line, or about racing toward it," said Griff

"What in the hell *do* you feel passionate about?" said Alex. "I haven't seen any signs of it."

"Living," said Griff. "I feel passionate about living."

"That's a fucking copout," said Alex.

"I don't think so," said Bernard, from his easy chair. "I'm feeling passionate about living right at this moment."

Alex turned to him; then, seeing him so comfortable, so relaxed, so alert, he laughed. They all laughed, somewhat uneasily, remembering why they were there, the solemnity of the occasion having been forgotten under the influence of the liquor, and the old dispute between Alex and Griff.

"Someday, you two are going to have to duke it out," said Bernard. "I'd like to be there to see it. Just to be on the safe side, would you like to have a go at it right now?"

"You know we'd do anything for you, Gramps," said Alex. "But I'm too old, too tired, and too drunk for a fist fight."

"You don't know what it is to feel old and tired," said Bernard. "Drunk, yes."

Selene shivered, as if to shake off the hostility. She got up, poured a little more whiskey in her glass. She wanted to look at Griff, but she felt Alex was watching her. Alex nodded when she held up the bottle. She took his glass, filled it with ice, poured whiskey over the ice.

"Diluting the sauce, are you?" he said, when she handed the tumbler to him.

She sat down beside him on the couch, where she could see Griff, who sat directly across from Alex, close to Bernard. Alex put his arm around her. He said, the words low and a little slurred, "My one and only wife."

Selene pulled away. "Why did you say that?"

"Say what?"

"What you just said."

"What did I just say?"

Selene shrugged. "Never mind."

"Nan," said Bernard. "We can't call this a real party without some music. Will you play for us?"

"I haven't played for such a long time, Dad," said Nan.

"Please do," said Selene.

"Play for us, Mom," said Alex, pulling Selene close to him again.

Nan got up and went to the piano. Opening Bernard's favorite songbooks, mostly old standards from early in the century, she began to play—hesitantly at first, but, as they applauded her every effort, she gradually relaxed, began to enjoy herself, sipping at her glass of whiskey between selections. She played the songs she knew Bernard would enjoy, old tunes and light classical: "By the Light of the Silvery Moon," "The Merry Widow Waltz," "Peg O' My Heart," "Last Night on the Back Porch," "Humoresque," "My Melancholy Baby," "A Bird in a Gilded Cage," "Moonlight Bay."

Bernard sang along with her, Selene joining in, humming when she couldn't remember the words. Alex and Griff were silent.

"Ah, that was good," said Bernard, when Nan stopped playing. "I want it back, you know. Those years. My time with Anna. The middle years."

"Why the middle years?" said Selene, getting up from the couch, going over to Bernard. She crouched next to his chair, close to Griff. She felt Griff's thigh brush against her as she took Bernard's hand. The old man squeezed her hand gratefully.

"They were solid," said Bernard. "Brick solid. In marriage, you know, you start out with a house of straw. But if it's a good marriage—" He paused. "We built a good solid brick house, Anna and I." He paused, pulled himself up, sipped his whiskey. "Don't get me wrong. We had plenty of problems. Mostly, my problems. But we got through it. And those middle years were—"

He stopped, looking back. Selene waited. They all waited.

"They were grand," he said. "And they're gone. Maybe I dreamed it—all the years we were given."

He looked at Nan, still sitting at the piano. "Play for us, Nan."

She played: "Cruising Down the River," "Silver Threads Among the Gold," "In the Good Old Summer Time," "I Wonder Who's Kissing Her Now."

Bernard said to Selene, holding out his glass, "Bring me another, will you, my dear?"

Selene stood up. "I'll see if there's more where this came from."

She looked at Nan, who nodded toward the kitchen but kept on playing. Alex leaned back on the couch, closing his eyes. Griff turned to Bernard to say something Selene could not hear.

She went out to the kitchen, poking around in the pantry until she found another bottle of whiskey. It was in the back of one of the higher cupboards. As she reached for it, another, longer, arm reached beyond her and took the bottle from the shelf. She looked over her shoulder. Griff was standing behind her.

He put the bottle on the narrow counter beneath the wall of cupboards, switched off the pantry light. Selene took a step back, startled by his sudden appearance, the darkness of the pantry after the glaring overhead light. The light from the kitchen made him look enormous, but she couldn't see his face. Then she felt him, the weight of his body pushing her against the opposite wall, his mouth pressing against her, forcing it open, his tongue inside her mouth, his hands everywhere. Her legs trembled, the tremor moving up her body.

Her voice was a hoarse whisper, saying, "Take me."

*   *   *

TONI FUHRMAN

He was gone. Selene stood in the darkened pantry, her breath coming in gasps, pressing her hands against her mouth to keep from calling him, begging him, to come back. She heard Nan finish a tune, "Let Me Call You Sweetheart." She heard the buzz of talk. She wasn't sure if she heard Griff's voice. She put her hands on the counter, one on either side of the whiskey bottle, leaning forward, her eyes shut, waiting for her head to clear, for her body to be still. How long had he been there with her? How many seconds? Yet Selene felt her life shift under her, as it had the day she saw him at the door of her house, with Alex. He had fixed himself in her mind, then. She had wanted him, then. But now—

She waited to feel outrage, but she felt only the joy of those moments with him—and a desperate need.

*   *   *

"Selene? Are you all right?"

She looked up, startled. Nan was in the doorway.

"Yes. Yes." Selene rubbed her hands against her face, so that Nan wouldn't see her expression.

Nan put her hands on Selene's shoulders, pulled her close, said, "What's wrong, dear? Tell me what's wrong."

"I think—I'm sure—it's the whiskey," Selene said. "I'm not used to it. And Bernard. I'm so— He's so—"

Nan nodded. "I'm glad we're here together. But it's taking a toll on all of us. I'll make some more coffee. Would you like to lie down?"

"No. I'm fine. Thank you." Selene handed the whiskey to Nan. "Will you take care of this? I'm going to wash my face."

In the bathroom off Bernard's bedroom, she splashed cold water on her face, then examined her face in the mirror. It was familiar, yet strange, as though she were looking at someone she hadn't seen for a long time.

He's using me, she thought, staring at her reflection, *and I don't care. Let him get back at Alex through me. I don't care. I don't care how it happens, why it happens. I don't care!*

When she returned to the living room, Griff was sitting beside Bernard, as though he had never left. Nan was refilling their glasses. Alex was still leaning back on the couch with his eyes closed, Nippy curled up beside him. He opened his eyes when he heard her talking to Nan.

"I think I dozed off," he said. "Did I miss anything?"

"No. Nothing," said Selene. "Would you like a refill?"

"Only if you're the designated driver," he said.

She refilled his glass with ice and whiskey, handed it to him.

"I'll drive," she said, wanting him drunk, wanting to be as clear in her mind as she could be. "Nan started some coffee."

"Just for those of you who want it," said Nan. "I don't want to spoil the party."

"It's a grand party," said Bernard, saluting her with his tumbler. "Best wake I've ever been to."

"I never thought I'd hear myself saying it about a 'wake,'" said Nan, returning his salute, "but I agree."

"Here's to your wake, Gramps," said Griff.

"Hear, hear," said Alex, sleepily.

They all raised their glasses and drank. Bernard rested his head on the back of the chair, sighed, closed his eyes. "I think I can go now," he said. "It's not so bad, letting go. We all have to do it sooner or later."

"Wait a little, won't you, Gramps?" said Selene, going to him, crouching beside his chair, careful not to touch Griff, because the need to touch him was so great. "You may be ready, but we're not. Think of us."

"I'll think of you with pleasure, my dear, for as long as I can," said Bernard, opening his eyes.

She stood up, kissing him, lightly, on the mouth. "Ah," he said. "Thank you for that."

She sat down beside Alex, Nippy resting his muzzle on her thigh. Selene stroked the dog's head and looked at Alex. He was looking back at her. She shook her head, not knowing why. He reached up, took her chin between his thumb and forefinger. She was frightened by the intensity in his eyes, but she didn't look away. He released her, leaning back, as if he had already forgotten the gesture.

Nan and Griff were talking quietly. Selene heard her say, "But you must stay here. With us."

Bernard roused himself, said, "Of course. You'll stay, Griff. You'll all stay. There's been too damn much going away and coming back again. I won't keep you long, my boy. Bernard Cavillon will be resting beside Anna Griffith Cavillon before you know it."

"I'll stay, Gramps," said Griff. "Don't worry. I'll stay."

"I'm not worried. After all, we're having a party here. Good company. Good booze. Good music. What we need to round out the evening is some good poetry. Dylan Thomas comes to mind. You know the one, Griff. Read it to me. Read it to all of us."

Griff nodded and looked at Nan, who got up and went to the bookshelf at the far end of the room. She returned with a small, well-worn volume, which she handed to Griff. There was a hush as he leafed through the book. He glanced at Nan, then at Alex and Selene. He began.

Now as I was young and easy under the apple boughs
About the lilting house and happy as the grass was green,
The night above the dingle starry,
Time let me hail and climb
Golden in the heyday of his eyes,

And honoured among wagons I was prince of the apple towns
And once below a time I lordly had the trees and leaves
Trail with daisies and barley
Down the rivers of the windfall light.

"That's it," said Bernard. "That's the one. "Fern Hill." Didn't he know how to say it, and just a young squirt when he wrote it. Read on. Read on."

Selene, unprepared for the words, turned to Nan, who was smiling as she took the book from Griff and read the next stanza.

And as I was green and carefree, famous among the barns
About the happy yard and singing as the farm was home,
In the sun that is young once only,
Time let me play and be
Golden in the mercy of his means,
And green and golden I was huntsman and herdsman,
the calves
Sang to my horn, the foxes on the hills barked clear and cold,
And the sabbath rang slowly
In the pebbles of the holy streams.

Nan got up from her chair and brought the book to Alex, putting her hand against Selene's cheek reassuringly before she sat down again. Selene nodded, beginning to feel the soothing rhythm of their round-robin reading. Alex sat up, cleared his throat, fixed his eyes on the page, frowning in concentration, his deep voice resonant.

All the sun long it was running, it was lovely, the hay
Fields high as the house, the tunes from the chimneys, it was air
And playing, lovely and watery

And fire green as grass
And nightly under the simple stars
As I rode to sleep the owls were bearing the farm away,
All the moon long I heard, blessed among stables, the nightjars
Flying with the ricks, and the horses
Flashing into the dark.

Alex looked at Selene, questioning her with his eyes. She took the volume from him. Her voice trembled as she read.

And then to awake, and the farm, like a wanderer white
With the dew, come back, the cock on his shoulder: it was all
Shining, it was Adam and maiden,
The sky gathered again
And the sun grew round that very day.
So it must have been after the birth of the simple light
In the first, spinning place, the spellbound horses walking warm
Out of the whinnying green stable
On to the fields of praise.

"Ah, I like that one," sighed Bernard. "You did it well. Give it to me."

He held out his hand. Selene went to him, gave him the book, sat down again beside Alex, so that she could watch Bernard as he read. His sharp old eyes glanced down the page. He put his finger at his place. "Yes, this is for me," he said, glancing up at Selene, winking at her.

And honored among foxes and pheasants by the gay house
Under the new made clouds and happy as the heart was long,
In the sun born over and over,

I ran my heedless ways,
My wishes raced through the house high hay
And nothing I cared, at my sky blue trades, that time allows
In all his tuneful turning so few and such morning songs
Before the children green and golden
Follow him out of grace,

He said, reflectively, as though he were sipping the words like whiskey, rolling them on his tongue to extract the taste of them, "*Before the children green and golden/Follow him out of grace.*"

He laughed, suddenly. "By God, no one says it better. Here, my boy. Polish it off for us." He handed the book to Griff.

Griff waited, looking down at the verse, then he spoke. Selene, hearing the rasp of his voice, shut her eyes against her longing, her sadness.

Nothing I cared, in the lamb white days, that time would take me
Up to the swallow thronged loft by the shadow of my hand,
In the moon that is always rising,
Nor that riding to sleep
I should hear him fly with the high fields
And wake to the farm forever fled from the childless land.
Oh as I was young and easy in the mercy of his means,
Time held me green and dying
Though I sang in my chains like the sea.

There was a silence.

Selene said, before she had time to think about it, "Are you afraid?"

"The answer," said Bernard without hesitation, "is yes and no."

"I'm sorry. I didn't—"

"Why should you be sorry? If I went out like a light this evening, with all of you here, I'd count myself damned lucky. I'm well into my eighth decade, after all. I've been losing friends and family for twenty years and more. How much time can we ask for?"

"As much as we can get," said Alex. "More, if we can manage it."

"That's your problem," said Griff. "You always want more than you've got."

"At least I've got it," said Alex, "or some part of it."

"What the fuck is that supposed to mean?"

"It means you want what I've got."

"There's nothing you've got that I want," said Griff.

He stood up, said, "I'm going out for a smoke," then walked out of the room.

Selene sat motionless, the words, "There's nothing you've got that I want," hitting her again and again. She began to shudder, uncontrollably. Nan came and sat beside her, taking her hand, murmuring her name. Selene heard her as if from a great distance. Alex leaned his head back against the couch, closing his eyes. Nippy yawned, stretched, sat up.

"Nippy, come here, pal," said Bernard.

Nippy jumped off the couch, leaping up on his lap in two quick bounds.

"We've got a situation here," said Bernard, "and I think the party's over. But it was a good one, wasn't it, pal?"

Nippy frisked momentarily, then settled down on his lap, not willing to expend too much energy this late at night. He put his head down, sighed. Bernard fondled his ears.

"Nan, I think I can sleep now," he said. "Even in the midst of the fray, I'm just an onlooker. Can't even referee those two hotheads anymore. Too old. Too tired."

He drank down the last of his whiskey, the half-melted ice clinking against his teeth. He put the glass down on the side table. Resting his head against the back of the chair, he closed his eyes.

Selene, trying to focus on his words, trying to stop the trembling, was alarmed by his pale face, his stillness. She began to get up, to go to him, but Nan held her back.

"He's just sleeping," Nan said. "He's had a good time, and a lot of whiskey."

"But he looks so—"

Bernard took a deep breath. He said, to no one in particular, his eyes still closed, "Poetry, you know. It's for the very young and the very old. Before you set sail, or after you anchor for good. For the rest of you, it's like talking to the wind. You're not ready to hear. Remember hearing him recite, Nan? Remember his voice on the radio? Remember him saying, *Time held me green and dying/Though I sang in my chains like the sea.*"

He began to snore, gently at first, then more and more audibly.

CHAPTER 15

There was no moon. Nan looked for the glow of Griff's cigarette. He had walked out to his truck. He was leaning against it, ankles crossed, left hand gripping right elbow, cigarette dangling from his drooping right hand. He didn't turn as she approached, but she knew he was aware of her.

"I don't fit in this house, Mom," he said, when she was close to him. "I don't fit in this family."

"If you leave," said Nan, her voice low, "I don't know what I'll do."

"I'll stay until—I'll stay for Gramps."

"Stay for me, too."

"You do just fine without me, Mom."

"No, Griff. That's not right. I do without you, but I don't do 'just fine' without you."

Griff shifted, walked a few steps away from her, flicked his cigarette into the dark, and walked back. "That's my last cigarette," he said. "Ever."

Nan smiled. "I rarely see you with a cigarette."

"I rarely have one," he said. "I hate the filthy things."

Griff leaned against the truck again, his movements less tense, more natural.

"Here's the thing, Mom," he said. "I'm angry. When I'm here, in this house, in this town, in this fucking state, I'm angry." He stopped. "I'm sorry. I shouldn't have said that."

"Do you think I don't feel your anger? Do you think I don't feel what you're feeling?" Nan's voice rose. "I know you came back for Dad, and that his being alive is all that's keeping you here. Not me. Never me. That and—something else we won't discuss now." She paused. Griff shifted uncomfortably. "I know you can't forgive me, for making you—different. Different from Alex, not quite—belonging—to Howard. Never quite easy within the family and not knowing why, until—"

"That's not—I'm not blaming you."

Nan waved her arm dismissively. "I can fool myself into believing that most of the time but not now. Not tonight. Not when I see and hear all of the resentment you're feeling toward me, all the resentment you're pushing and shoving at Alex."

"What's that supposed to mean?"

"It means Alex is not at fault. I am. If you have to throw knives, aim them at me. Don't you see? I'm the one you're angry with, not him, not the house, not the town."

"I'm not angry with you. I never was, even when I found out—Howard wasn't my father."

"He was your father—as much as he could be. And I loved him, as much as I could. It's the same way I love Alex. As much as I can. Don't you see? Only you can break my heart, every time you go away."

"But you know I'll come back."

Nan shook her head. Griff could see her face, white, almost ghostly, as the light from an oncoming car caught her image for a moment, then passed down the street.

"I don't know that," she said. "I never know that. Every time you disappear it's like the time your father disappeared from my life forever. I feel it all again, and I want to die."

"I'm not the bad guy here," Griff said. Hearing the words carry across the dewy grass into the darkness of the quiet street, Griff lowered his voice. "I came back because I heard Gramps calling out for me. I heard it, even though I was running away again. And because—because—"

He stopped, confused.

Nan's voice, low again, murmured, "Because you can't make up your mind about Selene."

"I don't— I can't—"

Griff stopped, unable to complete whatever thought he had started.

"Every generation thinks the world was created by them, for them," said Nan. She had turned so that Griff could not see her face clearly, could only hear her voice. "When I fell in love with your father, I was sure no one had ever felt what I felt for him, that whatever happened was inevitable, preordained. I didn't consider Howard, or Alex—much. I didn't consider much of anything. I wanted him. And when he left, and he left me with you, I patched together a life with my husband and my son so I could have you, raise you. I compromised everything so I could have what he gave me. And he gave me, I believed then and still believe, all that he was capable of giving me. But, Griff—"

She paused, searching his face in the dark which had become, for them, for now, a screen, a sort of shadowy confessional. "Consider this. She is Alex's wife, his second wife, and he cut a path of destruction to get to her. I have a grandson I never see. A granddaughter I almost never see. An ex-daughter-in-law I no longer know." She took a breath. "Alex is—he's my son too. Stronger than you, in a way. But you can hurt him. You know how."

They stood in the darkness, in the silence. Her words seemed to echo in the air.

You know how.

Nan turned away from him and walked back to the house.

* * *

Bernard was still snoring, loudly now. Alex was sleeping, his long body stretched the length of the couch. Selene was pacing. She stopped, abruptly, when Nan opened the front door and came back into the living room.

Selene said, in a whisper, "We'd better go."

She roused Alex, who sat up reluctantly, murmuring, "Party all over? What'd I miss?"

"We took a vote and decided to call it quits for tonight," said Selene.

She sat beside him, put her head on his shoulder. His arm went around her, automatically. They sat close together, not speaking, while Nan coaxed Bernard into wakefulness.

"What the— Where's Griff?" Bernard said, waking up suddenly, completely, looking around the room.

"He'll be back by the time you wake up," said Nan.

"Come on, you old fart," said Alex. "I'll help you if you can't make it on your own."

"Speak for yourself," said Bernard, heaving himself out of the chair. "You youngsters just can't take a good old-fashioned wake, can you? I feel fit as a fiddle."

Alex laughed. "You may be right, Gramps. You drank us all under the table."

"And lived to hear about it," said Bernard.

He saluted them, blew Selene a kiss, which she returned, and walked slowly out of the room.

"Best goddamned wake I've ever been to," they heard him say as he walked down the hall to his bedroom.

Nan looked after him, shaking her head. "Do you think he'll be all right?"

"For now, Mom," said Alex, "I think he will be." He looked at Selene. "Ready to go?"

Selene shook her head. "Nan, can we stay—"

"I'm not frightened any more," said Nan. "I'm really not. And Griff is here."

"Or maybe not," said Alex.

"He is. He'll be back," said Nan.

"Roll of the dice," said Alex.

"Alex, don't," said Selene.

Alex got up, stretched, yawned. He went to Nan, hugged her, kissed her on the cheek. "We're here for you, Mom," he said. "We'll pick up Selene's car tomorrow."

Alex and Selene walked outside, into the dark, moonless night, Nippy bounding out ahead of them to lift his leg against a bush. Selene searched for Griff's truck, not seeing it. Suddenly, he walked across the lawn toward them, out of the darkness. He lifted his arm, in a silent salute, walked up to the door, disappeared inside.

"So, he decided to come back," muttered Alex, unlocking his car door, allowing Nippy to jump in ahead of him.

"Did you think he wouldn't?" said Selene, looking back, wanting to follow him inside, wanting to take his hand, roam her body with it.

"I think he'll hang around as long as Gramps is alive," said Alex.

He tossed the keys at Selene, got in on the passenger side, slammed the door. Selene got in on the driver's side, turned the key in the ignition, took a last look at the house. She thought she saw a shadow at the living room window, but she couldn't be sure.

If you live to be a hundred, Bernard, she thought, as she drove slowly down the dark street, away from the house, *it may just be enough time for me to figure out that bastard.*

* * *

Bernard, however, didn't extend his stay much beyond his wake. A few days later, he had a stroke, woke up in the Intensive Care Unit at Sylvan Springs Memorial Hospital, recognizing them but unable to speak, and let the life seep out of him, without sound, without resistance.

They stood around his bed, the same group that had assembled for his "wake," and wondered at his timing.

"Did he know, do you think?" said Selene.

"I think he did," said Nan.

"I know he did," said Griff.

"It was just a coincidence," said Alex.

Nan shook her head at Griff, almost imperceptibly. He turned away, clamping his jaw.

Nan held Bernard's right hand. Griff, on the other side of the bed, held his other hand. Alex and Selene stood at the foot of the bed, Selene both comforted and repelled by the arm Alex wrapped around her, his need to be close to her. They talked to Bernard, to each other, as though he were fully aware of them, of what they were saying.

"If you need attention that bad, we'll throw you another wake, you old fart," said Alex. "How about it? I'll personally restock the booze."

They thought they saw a whisper of movement at the ends of his mouth, but they couldn't be sure. The life support system that fed into his veins and his nostrils all but obliterated movement and expression.

"Is Wendy on her way?" said Nan.

Alex nodded. "She'll be at Carolyn's tonight."

"And—Kevin?"

"Can't locate him," said Alex. "My son has chosen to disappear completely. Seems to run in the family."

"Alex, don't," said Nan.

"Sorry," said Alex, but they could all hear the bitter edge in his voice. Selene had found him increasingly defensive in the few days since they'd been at Nan's, as though he were fending off invisible blows.

"Gramps?"

The question in Griff's voice made them all turn their attention to the old man in the hospital bed, wired like a reluctant puppet to the tubes and monitors surrounding him. Two nurses stood quietly behind them. Nan bowed her head and cried. Selene gripped Alex's arm, suddenly grateful for his nearness.

"He's gone," said Griff.

The nurses, and the monitors, confirmed it.

"I'm glad we had our p-party," said Selene, looking up at Alex.

Alex nodded, pulled her close, then went to Nan. Griff was still holding Bernard's hand. After a while, he turned his head toward Selene and she saw, before he turned away, the devastation in his eyes.

* * *

"I miss him so much already," said Nan, weeping, as Selene held her close. Alex and Griff were conferring quietly with the nurses. Alex nodded to Selene. She led Nan away from the bed where Bernard lay, the apparatuses of support as still as he was.

"Let's go home, Mom," said Alex. "There's nothing else to do here."

"No," said Nan. "I'm going to say goodbye. You go ahead without me."

"Mom," said Alex, "don't you think—"

"Go away, all of you," said Nan, her normally soft voice harsh, gritty. "I have to do this."

*   *   *

Nan went back inside the unit, pulling the curtain across the opening. She had seen death before. She wasn't afraid of it. She could be alone with it. She didn't want to wait for the funeral rites, when he would be tucked into a casket, his face coaxed into a semblance of life. She would say goodbye now, while the spirit of life still hovered close to him, not quite gone.

"You did, after all, go gently into that good night," she said, her voice barely a whisper. "You gave up and, maybe, when I've lived as long as you have, I will, too. But, Dad, you were our center, you kept us together. Now, they'll know that I can't do what you did—that I'm too divided between them. I'm so afraid, Dad. When I got us all together the other night, it wasn't because I was afraid you would die—it was because I was afraid of this—this *unraveling*. I feel it already. It's happening, Dad, it's happening. And I have no one to guide me through it."

She sat beside him, her hands crossed on her lap, her eyes dry, watching her father's facial features imperceptibly recede, as though they were being erased.

*   *   *

The funeral rites performed, friends and fellow mourners departed, they sat uneasily in Nan's living room. Alex and Selene. Carolyn and Wendy. Griff and Sue Smoller.

Nan looked around at them, biting her bottom lip to keep her mouth from twitching upward in a kind of manic grin. She had been through this before. With her mother. With Howard. Always, always, there were moments when to laugh seemed the only possible defense. But would they understand her laughter, this group of seeming adults assembled in her living room to mourn Bernard? Only Bernard would laugh, but he had just been lowered into the soft summer earth. Only Bernard could understand. He had grown past seriousness as he had grown older. It seemed she was about to do the same.

Wendy, the youngest present, was perhaps the most serious of all. In her current college uniform of dun-colored longish skirt, loose, button-down top, flat-soled shoes, her long brown hair swinging close to her face, she looked prim, yet alluring, as though she were covering up all that made her specifically female. She seemed unable to make eye contact with anyone. She ducked her head if anyone happened to look directly at her.

"Are you liking it in Texas?" said Nan. Seeing she would get only a nod, she added, "What is it like there, my dear?"

"It's—brown," said Wendy, after a moment's reflection.

"And your studies? You're in—?"

"Computer programming. I like it a lot, Nana."

She actually smiled when she said this. Nan was more than satisfied. After this, there was a little flurry of questions and comments about Wendy's studies at Texas A&M, her life in Texas, but it was short-lived. Nan's urge to laugh returned. Again, she suppressed it.

"Coffee, anyone?" she said. The lilt in her voice brought everyone's attention to her face, to the coffee table in front of her.

"I'll have one, if you don't mind," said Sue. "Just lay on the cream and sugar as thick as you please."

Griff's decision to bring Sue to the funeral and reception had mystified Nan, but she was not sorry she was there. There was something about her eyes, her dark, stiffly curled hair, that lightened the occasion. When she spoke, Nan noticed her eyes tilted up slightly, as though she were perpetually smiling. Her hands, carefully manicured, the nails long and possibly false, flew about like birds let loose for a moment, then curbed into reluctant stillness.

"I could live on coffee," said Sue, when Nan handed her the cup. "In fact, I mostly do, don't I, Griff? You used to say to me—"

She stopped, as though what she was about to say was too intimate. Her free hand fluttered to the handle of the cup. She sipped the coffee, as though swallowing the thought.

Nan looked around the room, her offer of coffee conferring the right to survey each face. Selene sat beside Alex, only her eyes moving, bouncing from Griff to Sue and back again, as though unable to fathom their proximity to each other. Alex was relaxed, his arm across the back of the couch on which they sat, claiming Selene, perhaps protecting her, but not touching her. His expression, when he looked at Wendy, was pleading—asking for recognition, for the attention a daughter might give her father—but she would not meet his eyes.

Carolyn, trim and well turned out, looked strangely at ease. She nodded when Nan turned to her. Nan, remembering her preference, stirred a level teaspoonful of sugar in her coffee before handing her the cup. Carolyn got up, smiled her thanks, sat down again beside Wendy.

Griff, catching Nan's eye as she turned to him, shook his head. Only Griff seemed to notice, with something like delight, that she was on the verge of laughing. Only Griff seemed to see the humor in their oddly assorted, yet closely connected, company. He had introduced her to Sue almost defiantly, but he was unembarrassed by her presence, obviously relishing what she had to say. As far as Nan knew, Griff no longer saw Sue, but had pulled her out of her obscurity especially for the occasion. He owed Nan no explanation, and he had given her none.

Nan poured herself a cup of coffee. "I think it went well," she said. "Considering."

"Considering what?" said Alex.

"Considering Bernard wasn't here to enjoy it," said Nan.

She looked around the room, her voice edged with laughter. Seeing the disbelief in Wendy's brief glance, she added, "He loved a good party, didn't he, Alex? And he would have loved to see you, Wendy."

"He asked me about you all the time," said Alex, pulling away from Selene, leaning forward, toward Wendy. "He would say, 'How's the little Wendy great-grandchild? How's she doing out there in Texas?'"

"I missed him, too, Dad," said Wendy. Then she ducked her head again.

"I had a cousin in Texas," said Sue. "He said he had so many acres, the acres had acres." She paused. "Whenever he visited us, he used to put me on his knee and tell me stories about Texas." She laughed. "Of course, I was just a kid then. I believed every word. I thought Texas was this far-off, magical land. I had no idea it was right here in the good old U. S. of A. When I found out, I cried. It was like hearing there was no Santa Claus."

"Our illusions are very important to us," said Selene.

Everyone looked at her expectantly, but she seemed to have encompassed everything she had to say, and was silent again.

"Damned straight," said Sue. "Take my kid, for example. He used to think he was king of the road. Then, he fell off his motorcycle and found out he was helpless as a baby."

"How is your son?" said Nan.

"Not bad," said Sue. "Thank you kindly for asking, Mrs. Price. He was hurt pretty bad. His leg was crushed under the motorcycle. We thought for a while he'd lose it—the leg, I mean. I thought I'd sink under all the worry. Griff here will tell you. But they saved it—the docs over at Clearview—and Jimbo is getting so he can walk around a little. He won't be riding a motorcycle again, though."

"I'm so glad," said Nan. "I mean, that he's walking."

"I know what you mean," said Sue, "and I thank you. I'm glad he's off that bike for good, too. I was always scared shitless—I mean scared to death—something like this would happen."

Like a suppressed sob, the urge to laugh rose up again. Nan put her coffee cup to her lips.

"Have you heard from Kevin?" said Alex, still leaning forward, toward Wendy, as if to capture her attention.

"Not since—not for a long time," said Wendy. "I'm not sure where he is, Dad."

Alex nodded, folding his hands between his knees. "I wish he could have been here."

"I'm sure he would have been—if he'd known," said Carolyn.

Alex looked at her reflectively. "Maybe," he said. Glancing at Wendy, he added, "I'm sure you're right."

"He's just—being Kevin," said Carolyn. "He'll come around, when he's ready."

She gave Selene a brief, defiant glance as she said this, but Selene didn't notice. She was still focused on Griff and Sue. Nan hoped everyone else was too preoccupied to see this, but she noticed Carolyn lifting her eyebrows as she looked at Selene. Carolyn, Nan remembered, was always keenly observant of other women.

"What was Kevin up to, last you heard?" said Griff, looking at Carolyn, forcing her glance away from Selene.

"Why, I'm not sure, exactly," said Carolyn, smiling at Griff. "He's kind of like you, Griff. He just does what he likes and likes what he does. Odd jobs, I think. Just enough to get by."

"If that's a family trait," said Alex, irritably, "I think it's a damned poor excuse for one."

Griff looked at him coolly. "I guess Kevin, like me, doesn't give a flying fart what you think."

Nan laughed. She couldn't help it. Despite the solemnity of the occasion, despite all of her efforts at control, she laughed until the tears came, the laughter releasing something tight in her chest, something lodged in her throat.

Carolyn came to her with a box of tissues. Selene stared at her in astonishment. Alex shook his head and leaned back. Wendy looked mystified; she got up, hesitated, started to go to Nan. Instead, she waited for Carolyn to return to her seat, then sat down again.

Nan, focusing on Griff's face, knowing at least one person in the room understood, pulled out a tissue, wiped her eyes, took a deep breath.

Sue, as if shaking off some invisible shackle, some presumed etiquette that had held her back, began to talk.

"You know, I always say, a good laugh can set you free. Now, Jimbo and me, we've been laughing a lot lately. Especially when he tries to walk and falls all over himself. It can get to be pretty funny. Of course, if you look at it another way, it's pretty sad. His leg will never be what it was. And your father, of course— But, hey, what the hell. He had a good long life, and Griff told me he liked having a good time, belting down a few— Didn't you tell me you had a whopping good party just a few nights before he died?"

Griff nodded. Sue went on.

"I only met the old gentleman once, and that was years ago. Griff and me, we were, you know, seeing each other, and Griff saw him and his missus—your mother, Mrs. Price—on the street downtown. They were just walking down the street, and Griff said—do you remember, Griff?—he said, 'See that couple walking down the street there? That's my Grampa Bernard and my Grandma Anna. They're the best people I know, the only couple I know who really love each other.'"

Nan listened with rapt attention. The others had turned their attention from Nan to Sue, who went on as though unconscious of the others, as though she were alone with Nan and Griff.

"I was just a young kid, then, Mrs. Price, but I already knew enough to know there weren't that many good people in the world, and even fewer happily married couples, so when he asked me if I'd like to meet them, I right away said yes. Besides, he was Griff's family, and I had a thing for your son—back then."

She stopped, winked at Griff. Nan swung her eyes over to Selene. She saw her shudder.

"So me and Griff, we crossed the street and walked right up to them, and Griff introduced us. Mrs. Cavillon, she was just as nice as you please, and Mr. Cavillon, he looked at me like he was studying a picture, with his head cocked to one side and his thumb and forefinger pressed against his chin, like this—" Sue demonstrated the gesture, "—and then he said, 'Young lady, I can see why Griff here has taken a fancy to you, but watch out for him. He's slippery as a fresh-caught fish and twice as squirmy. I'd throw him back in the water if I were you, and have you some steak and potatoes.' Well, I laughed at that, and Mrs. Cavillon, she poked him, told him to hush his mouth. We talked for a while longer, then Mr. Cavillon tipped his hat at me—he wasn't wearing a hat, but he tipped it anyways—he said, 'Remember what I said, young lady,' and off they went."

Sue paused.

"Not long after that, off went Griff, just like the old man said. He was a wise old guy, wasn't he, Griff?"

Wendy said, into the silence, "He always said what he thought. He didn't think about what he said before he said it, and sometimes it was beautiful, what he said."

She turned to her mother. "Remember when he told me I'd be good at what I did because I was a natural-born chess player?"

Carolyn nodded. "I also remember he told Kevin not to play games at all because he couldn't stand to lose, and felt sorry for the losers when he won."

Nan laughed, freely now, sensing the shift in mood since Sue's reminiscence.

"Dad was exactly the same as Kevin," she said. "He grumbled like an old bear when he lost, even when Kevin and Wendy were mere babies, and he lost to them. He mostly lost to you, Wendy. You were always good at games."

"Remember our poker challenge, Wendy?" said Alex. "You and Gramps. Me and Kevin. We played all one Sunday, I think it was over Christmas, while you both were still single digits. Kevin and Gramps kept falling out, and you and I kept upping the ante—"

"And Gramps started cheating," said Wendy, smiling at her father for the first time.

"Then Kevin blew the old man's cover," said Alex. "Gramps said, 'It's just a game, you little squirt,' and Kevin said, 'If it's just a game, why are you cheating?' And Gramps said—"

He stopped, searching his memory.

Wendy said, slowly, relishing the words, "He said, 'I cheat because I want to see if God is watching me. If I get away with it, I know that God has nodded off for a while. I like to keep Him on His toes.'"

CHAPTER 16

Selene climbed the stairs to Bernard's third-floor "eyrie." It had been almost two months since Bernard lived there, but she still thought of it as his. Tonight, however, it was Griff's. She was sure he wouldn't stay with Sue Smoller. She was sure he wouldn't leave Nan alone in the house on the day of Bernard's funeral.

If anyone besides Griff found her there, she would say she needed to lie down, to rest, after the exertions of the day. Alex had gone to Carolyn's house with Wendy, hoping to spend some time with his daughter. Selene was to drive his car home. Nan was lying on the couch, a damp towel over her eyes, her laughter succeeded by exhaustion. Griff had left some time ago to take that foul-mouthed creature home.

Selene paused at the second-story landing and looked out the window at the back yard. It was late afternoon. The small leaded-glass panes absorbed and reflected the rich summer light, turning the yard into a quilt of green and gold.

She had no plan. She had not thought of doing this earlier in the day, even an hour ago, when Sue Smoller was still in the house. How could he touch her? How could he have sex with her? She was coarse. Her voice was grainy, as were the pores on her face. Her hair was stiff and unnaturally dark, as though she were hiding gray. Everything she wore gaped, rose up, so that she was constantly adjusting her skirt over her thighs, the buttons and neckline of her blouse. And those nails!

She shook her head, running up the last flight of stairs. The door was ajar. She pushed it open without going inside. The light shone freely into the room from the huge window that dominated the dormer side of the apartment. It reflected off the hardwood floor, picking up little swirls of dust floating in the air. A single captain's chair was placed near the window, where Bernard had positioned his large easy chair, to capture every ray of sun. Griff probably sat there now, when he chose to spend the night, and perhaps Nan, when she wanted to escape from the worry and anxiety of the downstairs rooms.

She pushed the door open further and went inside. Her heels clicked on the hardwood floor. She reached down, pulling them off while she looked around the room. Two straight chairs were arranged around a small round table near the kitchen. Howard's desk, and the shelves of books that had occupied the study downstairs, were pushed carelessly against the wall across from the entrance. She glanced at the kitchen area, obviously unused since Bernard's occupancy, then turned to the open door of the bedroom.

There was Griff's large duffle bag, on the bed. A thick, chocolate-brown comforter had been pulled over the sheets and pillows. Next to the bed was an end table. A second captain's chair filled a corner of the room, beside the small, near-empty closet.

The duffle bag lay open, some of its contents strewn on the bed. Selene went up to the bed, touching his possessions hungrily. Two or three shirts, one plaid. Jockey shorts. T-shirts. Socks. A shaving kit, unzipped. She glanced in the small adjoining bathroom. Lining the back of the sink were his razor, shaving cream, a deodorant, toothbrush, toothpaste, a comb.

She picked up the plaid shirt and pressed her face against it, inhaling its slightly stale odor. Without thinking, she pushed the bag and the scattered items to one side of the bed, lying down on the other side, pillowing her head on the plaid shirt. There was an open window on the low wall that faced the back yard. A breeze licked at her body—warm from the climb up the stairs, her own nervous apprehension. She lay still, waiting for the next soothing puff of air, listening for the sound of footsteps on the stairs. Waiting for him ...

Some slight sound or movement woke her. She opened her eyes. He was standing by the side of the bed. He must have been looking down at her, but just then he was looking across the room toward the window, so that she was able to see him, unaware, for a moment. What she saw was the line of his jaw. It was clean-cut and square. He had clamped down on his teeth, so that the muscles of his jaw moved in a barely perceptible ripple. When he looked down at her, the fading light from the window making his eyes very blue, she raised her arms toward him.

He leaned over her. She put her hands lightly on either side of his face, bringing it close to her. Before she closed her eyes, a quick shudder—fear? apprehension?—crossed his face, making him tremble momentarily.

They came together urgently, almost violently. She had never felt so open, so vulnerable. The part of him that was thrusting inside her, so hard, so hurtful, so satiating, could kill her or redeem her, and she knew—she had always known—that she was indifferent to her fate.

*   *   *

They lay side by side, breathing hard, the duffle bag and its contents pushed unceremoniously off the side of the bed, the comforter on the floor. Selene was surprised to see the light still shining into the room. It seemed as if hours had passed, as if she had slipped seamlessly into another time zone. She was exhausted, yet supremely relaxed.

At the heart of their rough, almost savage, sexual encounter, at the center of it, was a calm, a place where Griff resided and she could see him, all of him, as he could see all of her. When he opened his eyes and they looked at each other—naked, sweaty, surfeited—it was as if his whole being lit up for her to see. Then he collapsed, with all his weight on her, and she surrendered to the sheer pleasure of it. She wanted only to stay where she was, restrained beneath him. But he moved off her, apologetically, as if he had bumped into her on the street and hurriedly stepped aside. He lay beside her, breathing hard. She wondered what she could say to make him feel her total assent, her complete capitulation. But they lay without touching, and no words came.

After a while, she realized his breathing had become rhythmic, as in a light sleep. Staring up at the ceiling, she listened to him for a while; then she slipped off the bed, picked up her discarded clothing, went in the living room area to dress. Her heels were by the captain's chair, where she had pulled them off. She scooped them up and, not hesitating, not looking back, went through the still-open door to the stairway, descending the stairs quickly, noiselessly.

In the kitchen, at the screen door, she listened for a few moments. There were no sounds but the whir of the refrigerator, a neighborhood lawnmower, birds winding down for the day, the far-off shouts of children at contentious play. She opened the door, guided it shut so that it didn't slam, ran for her car, feeling grass, then gravel, then warm concrete under her bare feet.

*   *   *

Nan lay on the couch, listening to the sounds of the car door shutting, the engine starting, the car backing out of the drive, then fading down the street. She took the wet cloth, now cold and clammy, away from her eyes and lay still, thinking of the day—of her father, so recently lowered into the earth; of

Wendy, remembering her great grandfather; of Sue Smoller's strangely compelling presence; of Carolyn studying Selene; of Selene, watching Griff and Sue with stealthy, catlike intensity.

What was there about death, and the rituals surrounding death, that seemed to loosen the tethers that otherwise bind us? Wendy, in her pride, would never in ordinary time have let Alex see the hurt beneath her anger. And perhaps Kevin, if he had come ...

But one child returned to her father was enough for one day and one funeral. Bernard would have considered his funeral a great success, had he been there to enjoy it.

And there was Selene. Selene—and Griff. What wise and witty spin would Bernard have put on their funeral-day union? What could it presage but another doomed marriage for Alex? Another misfortune for Griff, her child of misfortune?

Nan sat up and rubbed her eyes. She missed Bernard so much. Missed his wit and humor. Missed his generational shield. Now there was no one between her and death. Now it was her turn to shield her children, and her children's children. She wondered where she would find the strength, the courage, that had seemed so natural in Bernard.

She couldn't help Alex. She certainly couldn't help Griff and Selene. She, Nan, had rushed to her destiny, just as Griff and Alex's second wife were doing now. No wise advice, no warning, would have made it otherwise. They must play it through to its inevitable conclusion. She was sure Bernard would agree. He hadn't interfered in her life or with her choices.

She got up and walked slowly through the empty house to the kitchen. She turned on the tap, filled the teakettle, then stood at the sink while she waited for the friendly whistle. The window over the sink looked out on the back yard, where the pale light still clung to the day. September. The children had gone back to school, Bernard had gone quietly to his grave, and another sexual union had blessed the bed where she had lain with Griff's father, all those years ago. If it hadn't been for Griff, she may have looked back, questioning the reality of those encounters with a young man who had rented the apartment for a few months and who, despite their intimacy, she never really knew.

Griff was so like him. Why couldn't she say his name? Force of habit, she supposed. She had been so afraid she would give herself away just by uttering his name.

"Bill," she said aloud, over the whistling of the teakettle.

Such a simple name.

"Bill," she said again.

She had called the bed her "Only Bill Bed," but he never saw the humor of it, or of anything that wasn't immediately, almost painfully, obvious. He was acute and perceptive, as was Griff, but it was Howard who made her laugh, and laughed with her. It was Howard who, despite everything, made her feel comfortable. It was Howard who accepted Griff, and raised him as his own.

She measured tea into a small pot and poured water into it. The three most important men in her life were gone. Her husband. Her father. Her lover. There remained her two grown sons, who shared nothing except their desire for Selene, and their distaste for each other.

The phone rang. She took it quickly off its wall cradle so that it wouldn't disturb Griff, three stories above her. It was Alex, asking about Selene. She told him Selene had gone home.

He sighed, as if relieved.

"Are you alone?" he asked.

"Griff is here with me."

"That's good," he said. "Do you need anything?" Then, without waiting for her answer, "I'm going to stay at Carolyn's a little longer. Wendy and I are—we're actually talking to each other."

Soon after she had hung up, Griff came into the kitchen. He was wearing an old plaid shirt, absent a few buttons, and blue jeans. His hair was awry; his eyes were sleepy; his feet were bare. Nan looked at him for a moment, her love for him overwhelming her, then nodded for him to sit down. She took milk from the refrigerator, another mug from the cupboard, brought the sugar bowl, poured the tea. She watched him as he added generous amounts of milk and sugar, then stirred and sipped.

"Did the phone wake you?" she said.

He nodded. "The upstairs extension. Who called?"

"Alex. Looking for Selene. Checking up on me."

"Is he still at Carolyn's?"

"Yes. He and Wendy are paying tribute to your grandfather. Patching up their differences."

He nodded again, not seeing, as she did, a wry humor in the situation. How like his father he was. How like Bill.

"I don't think I can sit in the living room tonight," Griff said. "I don't think I can look at his—empty chair."

He leaned forward and bowed his head, his hands clasped. Nan put her hands over his.

"I know," she said. "You did all that you could, Griff. He was ready to go. He waited for you to come back, and then he was ready."

Griff got up suddenly, the chair scraping against the floor, the tea sloshing over the edge of his mug. He went to the back door, looking out at the waning light, clasping his elbows, his upper body rocking back and forth.

"I'm a screwup," he said, fiercely. "That's all I've ever been. Gramps—he just saw what he wanted to see, like you do. Alex is right about me. He sees me for what I am. So did Dad—Howard. He just never said it. Alex throws it in my face every chance he gets."

"No," said Nan. "No, Griff. That's not true. Your father loved you. Alex loves you."

"I have no father," he said quietly. "I had a grandfather, until a few days ago, and I have you. But don't tell me I have a father, and don't tell me I have a brother. I won't live with that lie."

*   *   *

When he dropped her off, Sue had known without asking that Griff would not come in the house with her. She patted his hand as it rested on the steering wheel, repeated her condolences, and got out of the car as fast as she could. He was gone before she turned her key in the front door lock.

It had been Selene all along, getting in the way, getting between them. Sue just hadn't known what it was, and who it was, until today. Here she'd been thinking it was something she did or didn't do, ready to take the blame, as she always did, but all the time she didn't even figure in the big picture. He had always been decent to her. He'd taken care of her when Jimbo was critical, but she was just a convenience store, where he picked up his bread and milk and a six-pack—until he got a chance to go to the supermarket.

She was sleek looking, Selene, with her smooth light hair and that light-colored, boxy little pant suit. And she couldn't keep her eyes off Griff, not that anybody noticed, except maybe that sharp-eyed ex-wife of Alex's. Just the way she crossed her legs and wiggled her foot in that strappy high heel was an invitation. Griff could hardly wait to give her his RSVP.

Jimbo's boom box filled the house with noise. She knew it would do no good to call up to him. They could back a van up to the front door, move out everything downstairs, and he still wouldn't hear a thing. She walked through the living room to the kitchen, where Jimbo had demolished its clean orderliness in his attempt to fix himself lunch. Well, at least he'd managed to hobble downstairs on his crutches. If he was hungry enough, he could look out for himself. She smiled as she put away bread, cold cuts, condiments; then she picked up the dirty dishes, soaking them in the sink. Her nursemaid days were almost over. She could go back to Hair Today full time. Her customers would be pleased. Hell, she was pleased. She wasn't cut out to be a nurse, especially to a surly teenager, even if he was her own flesh-and-blood teenager.

She looked around the kitchen, then stood in the doorway to the living room. Fucking tan. Everywhere she looked, fucking tan. She shook her head, pulled a cigarette and lighter out of the purse she had tossed on a chair. She took her place in the doorway and lit up. She exhaled luxuriously, leaning against the door frame. She couldn't complain. Griff had been good to her, better than most, even if he'd painted her walls the color of puke. It still smelled like fresh paint, and she liked that smell. It was a small house, kitchen and living room down, two bedrooms and a bath up, but it was hers, hers and Jimbo's. If she got back to work full time before her savings ran out, nobody could take her fucking tan home away from her.

The volume on the boom box diminished by a few decibels. Jimbo called down the stairs, "Hey, Ma, that you?"

"Yeah, baby, it's me," she called back, walking over to the foot of the stairs.

"You wanna bring me up some chips and a soda?" he yelled.

"Now why would I wanna do that?" she yelled back.

"I hate those freakin' stairs, Ma. Let's move to a ranch house."

"Get used to the stairs, cowboy. This is home sweet home for Jimbo the Gimp and his hardworking mom, and it ain't gonna change."

"Can we at least get an elevator?"

"Not in your lifetime. Now get your butt down here and wash up these dishes."

The volume rose to a deafening pitch. Sue stood at the foot of the stairs, smoking, closing her eyes in satisfaction as she exhaled.

* * *

For the first time in many years, Carolyn had three-quarters of her family in one room. Alex and Wendy—Gwendolyn at birth but soon shortened to Wendy—sat side by side on the couch in the living room of her condo, sipping sodas, eating chips and dip—actually talking to each other, like a family. A feeling of contentment swept over her. Except for the conversation, she might have forgotten it was a funeral that had brought them together.

"Do you think he's—somewhere near—that he can communicate with us?"

Alex took a chip, swept up an enormous mound of creamy spinach dip, chewed on it thoughtfully.

"Wendy, I don't."

Disappointed, she puckered up her face. Her features, small and regular, like Carolyn's, made her seem delicate, vulnerable. Alex shook his head.

"I know. That's not what you want to hear right now but, damn it, Wendy, you're an adult. I'm not going to pretend I can fix it for you, that I can make it all better with a few kind words. You and I and the rest of the family, we have to feel the hurt. Gramps Bernard is gone. We can't see him or touch him or talk to him or hear his voice. And what wouldn't I give right now to hear his voice."

He took a breath, then said, emphatically, "I miss him. We all miss him. Mom—Nana—she—well, she misses him most."

"It didn't seem so this afternoon," said Wendy. "The way she was laughing—"

"Don't be so judgmental," said Alex, rounding up another mouthful of chip and dip. "She's hurting. In fact, I probably should go over there—"

"Griff is there with her," said Carolyn.

"How do you know?" said Alex.

"I just—know," she said.

Alex looked at her thoughtfully. "He's a pain in the ass, but he can probably do more for her today than I can. After Mom, he was closer to Gramps than anybody else."

"I like Uncle Griff," said Wendy.

"You would," he said, cuffing her playfully on the arm. "Both of you appear and disappear whenever you please."

"I think I'll stay for a while this time," she said, shyly.

"That would make your old dad very happy," said Alex. He pulled her closer to him on the couch. Wendy kicked off her shoes, pulled her long brown mane of hair to one side and rested her head, tentatively, on her father's shoulder.

"I'm going to see what I can fix for supper," said Carolyn, getting up and going out to the kitchen.

She opened the refrigerator door, looked inside, called out, "How does fried chicken and a salad grab you?"

*　*　*

Selene turned the key in the lock and opened the back door. Nippy whimpered, then rushed to greet her. She cavorted with him, matching, even exceeding, his enthusiasm—then released him to the fresh air and freedom of the back yard, dusky now, replete with evening scents and shadows.

She leaned against the screen door, watching him, his tail like a small white flag moving in and out of the darkness as he marked his territory and assessed its circumference—"counting each blade of grass"—as Alex often said.

She surveyed her house from where she stood—the functional kitchen, the long dining room, the wide, street-facing living room.

"I love you," she said, dancing down the length of the house. "Mom and Dad, wherever you are, I love you, and I love every room of your house."

She ran up the stairs, then rushed down, arms held wide. "I love you, Bernard. I love your eyrie. I love your spirit, wherever it is now."

She collapsed on the couch, kicked off her heels, wriggled her toes. For now, just for now, there was no future, there were no consequences. She wanted only to think of Griff—the touch of him, the taste of him, the pure cellular response of her body to his body.

Minutes passed. Perhaps twenty minutes. Perhaps an hour. She lay motionless on the couch, her body throbbing as she remembered. She might have fallen asleep because she was startled by the sound of Nippy at the back door, scratching and whimpering to be let in.

She ran out to the kitchen, bare feet smacking against the floor, and opened the screen door. Nippy rushed in, sniffing the air, hoping for food scents. He followed her back to the living room, watching her as she lay back down on the couch, then jumped up at her feet, resting his head against her legs.

If I move again, I will lose it, she thought, lying motionless on the couch. *If I get up again, if I do something, anything, my body will begin to forget. And, oh, to remember! That's all I want right now. That's all I want.*

Getting up, leaving Griff, was the hardest thing she had ever done, but she knew she couldn't be there, solid and needy, when he woke up. She had to even the odds between them or he would never risk her again. Knowing that he would wake up wanting her—because she had eluded him—is, for now, *all* that she knows.

Unbidden, the thought of Alex rose in her mind, and she was frightened. She had betrayed him, had wanted to betray him for months, had schemed to betray him. She had pushed back, pushed aside, the thought of his hurt, the thought of his wrath. She drew her knees up to her chest, turning on her side.

She remembered that he was with his ex-wife, that his grandfather had just been buried, that his daughter was perhaps reaching out to him for comfort. She gleaned hope from this.

Oh, if only Alex and I had gone on loving each other without the resolution of marriage. If only we had left intact, or only damaged, the life that he and Carolyn built. If only I were free, as Griff is free ...

Selene sat up, suddenly, and switched on the lamp beside the couch. She thought she heard a car in the drive. Startled out of sleep, Nippy jumped to the floor, watching her face for cues. Selene strained forward; she listened. But there was no crunch of loose gravel on the drive, no sound of a car door slamming shut. She leaned back, heart pumping, feeling the fright she had pushed away.

Will he know? Will he look at me and know?

After a while, her heart slowed, soothed by the silence. She realized she was hungry. Famished. She had not thought to eat all day. There had been no room inside her for food. She stood up, stretching, calling to Nippy, "Come on, boy, let's fix something to eat."

Nippy bowed, front paws stretched forward, back end high in the air, before he propelled himself toward the kitchen, running back two or three times to urge her forward. Before she opened the refrigerator, she measured out his dry food, filled his bowl.

"Red meat, I think," she said to Nippy, who was crunching loudly at her feet. "Nothing but red meat will do tonight."

The steak was sizzling in the pan and Selene was tossing a salad when she heard a car in the drive. She stopped and listened, salad fork and spoon in midair. A car door slammed. Alex was talking to someone. Carolyn, probably. She must have driven him home. She heard him saying his goodbyes, approaching the back porch as the car backed out of the drive.

"Hello, there, boy," he said, pulling open the door, reaching down to Nippy, who was yipping excitedly. He looked up at Selene. "Hello, there."

Selene saw that he was unsure of his welcome. She scooped up the salad, tossed it with the wooden spoon and fork.

"Good evening," she said. "I wasn't sure if you were coming home."

Alex picked a piece of lettuce from the bowl and chewed on it, watching her.

"It's just that Wendy was so—well, so needy. I'm sorry, sweetheart. I didn't mean to just—leave you."

"It's all right," she said. She pecked him on the cheek.

My God, she thought, *it's all right. He's so involved with Wendy, and Carolyn, and his own guilt, he doesn't see mine.*

"It's all right." she said, again. "I was hoping you would get back in time to have dinner with me."

"I'm not very hungry," he said.

Selene sensed a new source of guilt.

"Carolyn, she—fixed us something. Wendy and me. But I'll sit with you. I'll have some salad."

Too easy, she thought. *Too easy.*

She put the steak and salad bowl on the table, which she had set for two.

"Yes, of course," she said. Indulgently. Sympathetically. "Sit with me, Alex. Have some salad. Tell me about your daughter. Tell me about Wendy."

CHAPTER 17

Selene can no longer think of the manuscript as belonging to Kirby Woods. *New Moon Dialogue: A Conversation about Possibilities* belongs to her. It is her research, her thought, her patient fitting together of the pieces, her dialogue between the believer and the skeptic.

"All that's left that belongs to him is his name," she says to Jeff at one of their meetings at Cotter Publishing. "Don't you see that? It's mine now. I've claimed it."

"I'll be goddamned if I'll go through a lawsuit for this baby," says Jeff. "And Kirby won't give it to you. You know him. What in the hell are you thinking? He's got clout in the industry. He's got a reputation. What do we have? What do you have?"

"I've got the manuscript," Selene says.

Jeff shakes his head, but he can't take his eyes off her. There is something electric in her; he's sure if he touches her arm he'll get a shock from the contact.

They continue to argue, until Jeff hits the desk with his fist, startling her into silence, and says, "Look, if Kirby Woods doesn't sue you, Cotter Publishing will. You work for us, goddamn it. You owe us that manuscript."

Selene gets up, walks to the wide window overlooking the parking lot. With her back to him, she sighs, shrugs, says, "I know. I read the contract. I don't mind turning it over to you, Jeff. I guess I can live with that. I just don't want to give it to—him."

"Why?"

She turns to him, arms crossed. "Besides the fact that he won't credit me? That as soon as he reads what I've written he'll forget I wrote it and take it as his? That he considers me a—a—researcher who makes notes on three-by-five cards so he can make sense of them, so he can make the magic connections, so he can write a Kirby Woods exclusive?"

"So he's an asshole," says Jeff, wearily. "So what? He owns you. He owns your ideas and your organizational skills. It's in the goddamn contract. Finish the book, then make your own baby. Make a dozen, for Christ's sake. Just not this one!"

Selene puts her hands up to her face. Jeff sees, with something like disbelief, that she is crying. He has never seen her cry. He stands up but he cannot move away from his desk. After a few moments, which seem much longer to Jeff, she stops shaking, her hands move away from her face. She gives Jeff a quick, apologetic look, reaches for her purse, extracts a tissue, wipes her face, blows her nose.

"I'm sorry," she says.

"Yeah," says Jeff. "Well."

He can't say anything more because he's thinking too hard. He's in love with her. Practically an old man, divorced, his wife remarried, his kids living their own lives, and he's in love with this young woman who's in love with her manuscript, who has a husband and who knows what else, who else, to fill up her life.

"Jeff, really." She moves away from the window, touches his arm. "I'm sorry. That was—"

"It's okay," he says. "Let's move on. This is a spring release, which means we should be pretty damned pregnant by now. I'll give you till the end of the year to make this baby viable."

He reaches across with his other arm, pats her hand where it rests on his arm. They stand like this for a moment. Then he releases her; she releases him. He wonders how much she knows. Probably all there is to know. Probably before he knew.

*　*　*

Selene and Griff meet wherever they can, whenever they can. Twice again, they meet in the eyrie, when Nan is gone for the day. They don't have much to say to each other. They meet to have sex, to relieve the terrible frustration of being away from each other. They meet in a motel but cannot adjust to the strange, sterile surroundings, so they leave after a quick encounter and have sex again in Selene's car. She coaxes him into her house, but he won't touch her on her and Alex's bed, so she leads him into the guest bedroom, where they have sex on her mother and father's old bed, then on the stairs, then in her office, her manuscript pushed carelessly off her desk.

She knows he's not in love with her, but she continues to wish for it, and to lust for him. She remembers, at times, her lustful love for Alex years ago, the need she felt to make him hers, to detach him from the claims of his wife and his children, to possess exclusive rights. She harbors no such delusion with Griff. She knows she cannot claim him. She wants only to be as close to him, physically, as it is possible to be.

When she pauses to consider the risk she is taking, the damage she is imposing on the foundations of her life and those close to her, she is appalled. She is not sorry, she is not ashamed, but she is horrified. She can see clearly that she is rudderless, but she has no will to go back, no notion of how to go forward. She needs all of her energy to stay afloat.

Alex is preoccupied with Wendy, and perhaps with Carolyn. Selene cannot tell. She wonders about Alex and Carolyn, when she can detach her thoughts from Griff. She tries to remember what they said to each other, how they looked at each other, at the funeral, but she can only recall Griff and Sue Smoller—the panic amounting almost to hysteria she felt when she looked at them sitting side by side. She wants to mourn Bernard, to comfort Nan, but his death and Nan's loss keep sliding away from her, like marbles on a slippery surface. Her only respite seems to be her manuscript, the research that absorbs her for a few hours each day, that allows her to turn her mind away from Griff.

She is jealous of the very air he breathes. She wants to pull that air into her lungs, to absorb it, as she absorbs him into her when they touch, when they fuck. She wants to call it love, making love, but she is determined to see him, to see them, clearly.

There is her guilt. It is like sticky paper. She can pull it off, like her clothes, when she is with Griff, but it is always there, waiting to adhere to her again in an unguarded moment, or when she is reaching for a new thought. She learns not to reflect, not to speculate. Best not to consider. Best not to invite pain. She is with him, for now.

Her work doesn't interest Griff. This does not surprise her. She does not resent it. He seems to be a man devoid of ambition, yet strong, energetic. He has worked in the months he has been in town—odd jobs that he doesn't talk about. But Nan has been aware; Nan has mentioned it. And there is his connection with Bernard—the sense he had of Bernard's need for him, the way he reappeared when Bernard needed him most. It is, perhaps, a gift, but when she hints at it, when she mentions it in connection with her book, her premise, he grows uncomfortable. He pulls away from her.

"I don't want to talk about it," he says to her.

So she is silent about her book, and his gift—this perception that may be the only thing, aside from their passion, that they have in common.

Before sex, he has little to say to her. After sex, he is restrained, almost shy. She thinks of the long, intimate, humorous talks she has with Alex after sex, his arm around her, her head tucked close to his. She wonders who she is when she is with Griff, who he is.

He seems to have no curiosity about her. He asks her nothing. It is as though he doesn't want to know her, that knowing her will trigger something he is holding at arm's length, something he is afraid of, something threatening. He communicates with her when he touches her, when he runs his rough hand along the length of her leg, when he touches her breasts and her nipples harden. She accepts that this is enough, but she persists.

* * *

"Was Howard good to you when you were growing up? Did he seem to favor Alex?"

"I don't know. I don't remember. What does it matter now?"

"Everything that happens to us as children matters. Our parents form us, make us who we are."

"Mom matters. He doesn't."

"But he did, when you were a child."

"Maybe. I don't remember."

They were in her home, on her parents' bed, where Selene had been conceived, where her mother and father had slept together, side by side, all of their adult lives, until they were separated by death. She was lying on her father's side of the bed, closest to the door. Griff was lying where her mother, Irene, slept, close to the window—where Irene could watch the moon travel across the sky at night, watch the first pink and blue rays of dawn. The last thing her mother did each night before she went to bed was to uncover this window.

"I adored my parents. They both died while I was in college."

She waited for the quick, sympathetic inhalation, the questions, the reassuring touch. Perhaps he had fallen asleep. It was mid-afternoon. The sex had been intense, frenetic. She turned her head to look at him. He was staring at the ceiling.

"I could use a cigarette," he said.

"Don't you want to know anything about me?" she said.

"You're my brother's wife. I know too much already."

His voice was mild, matter-of-fact.

"I—I don't think I love him anymore," she said in a small voice.

"When did you stop?"

"When I began to love you."

She had said this before she could censor the words.

He pulled himself up to a sitting position.

"I'd better get going," he said.

She fought back the panic she always felt at this moment, the fear that she wouldn't see him again, or that he would prolong their separation.

"When—when—?"

"Tomorrow."

She saw a flicker of sympathy in his eyes; he must have seen the relief in hers.

"I'll call you," he said.

He got up then. She looked at his broad back as he glanced out the window. She drank in the sight of his nakedness— the tender pink area just beneath his hairline, at the back of his neck (did Sue Smoller cut his hair?), the back of his ears, the outer lobes slightly reddened by the sun, or perhaps by a self-conscious blush, his shoulder blades moving slightly under his smooth, slightly browned, skin, the curve of his spine as he leaned to one side, his buttocks, his heavy, muscular thighs.

"Come here to me," she said, her voice husky.

He turned away from the window, toward her, as if responding to the intense longing in her voice.

"Come here to me," she said, again.

He came to her then, almost tenderly, so that she could sep-arate this encounter from the rest, so that she could remember it as the time—perhaps the only time—they made love.

* * *

She did not know that when he had come to her, almost tenderly, that afternoon, it would be for the last time. She cried after he left—not because she was prescient, or because he had touched her with any finality. She cried because he was able to leave her, and she was incapable of letting him go.

He had gotten up from the bed, put on his jeans and that soft, overwashed flannel shirt that matched his eyes, tied on those big, clumpy boots, said, "Later," and was gone.

Where did he go when he left her? She waited one agonizing day, then another, then called Nan—and was told Griff wasn't there, hadn't been there for some time, but he stopped by, peri-odically. So he was still in town. Alex had long since written him off, didn't expect to see him again, maybe not for years.

Several more days went by. The realization gradually crept over her, like the tread of an insect on her face in the dark. She brushed it away, again and again, but it was still there, hovering, waiting for an unguarded moment.

It's better, she thought, *that I didn't know it was the last time, just as I don't know when I will die. Knowing then would have been unbearable. Knowing—as I know now—that I will always want him, and he will always regret me.*

Alex was cheerful and affectionate. His tuneless whistling filled the house, driving Selene to distraction. But she tolerated it because she didn't want to draw his attention away from his happy thoughts. She didn't want him to watch her too closely.

"She's just not ready to see you, hon," he said, apologeti-cally. "Wendy's a stubborn kid. Not as stubborn as Kevin but still—"

"I understand," said Selene, grateful for Wendy's stubbornness. She had no room for Wendy. She had no room for affection for, or jealousy of, Alex's ex-family. She heard the names of "Wendy" and "Carolyn" and "Kevin" again and again, without emotion. She wanted to hear only one name, and there seemed to be only one person—Nan—for whom that name came comfortably, naturally.

*　*　*

"Griff has always been, if nothing else, elusive," said Nan, sitting in Selene's disorderly office, the corner of a low filing cabinet cleared to hold Nan's coffee mug.

Selene apologized for the mess, but Nan shrugged it off, saying it was good to get away from her house. She said she didn't want to disrupt Selene's work, so she hadn't bothered to call ahead.

Selene couldn't remember Nan's ever stopping by unannounced before. She had started talking about Griff of her own volition, as if he were the purpose for her being there, in Selene's office, in the middle of a work day; as if she needed to reassure Selene that her youngest son was acting in character, that she, Selene, was not to be overly concerned.

"I gave him all the love he would take. Howard gave him a rather distant affection and, when he died, a very small inheritance. Sometimes I think that pittance means more to him than anything else. Because it gives him freedom. Love is a burden, you see. It weighs one down."

Selene's eye's misted, and Nan looked away. Quickly. Too quickly.

"Dad used to say to me, when Griff was a boy, 'Leave him alone, Nan. Let him be. He won't give in, like the rest of us. He won't be dictated to. He'll tough it out, no matter what. He belongs to himself. *Period. End of story.*' Did you ever talk to Griff about your book?"

Selene blinked in astonishment at Nan's sudden shift. "My—book?"

Nan laughed, waving her hand around the office—the carelessly scattered reference books, loose files, stacks of manuscript pages, magazines, disks. "You know—your book."

"I don't think so. No. He didn't seem interested. Not in the book—and not in the subject of the extrasensory."

"I'm not surprised. For him, the extrasensory is too personal, too close to home. He has a gift, you know. I've known it since he was a boy. Nothing showy. Just a sensitivity—a quiet sort of perception. He sees into people, sometimes before they see it themselves. But he won't admit to it. I think he's afraid if he does it will go away. Or maybe he doesn't want anyone to know how sensitive he is."

"Does Alex know?"

Nan shook her head. "Griff made Bernard and me promise not to talk about it with Alex, or with Howard. He's ashamed of it, in a way."

"I would think he would be proud of it."

Nan shook her head again. "Not Griff. You see, he understands Alex, just as he understood Howard. He knows they would scorn that sort of ability. They would think of it as *vul-nerability*."

"Why—yes—you're right," said Selene, dazed by Nan's conversation. It was as though every word she said was carefully prepared. How much *did* she know? "I talk about my book with Alex all the time—but only as a business project. We never really talk about the premise, the research, the content."

"That's my Alex," said Nan. She picked up her coffee mug, sipping thoughtfully. "That's why he's good at what he does. That's why he's, quote unquote, 'successful.' He never lets the abstract, the philosophical, the contemplative, get in his way."

"No. No, he doesn't."

"My sons, you see, are as different as they can be. Dad used to say I grew two different fruit off the same tree. One local. One with a foreign flavor."

"Foreign—how?"

"Griff never seemed to belong to me. To us. It's true I didn't know his father all that well." Nan blushed slightly when she said this, and Selene realized this was more than she had ever said to her about Griff's father. "Perhaps he's mostly his father's child."

"He has your—empathy," said Selene.

"Empathy? Is that what you would call it? Except for one time, I don't remember his ever hurting anyone, physically. Even when he was bullied. He's very strong. Maybe he's afraid of his strength, were he to fight back."

"Why was he bullied?"

"For the usual reasons. For not being just like everyone else. Alex was—well, you already know all this. He was a football jock in high school. Quarterback. Very strong. Very fast. A team player. Griff admired him when he was a boy. Wanted to be just like him. He grew up to be very fast, and even stronger than Alex—but he wasn't a team player."

"So he didn't follow in Alex's footsteps?"

Nan shook her head. "He took up boxing, then martial arts. He still practices martial arts, or did the last time I asked." Nan sipped at her coffee. "He—hurt someone once. Someone he quarreled with. He was only a boy at the time. Still in his teens. But it had a profound effect on him."

"Did you love him?" said Selene.

"Did I love—?"

"Griff's father."

Nan smiled at Selene, as though she had been waiting for the question. She nodded. "Yes. Or so I thought at the time. Perhaps it was something else."

"Like what?"

"A sort of—suspension of reason, judgment, accountability. A willing suspension." She spoke slowly, quietly, thoughtfully. "A disregard for consequences. A yearning that's like—what you might feel if you had lost a limb and still felt it—the pain and the pleasure of it."

Selene looked away from her and said, after a silence, "How do you distinguish between love and—that other?"

"With 'that other,' as you call it, I felt I had no choice," said Nan. "I suppose—" She hesitated, then continued, "I suppose that's how you feel about Griff."

Selene opened her mouth to protest, then stopped herself.

So Nan knew. Of course. She had always known.

"Yes," she said.

There was a simplicity in Selene's response that Nan seemed to approve. She nodded.

"I—I don't know what to say," said Selene. "I feel so—"

"Never mind," said Nan. "I didn't come here to force a confession out of you, nor to get your promise of renunciation."

"Then what—?"

"I don't condemn, I don't condone, what you and Griff are doing. You know the danger. You know the consequences. You know you're headed down a dark path. I was there, remember? I was on that path."

Selene had only enough courage to keep her head up, to return Nan's gaze. She could not speak.

Nan got up then, looking around the cluttered office. "I'm keeping you from your work."

Selene got up also.

"I'm—I'm glad you came, Nan. I've missed you since Bernard—well, since Bernard was with us."

Nan pulled Selene close to her, hugging her long and affectionately. "I was worried about you, but I think—" She gripped Selene's shoulders, held her at arm's length. "I think you'll be all right."

Selene began to follow her to the office door, but Nan shook her head.

"Stay right here," said Nan. "I've taken enough of your time. I'll bring Nippy in from the back yard when I leave, and you can get back to work."

Selene sat down again at her desk. She heard the bustle of excitement as Nippy came inside, then the door closing.

Nippy trotted into the office and sat close to her.

"It's like this," said Selene, reaching down to rub his ears. "She came, she did what she came to do—and then she left."

Period. End of story.

CHAPTER 18

There are now only two major activities in Selene's life–the daily research and writing on her manuscript, and preparations for the party Alex is giving to impress his business associates at Stampler Communications. The latter is a task, an ordeal she approaches with determination and dread. Alex is almost pathetically grateful for her faux enthusiasm. Every evening and weekend they discuss her progress. Her work on the manuscript recedes in Alex's mind; the party emerges as the major, the only, project.

"Do it big, hon," he tells her. "Let's show 'em how it's done."

She brings in a professional cleaning service and turns them loose on every room in the house—except for the guest bedroom, formerly her parents' bedroom, and hopefully the room in which she conceived. It is too soon, but she carries herself as though there is a new life sprouting inside her. The guest bedroom must remain pristine, every dust mote undisturbed. So there is no mistake, she closes the door to the bedroom and locks it with an old skeleton key.

Selene convinced Griff, after their first hasty, unprotected encounter, that there was no need for condoms. He was reluctant, but he chose to trust her. There is a part of Griff, not evident to anyone except, perhaps, herself and Nan, that is childlike in its trustfulness. Unlike Alex, he accepts that people are what they say they are, until they betray him. Selene is prepared to betray him, and everyone close to her, to have what is Griff's.

Carefully, playfully, building on Alex's mood of buoyancy—with his daughter, Wendy, with the party planning, with release from the long tension of Bernard's illness and Griff's irritating presence—Selene reinstates herself as his young, sexy, affectionate wife and companion. On a Sunday morning, when the party is still some weeks away, she tries on the dress she has just purchased for the event, then goes downstairs to model it for him. The dress is long, black, clinging. In the living room, she paces back and forth in front of him, kicking the hem out of her way with her bare feet. He is sitting on the couch, reading the Sunday papers.

"It's from Spangleman's designer collection," she says. "It cost more than the catering service."

"Appetizing," he says, briskly folding the newspaper section he holds.

"It comes with a money-back guarantee," she says.

"Oh?"

"Yes. It's guaranteed to make you mad with desire."

"Or?"

"Back it goes to Spangleman's."

"Come here."

She comes close to him.

"Turn around."

She does. He unzips the dress. Selene releases herself from the dress. It drops to the floor. She wears nothing beneath it. She steps out of the dress and drapes herself over him. They make love quickly, intensely, a reunion without preliminaries after their long absence from each other.

Later, upstairs in their bedroom, she wraps Alex's terry cloth robe around her, then carefully drapes her party dress over a hanger.

"Done," she says out loud.

Hearing a slight sound, she turns and sees Nippy sitting in the doorway. He has followed her upstairs and, noiseless as a cat, is watching her every movement.

"It's my new policy," she says to him. He cocks his head to one side, to catch the tenor of her voice. "It's called, don't ask, don't tell."

*   *   *

"Don't do this to me again," said Sue Smoller.

"What am I doing?" said Griff.

"You're taking me down, and I'm not sure if I can get up again this time."

"Then I'll go."

"No. Don't go."

"Then I'll stay."

"Till you go back to her?"

"I won't go back. There's no going back."

They were sitting at Sue's small, wobbly kitchen table, two beer cans on its somewhat sticky, oilcloth-covered surface.

"What did she want with you?"

"What she got. Nothing more."

"I don't understand."

"You don't need to. It's over and done with."

"Then stay here. But don't touch me."

"I won't touch you."

"When will you leave again?"

"I don't know."

"But you will leave again."

"Yes."

"Then leave now."

"Okay."

"No. Don't leave now. Shit. I'm such a goddamned fucking screwup."

Griff smiled. "I guess we're two of a kind."

"I'm so glad to see you I could shit my pants," she said.

Sue picked up her beer, drank from the can. When she put the can down again, her eyes were moist. She rubbed at them impatiently.

"How's Jimbo?" said Griff.

"Better all the time. Almost as obnoxious as he used to be."

"Back in school?"

Sue nodded. "Still on crutches, but doing pretty well for a gimp."

"He won't like me being here."

"Tough shit. He doesn't call the shots around here. Besides—"

"Besides what?"

Sue shook her head.

"Besides what?" Griff said again.

"Not that he said it in so many words, but I think he missed you. He kept saying things like, 'Where's the fuckhead? Did he get lost again? Do we need to tag the guy so he can find his way back here?'"

Griff leaned back in his chair until it creaked in protest.

"I shouldn't be here," he said. "And I shouldn't stay here. It's not fair to Jimbo, or to you."

"Jimbo can handle it," said Sue. "I can handle it."

"You're not as tough as you make yourself out to be," said Griff. "Neither is Jimbo."

Sue put her hand on his arm.

"Stay," she said. "We're tough enough."

Griff nodded, but he was still looking away from her.

"I don't mean to hurt you, Sue. I like—being with you. Being here. But you can boot me out the door any time you please."

Sue reached across the table, squeezed his arm, then released it.

"I've been thinking," said Sue. "While you were gone. I've been thinking about—what we need from each other, and what we actually get. I don't mean just you and me. I mean every fucking one of us. We kind of go shopping, you know? But we can't find everything we want in one store, so we go on to the next store. And the next. But we're just putting on, then discarding each other. Like clothes. We're just using each other. We shop and we shop—we don't even realize, most of us, that no one person can make the grade. So, we're all going to be returned or discarded or put away and forgotten. None of us are good enough, Griff. Not if you examine the merchandise too closely."

Griff leaned forward, elbow on the table, left hand fisted under his chin. He stared at her.

"I think I may love you, Sue Smoller."

"Fuck you," she said, amicably.

*   *   *

On the morning of the party for Alex's business associates, a Saturday morning, Selene woke up feeling ill. Alex lay beside her, snoring lightly. Sunlight oozed through the curtains, warming her face. She smiled, lifting her chin. She would tell him tomorrow, after the party. She would take a test, but she was already sure.

She cupped her breasts, to feel their swelling.

"That's *my* job," said Alex.

Selene turned her head toward him. Alex was looking at her quizzically.

"You look like a Cheshire cat," he said.

She took his hand, sliding it across her breasts.

"Think of these inside my party dress," she said.

"Is that what you're thinking of?"

"Of course."

She swung her feet to the floor, sat on the side of the bed. She felt him watching her as she sat there in her weightless nightgown, reaching, stretching, rotating her neck to work out the kinks.

"You have a beautiful back," he said. "I think I married you for your back."

She got up, put on his terry cloth robe.

"Where are you going?" he said.

"Things to do. Party tonight."

"That's my robe you're wearing."

"So it is."

"Can I look at your back again?"

"It will be on display all this evening."

"Selene?"

She turned to look at him. His head was still on the pillow. His eyes were dark, intense. She felt a sudden twinge—guilt—or fear.

"I think I might keep you," he said.

So he didn't know. He didn't even suspect. She came back to the bed, picked up her pillow, tossed it lightly at him.

"Let me know when you're sure," she said.

In the bathroom, she looked at her pale face in the mirror. She felt ill, but she wasn't disabled. She could make it through the day and evening. No one would know. She would put blusher on her cheeks and carry herself very upright. She allowed the nausea to surge up in her until it reached her throat, then she retched, turning on the water to muffle the sound. When the wave had passed, she turned off the water, listening. Alex had fallen asleep again. He was snoring. She opened the bathroom door noiselessly, walked softly past the bed in her bare feet, crept down the stairs to the kitchen.

She put Nippy out for his morning run and began to sketch out her day. She would sit at the kitchen table, munch dry crackers, make a list of what she had to do. The florist would arrive soon, then the cleaning company to make a final sweep of the house. The caterers were scheduled for late afternoon. Nippy would spend the night just down the street with a friendly Scottie and his family. She had plenty of time. She would be calm, relaxed. For Alex. She was doing this for Alex; then he would do this enormous thing for her. Without, she hoped, knowing it.

The phone rang. She picked it up, quickly, so as not to wake Alex. It was Nan, offering her help.

"Everything is under control for the party, Nan, but won't you change your mind and come tonight?"

"No. Thank you, Selene, but I would feel out of place with all of Alex's business cronies."

"As do I."

"Ah. But the difference is—I have a choice." Nan laughed softly. "Try to enjoy yourself, dear. You've worked hard to make this happen."

"I'll try."

"I'm sure you'll succeed, and I'm sure you'll look stunning in your new dress. I'll be thinking about you tonight. Griff is just pulling into the drive, so I must hang up. He's leaving town, you know."

Selene felt the nausea rising to her throat again.

"No. I didn't know. Where is he going?"

"The only place he ever goes, dear. Away."

Nan murmured a goodbye, then hung up. Selene stood clutching the phone until the dial tone ran its course. A recorded voice instructed her to hang up. She placed the phone on its wall cradle, pressed her stomach. The nausea, which had begun to recede, rolled over her again.

"Are you all right?"

Alex stood in the kitchen doorway.

"Just cramps, probably. I thought you fell asleep again."

"Phone woke me up. Who was it?"

"Your mother. She said Griff was coming over there to say goodbye. He's leaving town."

"Good riddance," said Alex.

"Oh? That's all you have to say?"

"Yes. That's all I have to say. How about if I make us an omelet for breakfast?"

Selene felt the strength in her legs dissolve. She sat down at the kitchen table.

"No. Thanks, but I'm not at all hungry."

Alex began preparing the omelet, whistling tunelessly. Selene wondered if he whistled at work, the way he whistled here whenever he was engrossed in an activity. She had to get away from the whistling, the cooking smells. She murmured something, some excuse for leaving, went outside.

She sat on the porch steps, watching Nippy as he inspected his territory. When he saw her, he came scampering toward her, his mouth stretched open in a grin of delight. He bounded up the steps to sit beside her, just touching her. They both looked out on the back lawn.

She had had the lawn manicured for the party: brought in a supply of candles and decorative lanterns; rented chairs, small tables. If the evening were pleasant, the guests would spill out onto the lawn. She had thought of everything, she felt sure— even bringing in a party planner for a consultation, hiring a valet to park cars. Alex's party would be a success. Alex could not fault her. He would still be flushed with success and pleasure tomorrow, when she told him she was pregnant.

"Sure you won't join me?" said Alex, from the door behind her.

"Sure," said Selene.

Nippy rushed for the opening in the door, tempted by the fragrant smells beyond. Selene sat alone, listening to the pleasant morning sounds of breakfast preparation, birds trilling, neighbors starting their day.

By this time tomorrow, she would have only two things to focus on—the child growing within her, and the manuscript that was evolving into a full-fledged book. They both belonged to her—to her alone. Alex's name would go on the birth certificate, and Kirby Woods' name would go on the book, but they were hers. She had given them life. She alone would bring them to fruition. She would nourish the lie of Alex's paternity; she would accept the lie of Kirby's authorship. She knew. It didn't matter that the rest of the world did not know.

Nan, of course, knew about Griff. But she would keep Selene's secret. After all, she had allowed her husband to raise Griff as his own. But Selene wouldn't let Alex distance himself from this child, as Howard had distanced himself from Griff.

He must believe the child to be his. He must want the child as she did.

She had planned this pregnancy as carefully as she had planned Kirby's book and Alex's party. She had worked out every detail. She could bear that Griff was gone from her. She could bear that Griff did not love her. She had taken from him that which he could not take back. He could not deny her the child who was already hers.

"At least—keep me company," said Alex, from the other side of the screen door.

She sighed.

"Okay," she said. "I'm coming."

The morning was perfect. She hated to turn her back on it. But Alex must be appeased. This was his day.

"When do the caterers come?" he said, as Selene joined him at the table, trying not to look at the omelet he was devouring. "Did you talk to them about the salmon? The tenderloin? What about the bar? Did we order enough wine? Did you tell them what I said about the booze? We may not live in the West Hills, but we're gonna have the best goddamned spread they ever saw. Right, hon?"

CHAPTER 19

In late afternoon of the day, which continued on its course of warm, bright, mild perfection, Selene stepped out of the bath, where she had soaked and dreamed for a few restful minutes. She patted herself dry with a thick towel; rubbed away a circle of steam on the mirror over the sink; studied her face. She still felt occasional waves of nausea, but the hot water had pumped blood into her complexion. She looked as if she had a healthy flush. She would underscore the flush with makeup, then spray some artificial glitter onto her face and hair.

Everything was proceeding according to her careful plan. Alex was in the bedroom, dressing for the evening. He had been cheerful all day, had started drinking Scotch and soda long before he took his shower. Selene wondered if she should caution him not to drink any more before the party. But what harm would it do? She would not impinge on his pleasure in the day.

The caterers, the bartender, and the valet had arrived, and the house was suffused with the scents of food being carried in from the van parked in the driveway. Selene had decided to play it safe with a vast assortment of canapés, warm hors d'oeuvres, and meat and seafood platters for those who came early and expected a full meal. She had left the caterers to finish laying out the food, finding the combined sight and smell of Swedish meatballs, crabmeat-stuffed mushrooms, beef tenderloin, and

275

chicken *roulade* were making her nauseous again. She leaned against the sink a moment as the vomity swelling in her throat thickened and then receded.

She opened the bathroom door to disperse the steam. Alex stood at the full-length mirror in their bedroom, shrugging himself into the closest possible communion with the new blazer he wore over a pale blue tieless silk shirt and charcoal gray trousers. He turned to her, still adjusting his broad shoulders.

"How do I look?" he said.

"Sensational."

"Not bad, if I do say so myself," he said, picking up his Scotch and sipping it as he admired himself in the mirror. "The ladies will be pleased."

Selene laughed. "They will have a feast just looking at you."

"I'm going to check on things downstairs. How long will it take you to pour yourself into that dress?"

"Not long. There's still plenty of time. Even the politically incorrect won't arrive for an hour or so."

"Don't count on it. Who's in charge of the music?"

"You are. But all the CDs are stacked up. Just put a few on and check it out now and then."

He tilted her chin up, kissed her lightly on the mouth. He smelled of soap, aftershave, and Scotch. For a moment, she loved him as she had all those years ago.

"Hurry up," he said, walking out with his drink in his hand.

She heard him whistling tunelessly as he went down the stairs.

A few minutes later, as she stood in front of the bathroom mirror making up her face, the music she had selected and pieced together for the opening portion of the party began to vibrate throughout her parents' staid old house. The stereo system Alex had installed filled the rooms with the sound of Queen's "Another One Bites the Dust." Selene danced in place.

"Good," she said to her image in the mirror. "A couple of hours of this, plus plenty of booze, and those cold corporate fish will be jumping out of the water."

She had invited a few couples that both she and Alex saw socially. Jeff Wolinski, her managing editor at Cotter Publishing, was coming with a date. But most of the people they'd invited to their party were colleagues of Alex, who had entertained them lavishly in the past, pulled Alex up the corporate ladder—or tried to push him off it. Among the guests were the CEO and his wife, and other 'C' level executives, a few board members, and almost every VP in the company. She was grateful that Jeff had agreed to come—to give her an encouraging nod now and then.

She thought she heard a car door slam, but she didn't hurry her preparations. Anyone rude enough to turn up this early could wait for the hostess. Alex would keep them occupied. She brushed her hair until it shot off sparks, then she pulled it back and up, pinning it, allowing tendrils along the sides and back to frame her face, curl down her neck.

Nothing fixed or sculpted, she thought, nodding at her image in approval. *More like I just stepped out of a bubble bath and into a drop-dead-gorgeous designer gown.*

Still naked under Alex's robe, she pulled it open, let it drop to the floor. Then she sprayed herself with Chanel No. 22, her favorite scent—light, flowery, and expensive. She kicked the robe out of her way and went into the bedroom, stopped in front of the full-length mirror.

This will go away for a while, she mused, admiring her reflection in the mirror. *Griff's child will grow inside me and distort me, swell my stomach, puff up my breasts and ankles, change all that is concave to convex. Griff's seed will transform every cell* in my body, make me languid and self-satisfied. I will probably neglect my book, as if it were an older child. Alex will frown at my preoccupation, be jealous of the child, though he wants it and thinks it is his.

A sudden cramp gripped at her stomach. She pressed against it.

"Don't worry, little one," she murmured. "All will be well. Grow and flourish. Devour whatever of me is nourishing to you."

She thought she heard raised voices over the pounding rhythm of the music—now the hard rock of AC/DC. She sighed and turned away from the mirror. It must be Alex arguing with someone—one of the caterers, or the bartender, or the valet. He was probably more than half drunk, suffering from pre-party jitters, and interfering with the smooth sequence of events she had set in motion before she came upstairs to take her bath.

She stepped into satiny black bikini panties, fastened a practically nonexistent lacy black bra around her swelling breasts, and sat down on the bed to spread a light, satiny lotion up her legs and around her stomach, which was still pulsating uncomfortably.

I'm sure it's normal this early in the pregnancy, she thought. Just like PMS, only different.

She took the black dress off its padded hanger, stepped into it, slid it up over her legs and hips, where it clung, outlining her body. She zipped up the back, stepped into high-heeled sandals. No jewelry, but she picked up a small spray can, stood at the mirror, and lightly sprayed her hair and shoulders with silver glitter. She put the spray can down, examining her image in the mirror. It occurred to her that she never again would look as beautiful as she did right now. She wanted Griff to see her. He could not see her as she looked now and not want her again.

The voices downstairs were louder now. She distinctly heard Alex—his voice unnaturally loud, angry. She turned away from the mirror, wondering what had gone wrong, but she followed her image, turning her head to look back, admiring the way the gown clung to her, yet moved and undulated as it flared out around her ankles.

"Now for it," she said.

As she started for the stairs, she heard Alex's voice over the music.

"—take your goddamned truck out of my drive and get the hell out of here."

"For Christ's sake, Alex, I'm just—"

Selene stopped near the top of the staircase. That was Griff's voice she heard over the rising crescendo of the music. Hadn't he left town? She had imagined him gone hours ago, after he said goodbye to Nan.

Had he come for her?

Without a moment's consideration, she knew she would go with him. She would walk down the stairs and out the door and go with him. Without a word. Without a backward glance at the house. Without a thought for the guests who were about to arrive, the comfortable certainty that had been her life with Alex. Without a twinge for Nan, and what it might do to her.

He'll see me, she thought. *I wanted him to see me as I look now, and he will. He'll see me.*

Then she realized that Alex must be drunk. The more he drank the more his tolerance for Griff seemed to wane. The anger in his voice throbbed like the beat of AC/DC's "Shot Down in Flames."

They were on the front porch. She couldn't see them until she reached the landing where the staircase took a left-angle turn, but she knew they weren't in the living room. She stepped down to the landing, then saw them through the open doorway. From the window on the landing, Selene could see the valet, a neatly dressed young man in white shirt, black vest and pants, leaning against Griff's red Chevy pickup truck, which was parked in the driveway.

Alex was standing very close to Griff, confronting him. Griff was taller than Alex, so his head was tilted down slightly, his chin pulled in, his hands lifted, palms out, in a conciliatory gesture.

"Look, man," said Griff, "I'm not trying to—"

"Shut up," said Alex. "Just shut up."

Alex stepped back, shrugged his shoulders, pulled at the cuffs of his shirt. Whatever they had said to each other, whatever had triggered his burst of temper, seemed to be subsiding as he remembered his appearance. He looked around at the valet, who was smoking a cigarette, watching Alex and Griff with great interest.

At that moment, with a final guitar riff, the CD selection ended. There was a pause before the next selection began. Selene walked down the stairs. She stood in the open doorway.

Griff saw her first, his mouth curling up in admiration. Then Alex looked from Griff to Selene. Something made him glance at the valet, who stamped out his cigarette and stepped away from the truck to get a better look at Selene, the same look of reflexive admiration crossing his face.

Selene saw Alex's fist shoot out and connect with Griff's chin. She shouted something—"Wait! Stop!"—but her voice was drowned out by the music, which began a new round just at that moment. She had chosen this particular sound to coincide with the arrival of the first guests. It was another rousing, throbbing, insinuating sound—Michael Jackson's "Black or White"—that Selene hoped would help disperse the crusty stiffness of early comers.

As she watched Griff fall back against the porch rails, shaking his head and rubbing his chin, the first couple—she thought she recognized them—pulled up in front of the house. The valet walked toward the car, still watching the porch. Selene moved to step between them but Alex was ahead of her. He grabbed Griff by the shoulders, stood him upright, and hit him again. Griff spun around, the force of the blow pushing him against the porch rails and almost over them. He grasped the rails, took a deep breath. When he turned around, he hit Alex in the face. Alex recoiled, then bent over. Griff hit him in the stomach, knocking the breath out of him.

Selene stood unmoving in the doorway, the music pounding behind her, the first arriving couple standing with the valet just outside their car. The nausea she had been feeling on and off all day rose again. Alex was gasping for breath. He moved a step or two toward her, turned his back to her, and hit Griff again.

Griff was caught off guard. He'd obviously thought the fight was over. With a shout, he lunged at Alex. They both fell against the rails, pulling each other off balance and onto the floor of the porch. For a few moments, Alex had the ascendancy. Selene saw him punching Griff's face mercilessly. Then Griff rolled out from under him, pulling him down the wooden stairs of the porch onto the sidewalk. They struggled, Griff pummeling Alex to the ground on the front lawn, neatly shaven for the party.

They got to their feet awkwardly, Alex shaking his head, looking stunned. Selene followed them down the steps. She stood between them, turning to Griff.

His face was cut and bleeding—from his nose and mouth, from just above his eye, from his cheekbone. As she looked at him, she realized that she was bleeding also. Blood was flowing out of her, onto her thighs, down her legs. Immense clots of blood. Seeping down her legs, trickling into her high-heeled sandals. She stood unmoving, feeling the blood drain out of her face and this other blood, that was to form and nourish his child and hers, flow out from between her legs. She could hear Alex breathing heavily behind her but she didn't look at him. Her eyes were fixed on Griff, who was wiping blood and sweat from his eyes.

"Sorry about this," he said, his voice cracked, his breath coming in short gasps. "I just came by to—I'm on my way out of town. I don't know what I said that—I don't know why—"

He shook his head, flung his hand out in a gesture of hopeless frustration.

"I'm out of here. Shouldn't have come. Should have left things as they were. Unfinished is better than—this."

He turned and walked to his truck. The valet moved eagerly across the yard so that he could open the door of the truck for Griff. Griff looked at the valet, looked across at Selene and Alex, shook his head, laughed—a brief, bitter laugh—then climbed into the truck. The valet closed the door behind him. Selene watched Griff as he started the motor, turned his head, backed out of the drive. She saw another car pull up in front of the house. The valet sprinted across the yard to open the passenger door. Griff backed his truck out on the street, gunned the motor, and drove away without looking back.

The first couple to arrive, the couple who had watched the fight, walked slowly toward them, as if uncertain of their welcome. It was Harry and his wife. Harry was the obnoxious VP who couldn't take his eyes off Selene at the party she and Alex had attended early in the summer—the party at which Selene had been defiant in her sheer dress.

Selene turned away from them, turned away from Alex, walked into the house and up the stairs, ignoring the caterers and the bartender, who had crowded into the hall to watch. The blood was cold on her thighs and hot as it oozed out of her. She felt she must be leaving a trail of blood behind her. She felt she couldn't bleed this much and still be conscious.

She went into the bathroom, ran bath water, took off her clothes. She unzipped the designer dress, sticky with blood, pulled it off, flung it in a heap on the tiled floor. She stepped out of her heels, peeled off her panties, unhooked her lacy black bra—the only thing she was wearing that wasn't stained with blood. As she stepped into the bathtub, easing herself into the warm water, she watched it turn pink. After a few minutes, she drained the water and filled the tub again. When the tub was half full, she turned off the water and listened. Over the music, she could hear the shower running in the guest bathroom down the hall. Alex was cleaning the blood off his body, as was she. She sat in the bathtub, very still, careful not to dampen her hair or face, while Alex finished his shower, came into the bedroom, and dressed again outside her bathroom door. After a few minutes, he turned the knob on the door, which she had locked when she came in. She waited.

"Selene?"

"Yes?"

"We have quite a few guests downstairs already. Will you be down soon?"

"Yes."

"Selene?"

"Yes?"

Selene could hear him breathing harshly. She watched the doorknob—old, brass, intricately designed—move back and forth, grating gently on its cylinder. After a long silence, Alex released the knob.

"I'm—so damned sorry."

CHAPTER 20

The next day, a bright, chilly Sunday, Selene woke up early, put on jeans, T-shirt, jeans jacket, and left the bedroom without waking Alex. Downstairs in the kitchen, she wrote him a note saying she was picking up Nippy and going for a ride. She closed and locked the back door soundlessly, walked to her silver Honda, which she had parked on the street, drove away.

She spent a few minutes politely thanking the neighbor down the street who had invited Nippy to a "sleepover" with the family's Scottie, then drove out of town. When she was on one of the quiet country roads that still edged the business hub and freeways, she slowed down, willing herself to take notice of where she was, to roll down the window, draw in the fresh October air, listen to the buzzing, humming, twittering country sounds, to enjoy the morning as Nippy was enjoying it. The little white terrier stood at the open passenger-side window, his front paws propped on the door, his head outside, mouth open, tongue dangling with pleasure, the black patch that circled his left eye like a permanent bruise.

* * *

The party had been a success. When Selene came back downstairs, after having changed into a long black velvet hostess skirt and a pink silk blouse, the early guests were chatting enthusiastically over the pounding, gravelly voice of Dr. John on the stereo, helping themselves to the lavish buffet that extended along the length of the dining room. They gathered around Alex, who looked clean and composed in suit and tie, which he had already loosened.

As Selene approached him, he drew her close to his side, saying, "Ah, here's my lovely—and forgiving—wife."

She saw then that his face was swollen, bruised on one side—the left side—his mouth was cut, his knuckles were bruised, red. But he saluted her with a glass of sparkling soda, his dark eyes exultant.

"We expected to be entertained, Alex, but not this well," said someone close to them. Selene saw that it was Harry, the VP she found so obnoxious. He and his wife had arrived while Alex and Griff were fighting.

Harry cuffed Alex. Alex winced in mock pain, evoking a round of laughter. The laughter, Selene observed, was genuine. Their guests were comfortable, relaxed. Somehow, Alex had turned a painfully embarrassing situation into the most effective icebreaker Corporate had ever experienced.

As she looked around, Selene saw that the other guests were talking about them, gesturing toward them. Incoming guests were greeted with some version of the fight. Selene, as she excused herself to circulate, heard Alex say, in a tone that already sounded as if it had been repeated a number of times, "Just a little brotherly spat. We've been fighting since we were kids. I even won a few times."

The party rode to the finish on the fight story, with version upgrades emerging as the evening lengthened. The background music mellowed. The guests, replete with food, liquor, and the excitement of the fight, gathered in groups in the living room, the dining room, the back yard. The night was clear, warm, and dry. The new moon was surrounded by a dazzling tiara of stars. Selene's clusters of lanterns and candles on small round tables drew many of the guests outside. Always, everywhere, the guests talked about the fight with which Alex had launched the party. Whether he was praised or vilified, there was no lessening of interest and speculation.

When the CEO and his wife arrived, both standing somewhat uncomfortably in the modest hallway, Alex took Selene by the elbow and walked up to him with his hand held out.

"Glad you could come, Steve," Alex said, grasping his hand in a hard grip, then rubbing his bruised fist. "As you can see from looking at me, you've missed the entertainment, but everybody's here, and there's still plenty of food and booze."

Selene moved through the evening like a well-programmed automaton, responding appropriately, offering food and drink, listening to Alex, listening to her guests talk about Alex and— whether they were complimentary or mildly insulting—not disagreeing.

"He's carrying it off like a champ."

"Yeah, he looks like he went at least nine rounds."

"Sibling rivalry gone haywire, wouldn't you say?"

"Boys will be boys."

"Beats any party I've been to lately."

"He's made himself look good, that's for sure."

"Wonder what the other guy has to say for himself."

"We'll never know. Price knocked him out cold."

"Monday-morning water-cooler talk will be juicy."

"Right. No way to hide the Rocky Balboa face."

"I always thought he was a son of a bitch."

*   *   *

Whenever she was in the kitchen, talking to the caterers or checking with the bartender, she glanced at the large wall clock. The hours seemed to crawl by. She excused herself several times to go upstairs, where she changed her tampon and sanitary pad—always soaked with fresh blood.

Once, late in the evening, she took a beer and a plate of food out to the young valet, who sat on the front porch steps, smoking, looking peaceful, relaxed, in his casual uniform of white shirt, black vest and pants. He stood up politely, accepting the plate and the beer, then sat down again, brushing back the straight blond hair that drifted across his forehead.

"That was some dress you had on," he said, as Selene impulsively sat down beside him, unable to resist the relative quiet of his company. "Why aren't you wearing it now?"

"It—didn't fit right."

"Could have fooled me," he said.

They were silent for a few minutes, while he ate from the plate Selene had heaped with food.

"How's your husband doing?" he said, after a long swallow of beer.

"Never been better," said Selene.

The valet nodded his head. "Yeah, well, the other guy, he got the worst of it. I don't suppose he's feeling very chipper right about now."

"I don't suppose he is."

After another minute or two, Selene got to her feet. "I'd better get back to my guests," she said.

The valet stood up. His young face was shadowy, but his voice was vibrant, sincere. "I sure do thank you for the food and beer—and for keeping me company for a while."

Selene nodded, wanting to sit down again, put her head on his shoulder.

"You're welcome," she said.

She went back into the house.

The guests stayed on and on, feeding on Alex's energy, and the endless supply of food and liquor that Selene had so carefully provided. She sent the bartender and the caterers home at midnight, switched the CD music to mellow and laid-back: Loreena McKennitt, Sarah McLachlan, George Winston. Still, the guests stayed on, picking at the food, refilling their own drinks.

Jeff Wolinski arrived late—and left early—having heard enough for him to say, when his date wasn't close enough to overhear, "Give me a call first thing Monday. You look like you could use a friend."

Selene squeezed his arm, nodded.

At last, well after 2:00 a.m., the CEO and his wife began to leave, creating a ripple effect, which caused the other guests to notice the lateness of the hour, as well as the exhaustion which was beginning to be evident in Selene's face.

To the end, up until the last guests said their goodbyes, Alex was energized, immensely affable, cancelling out his earlier drunkenness with total sobriety. He stuck with his sparkling soda throughout the evening.

*   *   *

Selene had been so preoccupied—with the child she believed she was carrying, with Griff, with the book she was ghostwriting for Kirby Woods, with the party—that autumn had come, reached its momentary zenith, and begun its long descent into winter before she took notice of it. Already, the October leaves had taken on their deceptively bright funereal hues and were floating in uncountable numbers from the trees which had given them a brief existence, to gather on the ground, to crackle and molder until they were swept away or buried beneath snow.

She felt as though she had missed an important appointment. She drove slowly, aimlessly, down dirt roads, looking for the turn that would take her wherever it was she needed to be.

She came to it without thought or the consciousness of having searched for it. There was the mill, solid and solitary, just ahead.

Griff had brought her there once, not long after Bernard died, in the first heat of their affair. She could call it an affair now, but only because she knew she was looking back on it. Because it was over.

* * *

It had been a weekday afternoon, hot and dry, buzzing with life. Griff had pulled his truck up to the mill and stopped the motor so that they could listen to the hum of insects, the unhurried stir of the river.

"We used to come here," he said. "Sunday picnics. Mom, Howard, Alex and me. I think Howard knew the guy who owns the property. I've never seen anybody else here. Nobody ever bothered us."

"You and Alex, were you ever close? When you were growing up, I mean?"

Griff had been silent for so long Selene had accepted that he wouldn't answer her. Then he said, "He was my hero. I always looked up to him. Wanted to be just like him. When we got older, and I got to be taller than him, I got into the habit of rounding my shoulders and stooping over. Mom kept after me for years to stand up straight, but Alex wouldn't look at me if he had to raise his head."

They had gotten out of the car, walked around the mill, along the rocky river, shallow and slow moving in the September heat, leaves and debris sailing along its smooth surface as if on an afternoon excursion.

"Alex never told me about this place," said Selene. "But then—it isn't the sort of thing we—do."

"Come on," said Griff.

He had taken her by the hand, led her away from the river, into the woods that skirted the mill property. It was a thick grove of trees—pine, ash, maple, alder. Selene soon felt lost, but Griff led her on. She was happy because he had never before held her hand. They came to an area that looked to Selene like all the rest of the wood. Griff had stopped, let go of her hand, leaned against a tree, then slid down until he was sitting on the ground, his knees bent.

"I used to come here when I wanted to be by myself," he said. "This is the only place I've ever claimed for myself—even though I have no claim on it at all."

She had knelt beside him, cupped his face with her hands, drew her fingers lingeringly across his mouth. He pushed her back toward the damp ground, onto a bed of freshly fallen leaves. She listened, for a moment, to the trees sighing; thought, for a moment, of the small, shy, watchful inhabitants of the woods—before inhibition dropped away and she was as one with the man penetrating her, as one with the unseen, unheard witnesses to their primordial union.

Later, when they were pulling on their clothes, Griff said, his back to her, "Don't ever come here without me."

"I won't," she said.

It had seemed to her, then, that they would return there again and again.

* * *

How deluded she had been. How blissfully deluded. But even now, as Selene sat in the car, she wondered if she should be here without him.

At last she opened the door and got out, Nippy prancing and scampering at his unexpected freedom. She walked past the mill to the river.

The river was deeper now, more resolute in its course. It mumbled and spat at the rocks that impeded it, sucked up the leaves that fell on its surface. She watched the dregs of nature float by, along with beer and soda cans, plastic bags, bits of paper, a lone sneaker.

I won't come here again, she thought. *Maybe he knew how I would feel. Maybe that's why he told me not to come back here ...*

She would never know him, any more than she would know this river, its source, its destination, the secrets it held beneath its churning surface, its changing moods, its relentless compulsion to keep moving. She was just a bit of debris he had picked up, moved along, then discarded on his way through. He was no more malicious and destructive than this river, or the creatures that inhabited the fields and woods around it. He used his gift—his unusual sensitivity—as any sentient animal might, to sense the approach of danger or the need to move on.

Selene sat down on the grassy river bank and wept. There was no one to see her or to hear her, so she wept copiously, loudly, as she had wanted to weep last night, when she saw Griff's bloody face, and felt the blood flowing down between her legs. She wept for the child that she believed had existed for a few weeks inside her, taking nourishment from her body, its cells growing and multiplying, its fishlike, miraculous body beginning to form. She wept for the life that might have bound Griff to her forever, wherever he was, for the joy she would never know of keeping what was his, what was theirs. She wept for Griff, because he was wounded, in pain—beaten up, beaten back—without Alex's ability to tough it out. Like a sick animal, he had run away from those who would heal him, comfort him. She wept for Bernard, because she had loved him, and she had not, until this moment, wept for him.

When there were no tears left, when her eyes were almost swollen shut and her throat ached, she looked around her. Nothing had changed. The morning was still bright, buzzing with life. Nippy lay on his belly close by, watching her intently. She laughed softly at his worried expression, his head tilted to one side. He moved slowly toward her, still on his belly, his legs splayed frog-like behind him. She laughed again. Nippy got up and bounced against her, knocking her off balance. She lay on her back where he had pushed her, her knees bent, one arm across her forehead, looking up at the cloudless sky, its blue less intense than it had been in September, its unpatterned vastness soothing. She fell asleep.

When she woke up, the buzzing sounds had changed, like an orchestral symphony well into its second, andante, movement. Even the river seemed less hurried. Nippy lay close to her, one eye open. She sat up, stiff from the hard ground. Nippy followed suit. As soon as she got to her feet, she felt the letdown of blood into her tampon and the thick pad she wore with it.

She sighed, stretched, looked around her. The sun was almost above her head; the river shimmered. A muskrat a few yards from her hesitated, then tunneled into the water, as though it were a warm, dry cave.

She moved closer to the river, wanting to tunnel into it herself, let it carry her downstream, just as it had the muskrat, and the debris of man and nature. Then, like a recording that is jolted and lands on another track, she thought of Bernard, not so many weeks ago, sitting in his armchair in Nan's living room, dozing, the noon sun shining on his face through the picture window, while Nan struggled to read the expiration date on one of his prescriptions. Finally, she'd handed the container to Selene, who read it out to her. There was a pause, then Bernard, his eyes still closed, said, "I hate expiration dates." Selene and Nan had looked at him, then at each other, then laughed. Bernard had smiled, satisfied, but kept his eyes closed, his head turned to the sun.

Again, Selene felt tears sliding down her cheeks. She wiped them away impatiently, surprised that she could shed still more tears.

"Come on, Nippy," she said, as he bounded toward her. "Let's go home."

She turned away from the river and walked past the mill, scarcely looking at it, not wanting to consider it—the solid permanence of its structure, its slow, picturesque decay.

CHAPTER 21

"*Where have you been?*"

"For a ride. I left you a note."

Selene threw the car keys on the kitchen table.

"I was worried about you."

"Well, you shouldn't have been. I'm a big girl now."

"Goddammit, Selene—"

Nippy was jumping at Alex's knees. He reached down, absently patting the dog as Selene walked past him.

"Wait a minute," he said, following her. "Where are you going?"

"I'm going upstairs. I'm bleeding."

"You're—"

"Menstruating. I told you last night."

"Yes. Your dress—"

"Ruined. Can't go back to Spangleman's now!"

She sang it out, triumphantly.

"I don't give a shit about the dress—although you looked—"

"Leave me alone, Alex. I did everything you wanted me to do. Now I want to be left alone."

His face, one side of which was garishly puffed up and blue, one eye almost swollen shut, a long cut just above his mouth, lifted in a comic parody of a smile. He winced and put a hand up to his mouth.

"Better put a cold pack on the Mr. Hyde side of your face," said Selene, as she walked through the dining room. "There's one in the freezer."

"Talk to me, Selene. Talk to me."

She was in the living room now, near the stairway and the front door. Selene glanced through the glass half of the door, then turned to face Alex, who had followed her.

"Why did you do it, Alex? Why did you hurt him so?"

"You know I was more than half drunk, and he said—"

"What?"

"Some stupid things. You know how he goads me."

"What? What did he say?"

"I don't—remember exactly, but—"

Selene turned away from him and ran up the stairs, but Alex was right behind her. At the landing, he grabbed her arm.

"I saw how he looked at you and I—"

"Don't say that," said Selene. "Don't use that. Men look at me plenty, and you don't beat their faces to a bloody pulp. You didn't beat up Harry last night, or at the Themes party this summer, when he was undressing me with his looks and innuendo."

"Innuendo be damned. We're not talking about Harry and his leers or his fucking innuendoes."

He released her arm to press his hand against his bruised, pulsating face. Selene ran up the short flight of stairs from the landing to their bedroom, went into their bathroom, locked the door. She pulled off her shoes, stripped off her jacket and jeans, and the panties holding the bloody pad between her legs. She wriggled out of her T-shirt and ran bath water. She thought she heard Alex say something on the other side of the door as she stepped into the tub, but the water muffled his voice. She made no effort to listen.

When she had cleaned off the blood, which continued to flow out of her, she stood up, turned off the faucet, drained the pinkish water. She inserted a fresh tampon and wrapped a towel around herself before she opened the door. Alex lay, fully clothed, on the unmade bed, the blue cold pack from the freezer over the bruised side of his face. He said nothing as she moved back and forth from the bedroom to the bathroom, girdling herself again with panty and thick pad, this time putting on an old gray sweatshirt and pants—familiar, warm, comfortable.

"Let's talk this out," said Alex, as she tied her running shoes, then stood up, pulling a brush through her hair with quick strokes.

She continued to brush her hair, then suddenly stopped mid-stroke, her brush in the air. She looked at his reflection in the mirror. She stared at him for so long that he lifted the cold pack off his face and sat up on the side of the bed.

"What is it?" he said. "What's wrong?"

"I won't let him have it," she said, still staring at his reflection. "I won't!"

With a sharp cry, she threw down the brush, started for the door.

"Hold on," Alex called out to her. "Where the hell are you going now?"

"I've got something to do," she called back, already halfway down the stairs.

Alex sighed, stood up carefully, followed her downstairs, cursing at every jolt.

She was in her office off the dining room, gathering papers and files, stacking them in neat piles on her desk. Evidence of her work—her research and manuscript pages for the book on extrasensory perception and psychic phenomena—was everywhere. Alex had often teased her about the state of her office. He kept his office and his desk in perfect order. But she said she knew where everything was; it was ordered in her mind. That was the only thing that mattered to her.

Now he stood leaning against the doorjamb as she moved around the small room, arranging papers and files precisely, tucking in corners, tapping them on the desk to align the pages.

When she was satisfied, when she had scanned the room for anything she may have missed, she turned on the shredder next to her desk, sat down, and began to feed the papers into it.

Alex, who was watching her with a puzzled but tolerant smile, moved toward her as she began to shred papers. He grabbed her shoulder.

"What in the name of Christ are you doing?"

"I'm not doing it in Christ's name," she answered calmly, shrugging off his hand. She continued to feed papers into the shredder, which chewed and buzzed and rumbled with satisfaction. "I'm doing it in my name. Mine. My work. My name."

"But this is your manuscript, isn't it? Isn't this your manuscript, your research?"

"Every bit of it."

He pulled the only other chair in the room close to her, sat down. She turned away from him. She continued to jam papers into the shredder, which coughed and stalled if she fed it too quickly.

"Selene, sweetheart, I'm so damned sorry about last night, and I know you're angry, but isn't this a little extreme?"

His voice was soft, soothing. It occurred to her that he might have been talking to a junior employee.

She paused, a sheaf of papers in her hand, squinting at him. Then she smiled, shook her head, pushed papers into the machine.

"Do you think I'm doing this because of you? Because you beat up Griff and sent him off with his tail between his legs? Think again."

He leaned back in the chair, crossing his arms.

"All right. You've made your point. But getting drunk and making a goddamned fool of myself didn't motivate this level of destruction. So why are you doing it? Why are you destroying your work?"

"Because."

She paused, but her hands were busy, the papers disappearing into the shredder with mechanical regularity. The shredder shrieked at each new bite, then sawed methodically, spitting out narrow ribbon lengths of paper. "Because I'd rather destroy it than give it to—him."

"'Him?' You mean Kirby Woods?"

"Yes."

"But it's your book as well as his."

"No. It's his. He told me so. It's his."

"For God's sake, Selene, that manuscript represents months of work—and a lot of money. Besides which, you could be sued."

"Let them sue. They can try for my money but they won't get the words. The words are gone."

She continued to feed papers into the shredder as fast as it would take them, pausing to lift the shredder off the container and overturn the shredded paper onto the floor when the container began to overflow. The shredded paper unbent and danced on the hardwood floor. "And the research is almost gone."

"Okay, Sele. If it makes you feel better."

Alex watched her, shaking his head.

After some time, he said, calmly, "Of course, you can retrieve most of this electronically, when you're so disposed."

Selene turned toward him, her gray eyes narrowed, intense. "Do you still think this is just a dramatic gesture?"

She opened the left-hand drawer of her desk, drew out two slim, square floppy disks. "To make me feel better?"

She pulled off the shutters, pried open the plastic casings with a letter opener, ripped out the flexible round magnetic disks; then, she fed the disks, one by one, to the shredder. They could hear the shredder whine as it digested this new material. "Because I'm in some sort of hormonal rage?"

She turned toward the computer, which she kept in sleep mode, and clicked it awake.

"You don't know me, Alex. I have a feeling we don't know each other at all."

In a few moments, she had opened her hard drive and was systematically deleting files. "Whether I killed it, or you killed it, or it never existed, *New Moon Dialogue: A Conversation about Possibilities*, is gone."

She turned away from the computer, pushing another batch of papers through the shredder. "This baby is gone."

"It was your baby, Sele," said Alex, leaning forward, looking at her intently. "And I'm sorry it's gone. I hope you don't regret it."

He got up to leave.

"Alex?"

He turned at the doorway, looking back at her. She sat at her desk, her hand hovering over the overflowing shredder, her face calm. Her gray eyes, hard as moonstone, narrowed, focused, as though he were a moving target.

"I'll never regret it."

* * *

It was November, a few days before Thanksgiving and the inevitable gravitational pull of the holidays. Carolyn Price's small condo was redolent with the scents of baked goods—cookies and fudge cooling on the counter, banana bread still in the oven. Carolyn, always ahead of the holidays, planning to freeze most of what she baked, hummed softly, or sang snatches of song under her breath, accompanying the radio selections, which were edging into the holidays with one Christmas favorite for every two or three non-seasonal selections.

Alex sat at the round kitchen table, tapping his fingers on the worn oak surface, paging through the newspaper, a sampling of sweets on a small plate at his elbow. Every few minutes he broke off a cookie or a piece of fudge and popped it into his mouth, chewing absently, as though he were trying to remember something. Carolyn couldn't help smiling whenever she looked at him, although she knew he didn't see her smile and wasn't thinking about her.

Although she had accepted that Alex was not going to leave Selene, she was less disappointed than she thought she would be. What she had was what she had missed the most before Alex began to come back to her—his companionship.

She didn't tell him this. They still had sex occasionally, and she enjoyed it when they did. But it was this that she relished—his being close to her, close enough to touch, close enough to talk to, should she have anything to say, or just comfortably, silently close by, as they were now. They were an old married couple, in a way that he and Selene most likely would never be.

She had heard Alex's version of the fight. She was sorry for Griff. He was stronger than Alex, but he had obviously chosen to be beaten—perhaps welcomed it. There was something in Griff that didn't want to win, just as there was something in Alex that couldn't bear to lose. She could imagine that fight, imagine Griff's goading Alex, Griff's ultimate physical restraint. She could imagine Alex's drunken anger, his will to punish, to triumph.

He did triumph. He sailed through that party on sheer bravado. "I had to think on my feet, Olyn. That crowd would have slaughtered me and eaten my liver, if I'd let them." Selene should have been proud of him. Instead, according to Alex, she avoided all mention of the party. Perhaps that was her way of punishing him, or perhaps—perhaps—

Carolyn stopped moving around the kitchen, stopped humming, leaned on the counter. She thought of Bernard's funeral, remembering the odd behavior of the group that remained after the funeral lunch: Sue Smoller, chatting about Bernard in her offhand, familiar way; Nan, laughing uncontrollably after Griff spat out an insult at Alex. And Selene—

Carolyn thought about Selene—her silence, the way she had looked at Sue, her eyes traveling back and forth between her and Griff, as though—

She closed her eyes, willing herself to remember.

It was as though Selene had claimed him.

Yes, that was it. She had thought it at the time. It was as though Selene had claimed him, as though she were putting a hex on Sue for being with him, for sitting next to him. She had noted it, then dismissed it. She hadn't consciously thought of it again, until now.

How close had they been, Selene and Griff?

"Olyn? You okay?"

Carolyn opened her eyes. Alex was looking at her over his newspaper. There was a film of powdered sugar at one corner of his mouth.

"I'm fine. Just thinking."

"About what?"

Carolyn hesitated. "About Griff, if you must know."

Alex groaned. "What about him?"

"Just—thinking. Do you think we'll hear from him?"

"Doubt it. He's not going to be dropping us a Christmas card, if that's what you mean."

Carolyn smiled, loving the unconscious "us." She said, casually, "He stays in touch with Nan, doesn't he?"

"Maybe. She doesn't tell me, and I don't ask."

"Is she still angry with you for—for—"

"Beating up her beloved second born? Yep. She doesn't say much about it but she's still fuming."

"Did she see him after you—"

"Nope. If I hadn't told her, if she hadn't seen my face, she never would have known."

Carolyn leaned over the table, wiped the powder off his mouth with a finger. Then she touched the scar above his lip, where Griff had hit him.

"You should have had this stitched," she said, tenderly.

He put his hand around her wrist, drew her close to him, kissing her. "Any coffee left?"

"I'll make some fresh."

She straightened up, put her hands on her hips. Her stance, her expression, were playful, teasing, familiar, as though she were hiding a surprise.

His voice eager, boyish, Alex said, "What? What is it?"

"I can't wait to see you and Wendy together again, over the holidays."

"Is she coming for sure?"

"Yes. She promised."

"And—Kevin?"

Carolyn turned away, not wanting to see his eyes dim with disappointment.

"She said she'd talk to him. We may get a phone call from him. I wouldn't count on more."

"I don't. I won't. All in good time. The kid's gotta grow up and accept his old man for the piss-poor father he is."

"Oh, but you're not—"

"I left them, didn't I? When I left you? Why should Kevin forgive me? Why should either of them forgive me?"

"Because I forgive you."

Alex pushed back his chair, stood up, began to pace. Carolyn measured coffee and water into the coffee maker, pressed the start button. She opened the oven, removed two loaves of sweet bread, put them on top of the stove, poking each of them with a toothpick to test their doneness. Satisfied, she leaned against the counter, watching him pace.

"I can't make it all better, Olyn. I can't undo what I've done."

"I know."

"Selene is—fragile. I told you what she did."

"Yes. I'm sorry for her. All that work. All that research. Do you think she regrets it?"

"No. No, I don't. It's as though, for her, it never existed. She's taken on another editing project, a textbook for middle school. You'd never know, from listening to her talk about it, that she'd ever taken on anything bigger, anything challenging and original."

"Maybe she's resting."

"Resting?"

Alex stopped pacing, frowned at her.

"That was her baby, sort of. You told me she used those words. And she lost it, destroyed it, prematurely, for whatever reason. Maybe she's resting now, like I did, after I had Wendy and Kevin."

Alex leaned against the counter, crossing his arms, shaking his head.

"Is that so far-fetched?" she said, thinking again of Selene at Bernard's funeral, the way she had looked from Griff to Sue Smoller. There was disbelief in that look, possessiveness, and—Carolyn searched for the word—an almost tangible panic, like a sweat she could see and smell. She had looked capable of anything—capable of wrestling Sue to the floor and beating her face, as Alex had beaten Griff.

"Maybe not," said Alex. "I don't know. She's lucky she got any project at all after that stunt. She's lucky she didn't get booted out of the publishing industry."

"How did she manage that?"

"Jeff what's-his-name. Her editor-in-chief. More than a business interest there, if you ask me. They worked up a story. Wastebasket caught on fire. Spread to her desk, files, computer. Everything gone before she could douse it with a fire extinguisher. The publisher bought it. The so-called author, Kirby Woods, ranted and raved, but he eventually bought it, too. He's still mumbling about bringing suit, but that would mean he'd have to go on record as having a ghostwriter, and he's not too keen on that. Not good for his reputation."

"By the way," Carolyn said, "I'll be substitute teaching again soon."

She was tired of Selene. She didn't want to think about her, about her bizarre behavior. She didn't want Alex to think about Selene, not while he was here, with her. This was their time. Let Selene deal with her loss, her angst, her itch for Griff. Alex would never know about Selene and Griff if she, Carolyn, were the only messenger. She wasn't about to re-glue his marriage to Selene with the adhesive of jealousy.

"I got a call from West Hills Elementary the other day. I start subbing right after the holidays. Somebody going on maternity leave."

"Good for you, Olyn. Are you thinking of teaching full-time again?"

"Yes. I am. I miss it. I've got too much time on my hands lately."

"Here. Let me see those hands."

He took her hands in his and studied them, looking first at the palms, then turning them over, rubbing the skin, following the lines of her veins. He kissed the back of her hands, first one, then the other.

"What's that for?" she said, cuffing his nose playfully.

"I'm grateful to you, Olyn."

"For what?"

"For putting up with me."

She turned away from him, so he couldn't see her face.

"You used to tell me I made the best banana bread you'd ever tasted. Care for a slice?"

* * *

Selene sat at her desk, Nippy at her feet, surrounded by research materials.

Today, like every day for weeks past, she has spent hours at the library, gathering material for her new editing and fact-checking project, a textbook for middle-school students on late twentieth-century American history. The work—Jeff Wolinski calls it Cotter Publishing's "bread and butter"—is just stimulating enough to keep her going from day to day, without tapping any vein of creativity, or rousing her to any original thought. Jeff is her only contact on the project. He thought it best, for a while, to shield her from the faculty committee.

* * *

"Just do the damn work," Jeff had said to her when they met at Cotter Publishing to discuss the textbook. "Let me deal with the big bad wolves."

"I can do it," she had said, stubbornly. "I can deal with them."

"Maybe. But it looks to me like you could use a rest."

"I do want to be—quiet for a while," she had admitted. Then, as if unable to hold it back, "Why do you men have to brawl, Jeff? Why do you have to draw blood? Why is it inevitable? Why?"

Jeff had shrugged. "You don't have to scratch very hard to find the answer to that one. We have a lot in common with the dog that pisses on the boundaries of his territory. Cross that invisible line, he bares his teeth and growls. Spit in his eye, he goes for the jugular."

"It was appalling and—and—unworthy of him."

"Maybe. But, from what I saw when I was there that night, and from the buzz I heard from other partygoers, he sure as hell carried it off well."

"You too?"

"Yeah, well. I gotta give him credit. It could have been a fiasco, but the son of a bitch wouldn't go down. He strutted around showing us his bruises like it was the latest thing in chic to warm up for a party with a fist fight. Now that's *chutzpah*."

"I can't make you understand."

"Maybe I understand more than you think."

She had hesitated. She knew he was edging closer to full disclosure of his feelings for her, feelings that were not just friendly and paternal. She knew she didn't want to hear any of it.

"You're my best friend in the world, Jeff. You're the only one who could have gotten me through this."

He had nodded, somewhat mortified. "Okay. Enough said. Let's tackle this magnificent opus of yours."

* * *

Selene sat at her desk, looking out on the driveway, the darkening street.

She tried not to think about Griff, or the child she had believed she was carrying—the child that would have been his. She tried not to think about Alex's primitive cruelty and smug satisfaction in defeating Griff.

Alex had mentioned recently that he was up for another promotion, that he wanted to buy a lot, build a house in the West Hills area. "I want the next party we give to be a house-warming," he had said to her, as if it were a settled issue. "This is a fine old house, but we can do better now."

When had her sentimental attachment to her parents' house, her childhood home, become a non-issue? When had Alex taken over their joint decision-making process?

He has been more confident since the party, particularly in their relationship—and Alex has always been notably confident. It is as though he has finally placed her, definitively, within the context of his life. She is his second wife, an attractive, desirable woman who works at home, earning a little money but not enough to embarrass him, independent but not flagrantly so, occasionally out of control, but she can be tethered by a skilled whisperer.

Looking ahead, she can't imagine her life with Alex—and she can't imagine her life without him.

If she and Alex are to continue together, she will have to leave the security of these walls, this neighborhood. Alex is ambitious. He is determined to have "CEO" after his name, whether it is here or in some other part of the country. If she is to continue to be part of the package, she will have to embrace the give-and-take of corporate entertainment, his frequent absence from home, his preoccupation when he is at home.

If he is seeing Carolyn ...

She is, oddly enough, not jealous of Carolyn. There was a time, before she and Alex were married, when she resented her very existence, when she wished that Carolyn and Wendy and Kevin would go away, would live their lives at a safe distance from her and Alex. Wendy and Kevin had done just that, but Carolyn had stuck close. Now Selene is grateful for her proximity. Even if Alex and Carolyn are having some sort of nostalgic, post-divorce affair, she can't sustain her anger. At some point, she knows, she and Alex will resume having sex, resume the normal course of their marriage, which includes mutual affection as well as mutual jealousy. Then she will know she has survived this terrible absence of feeling.

Even her feeling for Griff is receding, like the images she carries of him, of his body against her, inside her—of the way his blue eyes drew her in, yet distanced her—that look he sometimes had of not quite recognizing her—as though she were an old acquaintance whose name he can't remember. When she cannot avoid thinking about him, she sees him as she last saw him, in front of her house, his face bloodied, his eyes full of wrath and perplexity. If she had put her hand up to his face, he would have thrust her away from him. In those moments, Griff was unaware of her; he saw only Alex.

Selene thought about adultery, hers with Alex, then with Griff; Alex with Carolyn; Nan with Griff's father—even Bernard, in some brief betrayal that came back to haunt him in his last days.

Once, in the early days of Bernard's illness, Selene had taken him for a long afternoon ride. She had asked him to direct her to all his favorite country routes. He had complied, happily, confidently, taking them a hundred miles or so beyond the Sylvan Springs area. When dusk was approaching, and they were both weary, she had asked him to lead her back to a state route or a major artery, but he could not, nor would he admit to it. His confusion had been painful to witness.

"I know these roads as well as I know the back of my hand, as well as I knew Anna, and she knew me. Why, we—"

Selene had wanted only to find the way back, to credit him for finding the way, but she could not. She was as lost as he was, back roads leading to more back roads; endless acres of farmland, patchy woods, the rural mailboxes like sentinels. At last, when it was almost dark, she had stopped at a farmhouse, asked for directions. The farmer had been friendly, specific. She and Bernard were soon on a familiar route. But Bernard's humiliation had been complete.

He had barely spoken to her on the ride home, except to say, into the silence, "You know, no one can deceive us as completely as we deceive ourselves. I'm an old man, Selene. I can't even find my way home anymore."

* * *

Selene sat in the dark, thinking.

I can't find my way home anymore. I don't know where home is. I'm as lost, as rudderless, as Griff. Was he my lover, or did I invent him, imagine us as lovers?

But—No, she told herself. No. Griff was real. Her being with Griff was real. Her feelings had been real. Now that he was gone, out of her life, she could deny him, push him away, but she would not. She had not felt guilt then; she would not allow it to creep up on her now, to contaminate her memories of him, of them.

When I was with him, I bristled. I felt—everything. Everything impinged on me. Good or bad, I felt everything.

If she abandoned him, if she denied him, Griff—once again adrift, without a landing place—would eventually become as illusory as he was absent. Unless she allowed whatever he had changed in her to survive, intact, both Griff and she, Selene— the Selene who bristled with life—would be obliterated.

It was suddenly clear to her, those six months when Griff was in her life, and all the months of her life going forward. Even if she never saw or heard from him again, even without his child, she accepted what Griff had, in the end, given her: that part of himself that was lonely, vulnerable—and absolute.

*　*　*

She heard the crunch of loose gravel on the driveway. She looked out the window. It was Alex. She watched him as he turned off the ignition, gripped the steering wheel—as if uncertain what to do next.

She remembered watching Griff pull into her driveway; he hesitated in the same way. Once, he had come in. Once, he had driven away.

The light from the streetlight behind Alex was shining into the car, blacking out his features. He sat motionless for a few moments; then, abruptly, he got out of the car, slamming the door and rousing Nippy, who stirred, stretched, ran to the kitchen, whimpering in anticipation.

She listened. As if preternaturally alert, she heard everything—Alex's footsteps on the drive, then a brief silence as he crossed the lawn, then his footsteps again, ascending the back porch steps. His key scratched against the metal as he fumbled with the lock. There was a muffled click as the lock turned. The back door scraped and screeched as it was opened, then shut. She heard his keys jingling in his hand, then hitting the kitchen table. He murmured a greeting to Nippy.

As he came closer, as he left the kitchen and—not seeing her in the darkened office—headed for the living room, already lit up for the evening, she realized that she was hearing one thing more ...

He was whistling, tunelessly.

Writing a novel is a solo journey, but publishing a book is a collaboration. I'm very grateful to everyone who made this book possible.

Thank you, Lagoon House Press. I am so grateful to Barbara Crane, Marie Pal-Brown, Garrett M. Brown, and Bill Davis for supporting me every step of the way. Thanks also to Glenna Morrison for your excellent proofreading.

Thanks to the members of Holly Prado's writing workshop for working with me, chapter by chapter, as I edited the manuscript. A special thank you to Holly for inspiring me to "go farther, go deeper."

An across-the-pond thank you to Hannah Ellis, granddaughter of Dylan Thomas, who very generously facilitated my use of "Fern Hill" within the novel, with the kind permission of David Higham Associates and New Directions Publishing. Hannah Ellis is the Creative Director of the Dylan Thomas Literary Estate and presides over the official Dylan Thomas website at http://www.discoverdylanthomas.com.

As for the book itself, thank you, Marcia Barbour, designer extraordinaire, for the many hours and exceptional care you took to give this novel its distinctive look and feel. During the course of designing the cover and interior pages, you went far beyond the necessary. You have, indeed, imbued your own generous spirit into this book.

The text of this book was set in Goudy Old Style, a classic serif typeface originally created by Frederic W. Goudy (1865-1947) for American Type Founders (ATF) in 1915. A printer, artist, and type designer, Goudy designed more than 100 typefaces over the course of 50 years. He was the American master of type design in the first half of the twentieth century.

A graceful, balanced design with a few eccentricities, Goudy Old Style is the best known of Goudy's designs, and forms the basis for a large family of variants. Recognizable Goudy-isms include the upward pointing ear of the g, the diamond-shaped dots over the i and j, and the roundish upward swelling of the horizontal strokes at the base of the E and L. The italic, completed by Goudy in 1918, is notable for its minimal slope.

*　*　*

Special thanks to Marcia Barbour, whose love of, sensitivity to, and respect for the art of typography are reflected in the cover and interior design of this book.

Toni Fuhrman grew up in a small Ohio town – the fictional setting for her novel. Both *The Second Mrs. Price* and Toni's first novel, *One Who Loves*, are intensely personal explorations of intimacy and obsession within the context of strong family ties. Toni lives in Los Angeles and is working on her next novel. She publishes personal essays on writing and reading at *tonifuhrman.com.*

Printed in July 2019
by Rotomail Italia S.p.A., Vignate (MI) - Italy